SCATTERED HARVEST

a novel by

Thomas Ray Crowel

Success Press

Success Press, Highland, IN 46322
Copyright © 2006, 2015 by Thomas Ray Crowel

All rights reserved under International and Pan-American Copyright Conventions.
Published in the United States by Success Press, Highland, IN 46322

Library of Congress Catalog Card Number: 2006901830

ISBN-13: 978-0-9669917-3-4

Printed on recycled paper.

Second Printing

Behold, a sower went forth to sow;
And when he sowed, some seeds fell
by the way side, and the fowls came
and devoured them up:

Some fell upon stony places, where
they had not much earth: and forthwith
they sprung up, because they had no
deepness of earth:

And when the sun was up, they were
scorched; and because they had no root,
they withered away.

And some fell among thorns; and the thorns
sprung up, and choked them:

But other fell into good ground, and brought
forth fruit, some an hundredfold, some sixty-
fold, some thirtyfold.

Who hath ears to hear, let him hear.

Matthew 13:3-9

For those who believe

This novel is a work of fiction, although the historical elements match the times, the places, and the peoples. The story is based on real people and real locations, cloaked in fictitious names. In addition to my research, I've used family memories told to me through recollected events. However, over time memories fail, especially over the span of a hundred years. Therefore, any similarity to actual events or people is purely coincidental.

PROLOGUE

My story begins with a dream. In this dream, I was sitting at a table with my late uncle. He said to me, "Ray, there's someone who wants to talk to you."

My father, who is also deceased, walked into the room and sat down with us and said, "Son, go to the country and find your roots."

They were smiling and the room was so bright. "What am I looking for?" I asked them. My dad laughed and said, "Don't worry, you'll find out."

I wondered where my grandfather's farm used to be. Between bass fishing and working on writing a new novel, I was able to start my research. Because I didn't have the foggiest idea of how to go about this process, I sought help in a genealogy office in the same rural Indiana county that my relatives helped pioneer.

One cold winter day I found myself at the county courthouse. Once inside, I was told the records were in the basement of the old but well-preserved building.

Entering the basement, my nose told me I was in the right place, for the smell of old records is unmistakable-that telltale scent of a cardboard box full of old newspaper clippings and pictures that has gotten wet, dried, and then gotten wet all over again.

A young lady approached me. I held out my hand and said, "I'm Ray Krouse, and I'm looking for some information on my relatives."

She shook my hand. "I'm Malinda. I'm sure I can help you, Ray. I'll need some names and dates. Is there any person in particular that you want information on?"

"Yes, I'd like to see the records on my grandfather, Willard Aaron Krouse."

She excused herself and said that she would be back in a few minutes.

Upon her return, she explained that my grandfather's records were sealed away in a file cabinet labeled "Mentals" and they could not be opened without official approval. A chill ran down my spine.

PART I

The sun was beginning to rise. Frost from the night still coated the clay road. Every so often, the wagon would hit a deep rut. There had been major washouts along this road from the rain. It was going to be spring before these could be filled.

The sheriff looked over at his shackled prisoner and thought that this was going to be a rough trip in more ways than one.

No sound came from the gaunt, gray-faced man sitting next to him.

The sheriff tapped his shoulder. "I could've packed your ass in the back, but I thought I'd do you a favor and let you ride up front on the buckboard with me."

The prisoner's eyes remained fixed on the passing farmland.

Most of the corn had not been harvested because of the rain. There wasn't a slim chance that the farmers could get a wagon into the fields in their present condition, even if they used hardheaded mules or hard working Belgians.

Making sure the man next to him was awake, the sheriff tugged on the chain attached to his wrist cuffs. "Do you hear me?"

"Ow."

"At least you're still alive."

The sheriff took off his Stetson, replacing it in a slightly cocked position to block the sun from his eyes. If it weren't *for the hat and star pinned to his jacket, he would look like just another farmer.*

The man next to him managed to turn up the collar on his coat and continued his silent gaze.

"What's wrong? The mornin' air gettin' to you?"

No reply.

The sheriff followed suit turning up his own collar. "If we're lucky, we should reach Long Pointe before sunset."

His passenger shifted his body at the mention of Long Pointe and let out a deep breath. It wasn't the morning air that caused him to shiver.

"I want you talkin' to me before we get to that loony bin, or you won't get shit to eat tonight. How's that sound?"

The prisoner didn't know what to say. He was overwhelmed by the beauty of the farmland, the smell of the wet soil, even the ruinous signs of the damaged crops.

One of the grays whinnied. "Okay girl, you talk to me then."

The sheriff rubbed his kidneys each time the wagon's wheels hit a rut. "Let me know when you need to take a piss, and I'll pull up."

The man nodded.

They rode on in silence. It was difficult to tell the time of day because the sky was not only clouded over but dark and menacing. Unconsciously, the sheriff let the horses pick up their pace as they went down a hill, he wanted to make good time and maybe even avoid the rain.

At the bottom of the hill the wagon hit a deep rut. The horses reared up, pulling hard on the reins.

"Whoa there," yelled the sheriff, as the wagon tipped.

The prisoner grabbed for the iron ring his wrist cuffs were chained to. A flash of lightning shot across the sky and the wagon was on its side before the thunderous boom that followed. The prisoner fell off the seat and was hit hard by the frame of the wagon as it rolled over.

CHAPTER 1

Here at the beginning, if it were possible, Will Krouse would point to a photograph. In his mind's eye, he can see it all, the students of Hampton School, 1899. Next to them, Mister Longacher, their schoolmaster, would be standing straight and rigid, a clean-shaven Abe Lincoln minus his top hat, the deep-set eyes below his bushy brows probably angled toward the Kepler sisters. Longacher was the visible reminder of the old century that, even in America, was called by the name of an English Queen, *Victorian.*

Like Longacher, you'd notice Becky Kepler first, with her high cheekbones, long reddish hair, and bright eyes, too lean to be pretty yet. Her sister Callie, four years older, was on her way to being a great beauty. The two standing next to each other, identical except in height, dressed like twins from matching bonnets to black wool stockings on their long skinny legs.

You'd recognize Will Krouse the boy if you knew Will Krouse the man, his sandy hair tousled, his pale gray eyes playful, his mouth smiling but tight, a fine-featured boy, not tall, his arms already muscular from farm work.

Earl Slayer Jr. would be there, too, his wire-rimmed spectacles pushed back on his narrow, freckled nose. He is the only city kid in the group; his store-bought clothes — the only ones in the schoolhouse — give him away. Earl is the son of the local doctor.

Wendell Gates would make you smile. He is one of those boys who don't clean up well, whose clothes never fit him, his coarse hair is coal black, like an Indian's, though Wendell is the son of an Irish railroader.

Will would have liked to have had that picture to remind himself that they were all close once and so there would be a measure of how far they spun off in their own directions in a couple of decades.

There is no such picture, of course. Times were changing to be sure. Huge economic and political forces were stirring in the old countries that their grandparents had left behind. These forces would sweep through the world scattering everyone and everything. The children of these children would not grow up in their father's businesses and their grandfather's towns. They would not be friends and enemies for life as were these children in this imaginary photo. Will, Wendell, Earl, the Kepler girls, were part of the last generation that would stay put.

The great grandparents of the Krouses, and the Keplers, and the rest, left Europe at the beginning of the nineteenth century. Contrary to what has been said about them, they did not want a brand new world. They wanted a world much like the one they came from; a familiar world but one with less crowding, fewer restrictions.

The American branch of the Krouse family could trace its roots back to 1819, about the same time Indiana was officially declared a state.

Augusta D. Krouse and his wife, Anna, sailed from the old country, arriving in Virginia. Eventually, with other German immigrants, their covered wagon headed for Indiana territory. They had heard that the land there was perfect for farming and raising cattle.

Augusta and Anna Krouse settled in an area that later became Penn County. Pioneering was a test of survival. Augusta built the family's log cabin by hand, dug out fieldstones of all weights, sizes, and shapes — hundreds of them — so that he could plow in a straight line without breaking a blade.

It was colder on the prairie and windier than anything they'd ever dreamed of. The floods were wetter and the flies, bees, and mosquitoes of summertime were fierce. Nevertheless, the Krouses and a few others stayed.

Life on the prairie wasn't much easier for the later generations of Krouses who followed.

Willard A. "Will" Krouse was the great grandson of Augusta D. He never knew the old man, only of him, from the stories told by his grandfather Augusta W. Krouse, or 'Pop' as everyone called him. His grandmother, Gretchen, they all called 'Mom.'

Pop Krouse, had a gentle manner until something went haywire. Then he flew off the handle, as had every other Krouse when cornered or provoked. Whatever chore there was, it seemed to get done quicker if he was up against it. When moving fieldstones, they seemed to jump right out of the ground themselves once Pop got angry at them.

Pop was in his sixties and still driving hard when Will's father died. He didn't come in from the fields when he was supposed to and, as the shadows lengthened and dinner cooled, a member of the family went out to look and found him sprawled over a huge stone that was half out of the earth. With hard labor by Pop and a couple of mules, the stone became Willard R.'s gravestone.

Will's father had Will working at his side once Will

turned eight years old. After Willard died, Pop took over. Mom used to argue over what was best for the boy since Will's mother died soon after his father did. The family said that heartbreak carried her off. The records showed it was consumption. So Will was orphaned early. Like other boys who've seen a lot of trouble and passion young, Will became a man who looked to himself to get things done.

Pop loved his grandson deeply and showed this love, as Krouses did, by pushing Will hard. Mom fed her husband and her grandson the food of the body — berry pies were particular favorites. She also gave them the stories and songs that are the food of the spirit.

Fifteen years later, by 1914, not much had changed. There were new roads, new machinery, and an occasional telephone wire but most of that was yet to come. Will Krouse had remained on the Krouse property and married his childhood sweetheart, Becky Kepler.

Will still plowed with a team, but he did it in a grand old-country way, using a pair of huge Belgian mares, of which he was immensely proud. At 1,500 pounds each, the Belgians were powerful enough to pull a barn to its new location. He'd have them harnessed and in the field by sunrise, taking enormous pleasure in beating the sun to the work of the day.

Today, as he was turning under the sod before winter,

the sun inched over the treetops at the far end of the farm. The soil was still damp with dew. He could smell the earth's vapors as the newly plowed ground released them. A red-tailed hawk was circling high in the air above the team, hoping that the mare's heavy footfall would flush out some straggling field mouse for breakfast.

He watched the hawk swoop down on its prey, then he headed back toward the house. Becky would be cooking up breakfast. There was a little frost in the air, something you smelled more than felt and he wondered if he might not let his boy, Aaron, skip a day of school and work with him and the Belgians. Any day now, it could be too cold to sink the plow blade into the earth. It would be good to give the boy one last chance this season to handle the team.

Will's heart was stirred by the horses and the hawk, and his wife and children. He'd lost a lot and knew the value of what he'd kept. His spread was a large tract, compared to the surrounding properties. His father had been given over a thousand acres from Pop. He'd intended that the land he owned be divided in equal shares between his sons. It didn't turn out that way. Because of a "legal error," and for reasons Will didn't choose to wonder about, Will's older brother, Cecil, kept most of the land for himself. A section of one hundred-fifty acres was set aside for Will. As an adult, Will set out to buy back as much of the land as he could. He purchased it at a higher than market price from his brother because he set value on the things that Cecil had no thought for. Will owned the stone his father died on top of and under which he was buried. He ended up with the original Krouse log cabin and the worn-out barn that came with it. Cecil considered the land they sat on too poor for farming.

To Will, those decrepit buildings were filled with the tangible presence of what his ancestors were all about — hard work, chances taken, dreams visualized. He vowed never to tear them down and took care to repair them whenever they seemed to need it. Will and Becky built their new homestead a stone's throw from the log cabin.

Who says the departed can't influence our lives today? Because Cecil lacked feeling for the original Krouse place, he misjudged the true value of the land itself. Augusta knew it. He must have, Pop and Will decided. The old man had never told anyone about the hidden spring.

Will found this out by accident as a young boy hunting with his grandfather. They came upon a large pile of fieldstones. As fate would have it, Pop shot at a rabbit, hitting its hind leg. The rabbit ran under the pile for cover. Pop couldn't stomach leaving any animal to suffer, so he and Will began pulling aside the fieldstones that had been placed there over sixty years earlier.

They stopped when Pop yelled, "I'll be damned, if this

don't take the cake."

Underneath the stones was a small bubbling stream of clear running water. Without a word, they carefully put the stones back as they had found them. The find remained a secret between Pop and Will.

The spring was the old Krouse's gift to Will. It made it possible for him to get water to the additional 360 acres he eventually bought from the Pennsylvania Central Railroad — land that was once considered poorer dirt than that which his brother, Cecil, "allowed" him to purchase.

Technically speaking, Earl Slayer Jr. M.D. was a second-generation small-town dweller. His father, however, was such a country doctor, so pleased to be in open farmland in his rig, making house calls, so genuinely delighted at the gifts of eggs and butter given him by his patients that no one ever considered him anything but country.

Doc Slayer Jr. hated everything about the practice that his father had loved. Up early, eat breakfast, get ready to go to work. Same black wool suit; same stuffy office. Then there were the house calls. See them all, one by one ... the coughs, the colds, the sores, the bites, the births, the deaths, the diseases. Day in, day out.

Doc Jr. yearned for bigger things. He leaned against the high back of his father's brown leather chair, wondering how long he could stand to live in this jerkwater crossroads.

He was not his father, and all the townsfolk who had worshipped his father could attest to that fact. They already did attest to it, in fact. "Doc Senior's shoes are hard ones to fill," they would tell him, with an infuriating pity.

He did not want to fill Doc Senior's shoes. He'd hoped to advertise the fact by discarding all his father's old furniture, except this brown leather chair. He wanted to be some place where patients paid in cash, not pigs and chickens and baked goods tendered in pride.

His father had not liked hearing that Earl Jr. wanted to leave Penn County after medical school. He wasn't pleased that his son wanted to travel and see Europe, like so many of the people he had gone to school with back east. His father insisted he return to this lifeless farm town filled with people who thought Europe was a place you came from, not a place anyone went to for experience.

There was another reason, the only reason really, that brought him back to Hampton. It was something he didn't talk to his friends about. There was a girl — a girl he wanted — one that made his body burn with passion almost every night, unlike the sophisticated girls who gave themselves to him back east. She lived here in Penn County.

But when he returned to Hampton to claim her, someone had gotten to her first.

By the time the sun topped the trees, Will had the harnesses off and was knocking feed into the horses' trough. He pulled his watch out of his pocket, six thirty.

"How lucky can a man be?" Will said to no one in particular. "Out here among God's creations, working this Krouse land." They were the first words that had gone through his mind that day.

He opened the back door. "Will Krouse, don't you come in here with muddy boots," Becky said.

"I won't." Will stepped back out of the enclosed porch that led to the kitchen, untied his boots and kicked them off on the outside stairs.

Becky laughed her musical laugh at him until she nearly started coughing. "Caught ya," she said.

Her auburn hair looked almost red in the morning sun light shining through the kitchen window. A lock of it had fallen over her eyes, as if she were just half-awake. It was early; she was a little rumpled and wrinkled. At the sight of her husband — ten years and four kids later — she still brushed her hair in place with the back of her hand, wanting him to look at her. He did.

She smiled, picked up a fork, turned the sausage in the pan, and shot Aaron a fiery glance. The boy was at the bottom of the stairs dressed in patched overalls and his farm boots. "Will, talk to that boy of yours. He thinks that there's no school for him today."

He frowned as he stared at his mother. The boy had taken pains not to comb his hair.

There was going to be a struggle, Will could see. He took a deep breath and was distracted for a moment by the smells of the kitchen — sage spiced sausage, butter-milk biscuits, and even a hint of an apple pie that bub-bled over in the oven.

"Will ..." she said.

Aaron stood in the hallway, "Pa, remember, you said I could work the team."

Will walked over and wrapped his arms around his wife, who stood in front of the cooking stove. He didn't ask how a farmwoman, mother of four, could look so beauti-ful. He just knew that she was.

"Will, don't you come huggin' on me. Tell that spittin' image of yours he has to go to school."

Will gave her a pat on her backside and walked over to the sink. "Too hungry to talk, Becky." He pumped water over his hands. "You goin' to see your Mom today?" he asked.

"I'm going to see Callie," she said in a small voice. Callie was gone. Like Will's mother, she had been taken by consumption.

"You sure?" he asked. The trips to the graveyard always left Becky exhausted.

"Got to," said Becky in a voice so small and so absolute that there was no arguing. "I miss her so."

Many young men would have married Becky for her looks or even for her cooking, something she learned from her mother. Will married her because she was Rebecca Kepler, a determined woman with a big heart.

The boys and he sat down and skidded their chairs to the table. Will surveyed them with the same pleasure and more he took in the Belgians, the red-tailed hawk, and the sunrise.

Becky stood behind them and cleared her throat.

Will bowed his head. "Lord, thank you for all our blessings and grant us spiritual wisdom. Amen."

Wendell Gates was a big man. He had a two inch scar etched across his eyebrow to prove it. A root cellar door "ran into" him while he was horsing around with a couple of pals back in high school. They were looking for some "shine" Wendell had stashed away.

This morning, as he stood in front of the long mirror behind the bedroom door, Wendell couldn't help noticing that his skin was blotchy, his eyes bleary — signs of another late night at Honey Boy's.

"Piss on the shave," he mumbled as he rubbed

his unshaven face. There hadn't been a major political figure in the country who shaved since before Lincoln. Not till now, when the sitting President was an east coast Princeton man with a smooth face.

Wendell didn't look like many of the political figures who danced in his head. His dark complexion and solid build gave him the look of a Potawatomi Indian. He watched his muscles flex as he rubbed some Wild Rose tonic on his scalp. Parting his hair down the middle, he noticed the sides were long. He needed a haircut.

He turned sideways and gazed at himself. Except for a couple of small love handles, he was, as he usually said, in fightin' or fuckin' shape. His eyes still foggy, he struggled with the last two buttons of his shirt.

"You up, Wendell?" Mildred called from the kitchen.

He held onto the door jamb as he pulled on his overalls, then looked over at the still-made bed. His pillow was on the floor, apparently where he had slept.

"Wendell?" Mildred whined. He liked her so much better with her mouth shut.

"Just coffee," Wendell said.

Mildred grimaced as she put the pot on the stove. He'd been "campaigning" again at Honey Boy's. How late? Who knew? She remembered the old grandfather clock striking twelve before she finally fell asleep. Too drunk to think about waking me up. Lucky me.

Mildred stood at the bottom of the stairs as Wendell came down.

"You might as well have breakfast," she said. "There's no hurry."

"What are you talkin' about?" he asked. "I'm goin' to work."

"You're late for work. The railroad sent a puddle jumper over to get you," she said. "Why don't they just call them errand boys?"

"What did you tell him?"

"That you were still in bed."

"Thanks a lot."

"Will they fire you?"

"Who gives a shit," he said. Once he was sheriff, he'd be entirely out of their league.

"Where's my coat?" he asked, but she was gone. "Mildred," he shouted.

"It's too warm for a coat."

He followed her into the kitchen. The coat was hanging on a peg. He carefully removed the badge and pinned it on the strap of his overalls, then took the chipped tin cup she offered. Wendell could drink coffee hot enough to boil eggs. He knocked it down like a shot of medicine, which in a way it was, turned, and slammed out the door.

Will walked to the barn where he had left the horses. He

took the Belgians' harnesses and handed them to Aaron.

Aaron was amazed, every time he looked at them up close, at how big and powerful they were. The horses were heavily muscled, with deep chests and wide barrels. The harnesses draped across his arms, mostly touching the ground. "Pa, these are the greatest plow horses there are."

Will nodded. "Aaron, you're going to have to climb up on their stall to get that rig on them."

Aaron had watched his father hitch the team so often over the last year that he didn't have to worry about getting it wrong. Every once in a while, he patted the animals. Their coats were softer than that of the bull he was raising. He knew how to scratch the horses; they turned their heads in approval.

Will glanced over at his son. "Now remember, it's not the Belgians you have to be concerned about when plowing. It's the surrey seat that you'll be sitting on."

"I know, Pa."

"Good, then you'll understand why you'll be sitting on my lap at first."

"But, Pa ..."

"Come on." Will turned hard away from the barn and set the boy on his lap. He could tell that his son wasn't pleased at the arrangement. Will had never forgotten the boyhood incident when a neighbor's team of mules hit a half buried fieldstone, tipping over the surrey, throwing the neighbor off. The man lost his life and his family that day. His daughter was forced into marriage and his four sons were split up. The two oldest ended up somewhere out West; the other two nobody seemed to know. That winter, his wife sat out on the fieldstone that took her husband's life until she froze to death. The story told around the countryside was that the tears on her cheeks were still frozen when she was found days later.

Will swallowed hard. He knew what it was like without his ma and pa, but Becky and the kids? The boy in his lap, Will worked the team, his arms around his son, as the earth turned beneath them.

"Pa, do you have to hold me so tight?"

Hattie Wallace started out cleaning tables and serving drinks downstairs, but once Honey Boy convinced her how easy the work upstairs was, she changed her arrangement with him. No, "flat-backin'" wasn't honest work, but compared with her life in Beaver Hollow, Honey Boy's was heaven.

When she reached the top of the narrow staircase, Hattie heard two familiar voices coming from one of the rooms on the left. She peeked in. "Am I disturbing anything?"

"No, dearie," Ruby said. "Come on in."

Ruby and Prudy Garner sat facing each other, legs crossed, on opposite ends of the small sofa beneath the window. Their matching red bathrobes clashed with both their thick strawberry blonde hair and with the somewhat tattered wine-colored curtains hanging down behind them, but the overall look was colorful ... as were the Garner twins.

Hattie always marveled at their humor, their kindness ... and how difficult it was to tell them apart. Time — and their constant partnership — made the process even harder by endowing them with identical mannerisms and matching laugh lines.

"Can I sit on your work bench, Ruby?" Hattie asked, patting the thin mattress on the old iron barred bed.

"Put your ass wherever you like, honey," Ruby said. "What's on your pretty mind?"

Hattie was pretty. Very pretty. Her straight hair was coal black like her younger sister, Stella's. The Wallace daughter's eyes were brown and large, setting off their narrow noses. Everyone said their good looks came from their ma, but the family's craziness definitely came from their pa, Homer Wallace.

"Oh, I was getting a little lonesome and thought if you two didn't mind, I could use a little company before my beau shows."

"Beau. I *like* that word, Hattie," Ruby exclaimed.

"What do you think, Prudy?"

"Beau," Prudy repeated, clasping her hands together. "I'll use that. Sure beats real people's names." She looked at her sister and rolled her eyes. "Like 'Daniel Norton,' for example."

"Ohhh ..." Hattie groaned, making a face. "I had Dan Norton last night. Where does that man hang out that makes him smell so bad?"

"More like where hasn't he hung out?" Ruby said. "A smell that bad takes years to build up."

"Look on the bright side," Prudy interjected, "You always know with Dan Norton you won't have to smell it long."

"He is a quickie," Hattie said.

"He comes and goes," Ruby squealed, bursting into giggles.

The other two laughed with her.

"He tried to kiss me last night," Hattie said.

"Dan Norton?" Prudy looked at Ruby. "What did you say to him?"

"Didn't say anything." Hattie leaned back against the head of the bed, examining her long fingernails. "Squeeze their seeds hard enough and they forget about kissing."

"I'm never going to kiss them," Ruby said.

"But how about if they get rough?" Prudy asked.

Hattie blew on her freshly polished nails. "Honey Boy

will take care of the roughhousers."

The twins agreed.

"Where's your baby sister been, Hattie?" Ruby asked.

"Stella? She's still got that job working out at Long Pointe."

"With all the crazies?"

"Hell, we work with crazies, too," Hattie said. "At least hers are locked up." She shot her friends a look.

"But don't you still see her?" Ruby asked. "She's got to come home at night to sleep."

"It'd take a day to drive out there," Prudy said. "What are you talkin' about?"

"I guess you're right," said Ruby.

"You guess ...," they both giggled.

"She don't come home that often," Hattie shrugged. "Not even on days off. They have rooms for the help to stay in out there."

Prudy made a face. "She lives right there?"

"It's a better place for Stella than Pa's." Hattie clenched her jaw and stared into space with such a pained expression it took Prudy's breath away.

Doctor Earl Slayer Jr. lived in the frame house that his folks left to him. It was where he was born and, the way things were going, it was where he would die. Though it was not where he planned to spend this evening. When he'd stopped by to change his shirt, Pansy was there. She was a legitimate cause for detour.

Earl squinted, watching Pansy undress in the flickering light coming from the kerosene lamp on the table next to him.

"Are you just going to lay there and watch me, again?" she asked.

"Yes," he said. He loosened one of his lace-ups with the other and shook his feet until both shoes fell with a thump onto the hardwood floor. "Come over to this side of the bed where I can see you better."

"In front of the window?"

"So what, we're upstairs."

"That don't mean someone from the street can't see in."

"Who cares?"

"I do."

"Why? You have nothing to be ashamed of."

She smiled as she untied the ribbon holding her petticoat and slipped it off, then carefully laid it on the high back chair along with her dress. She giggled.

"What's so damn funny?"

"You should see yourself laying there in nothing but your socks."

"Step out where I can see you better."

"Would you please dim that lamp?"

Doc leaned over and turned the brass knob on the base, lowering the wick.

Pansy stepped to the side of the spindled bed.

"Hmm, much better, Rebecca," he said.

She turned her back to him and bit down on her lip as the name "Rebecca" rang through her head. She tasted the small droplet of blood as it formed on her lower lip. She stepped out of her pantaloons and removed her stockings, then finally her camisole.

"Now what are you going to do, just stand there?" he asked.

She laid the rest of her undergarments on the chair and turned to face him.

"Part your legs," Doc said.

She parted her lips, wetting them with her tongue, soothing the tiny pierce. She spread her long legs. Doc's eyes fixed on her silhouette. Then she pulled the ribbon from her long black hair, letting it fall over her breasts.

"Push your hair back, Rebecca."

She knew everything she would have to do for him before she could join him in bed. Doc watched her every move. He reached over and turned the lamp back up.

"Get me my black bag."

"You going to hurt me?" Pansy asked.

"Just do what I say."

She picked up his bag and set it on the bed, then climbed on top of him. He felt around inside for the tiny vial before placing his hand between her breasts, savoring for a moment her skin against his. Pulling down hard on her hair, he let a small amount of opiate drain into her mouth. Her back arched as he thrust himself inside her.

"Oh, Doc, I can be her," Pansy said.

Supper finished, Will took Samuel and Jacob into the parlor to read them a story from his old *Grimm's Fairy Tale* book. Aaron followed. The book was written in German in the black ornate fonts of the old country. The children were only interested in the pictures. Becky put Adeline to bed and went into the parlor. Aaron lay on the floor half-asleep.

"Will Krouse, you've worn your son out. He's barely got enough strength to do his sums."

"Aw, Ma," Aaron said, getting to his feet.

Becky paused in the kitchen doorway. "Didn't I get you a Grimm's that's written in English?"

Will looked at her over the top of the book. "I told you that my father read to me out of this book, just like his father did him."

Little was he to know that in less than three years, his children's generation and future Krouses of Penn County would be forbidden from speaking their native tongue any longer.

"Well, I would like our children to read out of the new book."

"Okay, I am reading it in English," Will said, before hiding his face behind the book.

"That's funny, I thought I heard some German when I came downstairs a minute ago."

"No you didn't," he said. Most of the time he read aloud in English, only slipping occasionally. Will didn't have his grandfather's accent.

He turned the pages and thought about the old country. Then he tried to remember the names of some of the families that he'd see leave Penn County. Was it the hard winters? Or the hard life, in general? With the rails and the roads, would more of them scatter?

Once in the kitchen, Becky took out the small chalkboard and started Aaron through his multiplication tables. Not more than ten minutes passed before Aaron asked, "Ma, would you like me to get us a slice of that good apple pie you baked?"

"That's not going to work, Aaron." Becky leaned across the table, lightly tapping her son's nose.

"Do I have to be the smartest boy in school?"

"No, but you needn't be the dumbest either."

Aaron had already picked up many of Will's mannerisms, one of which Becky observed right at that moment.

Aaron sat tapping his fingers on the table — thumb to pinky — sounding like a galloping horse.

"Stop that, Aaron."

"Stop what?"

"Don't you what me, son."

"Sorry, Ma."

Whenever Will got tired, bored, or thoughtful, he would tap his fingers. Most of the time it went unnoticed. Becky knew Aaron was trying with all he had to stay awake.

"Would you like to have a glass of cider and play twenty questions with me?" she asked.

"I'm really having fun doing my sums, Ma."

Becky gave him a kiss on the head and playfully tugged on his ear. "Nobody likes a fresh boy, Aaron."

She walked back into the parlor to see if the rest of her family wanted some. Will, Jacob, and Samuel were sound asleep and Mr. Grimm was lying face down where he landed after falling out of Will's hands. Becky smiled as she went back to the kitchen. Her smile turned into a laugh when she saw Aaron, head down on the table. She was among the living dead.

CHAPTER 2

Aaron was curious about Hampton and its landmarks because it was the only town he'd ever seen. Will didn't have answers to half the questions asked by his son. He didn't understand towns. Towns and people eventually betray their secrets. In time, Hampton would prove this to be true.

The first thing Will noticed as he stepped into Honey Boy's was the smell of whiskey and tobacco. It was always the same, first the whiskey, then the tobacco, and eventually the sweet smell of cheap perfume. When he was a younger man, before the kids, before Becky, when he had only needed to worry about himself, he was never aware of the aura that was Honey Boy's. Now, Will was like a man who had given up smoking and could smell tobacco a block away. He inhaled as he stepped inside.

The scent of perfume reached his nostrils when he heard a woman's voice. "Hey, Will."

He turned to see Prudy Garner with the rest of the regulars. She patted her leg above her exposed knee. "Come over and sit down."

Will smiled but continued to walk to the bar. His back was sore from a day in the fields and he plopped down on a stool. Looking over at his old friends gathered around a table, he spoke. "Hi, girls, Wendell, Doc."

"Too good to sit with us?" Doc said.

Will grinned. "I'm not staying long. Don't want to interrupt something important."

"Hey Will, what'll it be?"

Will swung around and found himself looking into the eyes of Honey Boy's scarred face. "Whiskey," Will answered.

The old man wiped down the worn oak bar and set a half-filled glass of whiskey in front of Will. Will raised it and gave it the once over. It was an old habit.

Honey Boy leaned in to talk. "How's Grandma Kepler doing since that daughter of hers passed on — Callie."

Will nodded. "You know the Keplers, Grandma will survive."

Honey Boy pushed his yellowish-gray hair back and rubbed his shabby beard. "That consumption is a killer. A lot of folks have fallen because of it."

Honey Boy saw Will's eyes sadden, his mouth turn down. He remembered, now, how Will's mother died. He walked back over to a shelf of bottles and began to wipe them down.

Will sipped his whiskey as he looked down the row of stools. Every so often, there was a brass spittoon in place to accommodate the tobacco chewers. Why? The hardwood floor was stained with the dark brown juice from one end of the bar to the other: telltale signs of the misses.

Will began to feel the whiskey and turned his ear toward his friends' table. Wendell Gates was bragging about how he was going to reform Penn County once he became sheriff.

"He's going to put an end to moonshining?" Will looked at his glass of whiskey. "That must be you doing Wendell's talking, Mister Whiskey."

It was one's love of money and the other's love of power that brought Wendell and Earl Slayer Jr. together, however different they were in every other respect.

Will nursed his drink. Glancing at the clock, he called to Honey Boy and ordered a round of drinks for Wendell's table. Whether he liked it or not, Will was stuck with *all* these old friends of his.

The clock began to chime. A cheer came from the table as Will turned to see Wendell and the twins raising their glasses in a toast. Doc's lips tightened as he set his jaw and glared.

Will turned back toward the bar and saw that Honey Boy had poured him another whiskey. He raised his eyebrows, looking into the deep-set eyes of the old man.

"Oh hell, Will, two whiskeys ain't gonna kill ya."

"I guess you're right. Becky wouldn't want me to fly on one wing, would she?"

About the time he'd settled himself down enough to ignore everything, Will felt a hand on his shoulder. Ruby.

Her hand slid to the back of his neck. "Will, I just heard about Callie. I'm so sorry. Did she suffer much?"

Will swung back around and the twin dropped her hand. "She did."

"And Becky, the poor thing, how's she takin' it? They say it's a lot like the black lung, ain't it, Will?"

Will studied Ruby's features as she spoke. He had a talent for telling Ruby and Prudy apart, but it remained his secret. The twins, he thought, must have seen a lot of lung disease being reared in coal mining country.

"They say black lung, brown lung, and consumption are all the same. The coughin' starts, gets worse, then the blood shows up little by little until the lungs are full of all the coal dust, cotton fibers, or whatever causes consumption, then the lungs can't get air and finally ..."

Will hung his head and stared at the stained floor.

Ruby sat down. She thought he needed the company. "I remember once when Becky, Prudy and me were down at the old covered bridge swimmin' hole when Callie caught us playin' hooky. Becky was in her pantaloons and Prudy and I were ... oh, you know. I thought Callie was goin' to blame Prudy and me, but Becky spoke up and said it was all her idea. Callie just looked at me and Sis and laughed and said, 'Get back in your bloomers.' Callie never told a soul. Did Becky ever tell you that story, Will?"

Will raised his head. "What's brown lung?"

Ruby patted his shoulder. "Just somethin' we should pray never to get."

"Hey, Ruby, get your pretty butt back over here," Wendell yelled from the table.

Ruby furrowed her brows and squinched her nose at him. She turned back to Will.

"I can't believe Callie's gone," she said.

Will reached in his back pocket and took out the faded red kerchief he tied around his neck on hot days in the field. "I know, Ruby." He wiped the tears from her cheek and handed her the hankie. "Take it."

"Ruby, you gone deaf?" a voice came from the table behind them.

"I better get back." She squeezed his knee, then felt a hand tighten around her arm. It was Doc.

"Didn't you hear Wendell telling you to get your ass back to the table?"

"There's no need for that, Doc," Will said. "Let her go."

Ruby twisted her arm loose at the same moment Doc threw a "haymaker" at Will's jaw. Ducking Doc's drunken swing, Will grabbed him by his lapels and shoved him. Doc stumbled backwards, finally landing square on his ass across the bar room. Will pushed his bar stool aside and headed over to where Doc had fallen down. He bent over to grab Doc up with his left hand as he made a fist with his right.

Doc looked up at Will wide-eyed, then started laughing. "Look, I didn't even spill a drop of my whiskey." He held out his still half-full glass.

Will tightened his lips and stared him down. "I'm too tired for your bullshit, Doc."

Doc staggered back to the table.

Doc's an asshole, Prudy mouthed in silence.

Ruby lipped, *I know.*

"I thought you was friendly with the Krouses, Doc," Wendell said.

Doc grimaced and made a tissing sound through his front teeth as if attempting to dislodge a piece of food. "I'll tell you something. There's a couple of stories that Becky would like to hear that took place when she was away at college."

Just then, Honey Boy strutted over with a round of drinks.

"These are on me, folks," Honey Boy said. "I want y'all to settle down before you piss me off." Honey Boy squinted and leaned forward, placing his hands on the table. "And if y'all hadn't noticed, Will left."

They looked over at the empty stool.

"You're a bunch of hayseeds," Doc said.

"And you're who?" Ruby asked as she tossed down her whiskey. She pushed her chair away from the table. "I'm going upstairs and rest awhile."

"Wait Sis, I'll join you," Prudy called after her.

Doc couldn't help but snort. "Is that what you call what you do upstairs? *Resting?*"

"Take it easy, Doc," Wendell said.

Doc smacked his lips and made a tissing sound again. What Becky ever saw in that rube was beyond him.

"Straighten your spectacles, Doc. One side's hangin' off your ear," Wendell said.

Doc pulled them from his face and fogged them. He snatched Will's kerchief from Ruby's hand and polished the lenses.

With the children already in bed, the house was quiet. Will saw a lamp on in the parlor and peeked his head around the corner.

"Fixing my old shirts again, Becky?"

"Waste not, want not," Becky said, cocking her ear toward the stairway. "Addie's fussing. I'm going to check on her."

"I'll go," Will said. He kicked off his boots and walked up the stairs in stocking feet. Addie had her own room next to theirs and he could hear her breathing hoarsely as he opened the door. He slipped inside.

His little girl sounded stuffy. Will knew the sound of deep congestion. He'd heard his mother's labored breathing in the weeks before she died. He'd heard Callie fighting for breath like a drowning person fighting to reach the surface. He put his fingertips on Addie's chest. He knew from experience that it was more likely a colt would die from a hard winter than a full grown mare. It was that way with all life. Why his little Addie? He put his hand on her chest. He always ended up checking for vibration. He moved his hand to her forehead. She didn't seem to have much of a fever. Will pulled the quilt back up over the child, then bent down and kissed the top of her head. "You'll be back bouncing around in no time, won't you baby girl?"

Will went back into the parlor and sat down in his chair.

"She all right? Did you get her back to sleep?" Becky asked.

"She was asleep already. She'll be fine."

She looked at him and grinned. "You're such a worrier," she said. "What gets into you?"

He rested his hands behind his head and leaned back, closing his eyes.

Becky stopped to re-thread her needle. "Do you think Earl Jr. will ever marry Pansy?"

"He's not over you yet."

"What's that supposed to mean?"

"Come on, Becky, he's always had his eye on you."

"That wasn't what I asked."

"If you ask me about Pansy, she's better off without him."

"Do you think he's sweet on one of the twins?"

"Men like Doc don't get sweet on girls like the twins. He doesn't care about Ruby or Prudy except what he can get from them."

He watched Becky as she went back to mending his shirt. The bright glow of the lamp accented her fine features.

"You know you're the most beautiful woman in the

world."

She blushed and then she laughed. "The whole world?"

"Well, in my world." He pulled his chair behind her stool and slipped his hands over her sides, folding them over her belly.

Becky put down her sewing and lowered her head. "What's on your mind, my dear husband?"

"What do you suppose?"

Will kissed her neck as he unbuttoned the back of her blouse. He slid his fingers through the straps of her camisole, placing his hands on her warm breasts. Becky reached up over her head and stretched her arms around his neck. He eluded her grasp, getting up and spinning her towards him as he picked her up and started up the stairway.

CHAPTER 3

It was February of 1915. To an outsider, there was nothing about it that would have predicted the end of winter. The snow had fallen for a week straight. The locals, rubbing snow between fingers and thumb, could feel it was wet — maybe the season's last chance for a party before the ice melted.

"Don't you think it's a bit cold for ice skating?" Will said as he slipped on his gloves.

"Maybe we should wait until spring," Becky said, tossing her braided hair outside her quilted jacket. "Don't be such a stick in the mud."

"There will be moonshine."

"Oh no, not moonshine." Becky threw up her hands.

Will grinned. He lifted her in his arms and carried her outside to the sleigh he had the Belgians hitched to.

"My, what strong arms you have," Becky whispered in his ear.

"Better to handle the Belgians with ... I mean better to handle you with." Will's smile turned into a laugh.

"Promise?" She nuzzled his neck.

Will settled Becky, picked up the reins, and started down the drive. There were exceptionally high drifts in the fields, but Will knew he could take the Belgians most anywhere.

"I like hearing the bells jingle. Did you put that harness on especially for me?"

"No, for the horses," he said. "In case they get lost."

"Oh, stop it. Try being romantic." Becky wrapped the blanket around herself as she snuggled closer to Will.

Except for a cloudbank to the west, the sky was crystal clear. With a full moon, the stars looked like candles reflecting off their shiny tin holders on a Christmas tree.

His white hair almost shoulder length, Homer Wallace — Pa Wallace — sat on a tree stump, strumming his banjo. He wore gloves on both hands with the fingertips cut off. A few of the folks who were gathered around the fire were singing. Wendell's bass voice could easily be heard above the others. Every once in a while, Homer would look up and smile through his broken front tooth. It was then the bright moon would illuminate his eyes, one brown and the other gray. It gave him a scary appearance.

Buck Wallace lumbered over, holding a harmonica in his large hands. He gave his pa a nod and started blowing out *Red River Valley.* They looked alike, except for their age and height — both were built broad and rugged. Both had heavy brows, each having been through his fair share of fist fights. So it seemed odd that they were both musical too, although neither one of them could read or write.

Will heard the Wallaces' music as he pulled the team into the clearing. Between them and the ice was a blazing bonfire where folks were laughing and drinking. Gathered around the fire were a mix of outsiders and Hollowers. The men standing around the fire looked beat up in their worn overalls and sweat stained felt hats pulled down to their eyebrows. Most of the women wore old feed sack dresses. Although many had deep lines in their faces, Will knew some of them and they were in their twenties and thirties.

There was a second, smaller fire, too, a few yards further off, in the direction of Pa Wallace's cabin. There was a spit there, its uprights pounded deep in the earth. Cooking on the spit was the whole carcass of a five-point buck. Stella Wallace, Pa's daughter, Hattie's sister, oversaw it. A number of skaters were already on the ice, among them Doc. He'd not taken his eyes off Becky since she arrived.

Stella Wallace stood next to the open flame.

"Need any help with that venison?"

Stella turned to see Hayward Kurtz grinning at her.

"It's about done, that's for sure."

"What do you want me to do?" he asked.

"Toss some snow on the flames."

Hayward obliged.

"That's good, Hayward." Kurtz moved up behind Stella. She felt him put one of his hands on her hip, then reach around with the other sliding it down the top of her overcoat.

"Hey..." Stella spun around and gave Kurtz a shove. "What the hell do you think you're doing?"

"I can do a lot of favors for you out at Long Pointe."

"Why don't you do one for me now and tell Hattie we need the plates."

"Yeah, maybe your big sister will be a little friendlier," Hayward spat, then strutted off.

Will took in the beauty surrounding him and Becky — the stars, the moon, the whiteness of the snow against the blackness of night. "Look at the snow on those pines," he said. "That would make a pretty picture."

Will put his hands on Becky's waist and started skating faster as he held onto her. He spun her around, then pulled her body close to his.

"Will, folks are ... We're not alone."

From across the ice, Doc watched Will steal a kiss from her.

"Mind if we cut in?" Doc called out, as he and Pansy skated up beside them.

Will and Becky turned and blinked. It was as though they had just woke up.

"Where have you two been?" Will asked.

"Pansy's been helping Stella cook and I've been over by the fire practicing medicine."

"Come on, Becky," Doc said, reaching out for her arm, "Let me show you some real skating."

Becky looked at Will.

"Go on honey, I'll show Pansy those deer we just saw." Will took Pansy's hand and skated off.

Doc took Becky's arm and led her in silence around the outer ring of the pond for several minutes. She felt his grip tighten.

"How would you like to try some dance moves?" he

asked.

"I'm not that good on the ice anymore."

"Follow me." Doc slipped away from the other skaters.

Doc moved as if he were born with blades on his feet. For a few moments, he skated alongside Becky, shifting his hand from her waist to underneath her arm. His hand edged to the side of her breast. Sensing his fingers exploring her, she began to wobble.

Doc spun around and started skating backwards, pulling her to him. She struggled to break free. Losing her balance, she fell to the ice.

"I'm sorry, Becky, are you all right? You've done that move before." Had he meant to make her fall?

"No, Doc, I'm not. And I'm not eighteen anymore either."

Doc stared into her eyes. Helping her up, he hesitated, then brushed off the front of her coat. "You still look eighteen to me, honey."

Becky felt her face flush and looked away.

"You feel good, too," he said.

Will and Pansy had not found the deer and on their way back they saw what happened. Will shoved Doc, causing him to fall on the ice. He and Becky skated away.

"You hurt?" Will asked.

"I'm all right," she said. "Do you want to leave,

Will?"

"No, he's not running me off." Will pulled off her mittens. "Your hands are cold." He blew on her fingers as he rubbed her hands. Prudy skated up to them with two pint jars half full of shine. They skated over to the fire.

From around the fire, the voices coming from the pond couldn't be heard — that is except for Doc's. Will took Becky back on the ice. Doc was barrel jumping. He had just cleared three, and a fourth was being dragged out.

Doc ignored Becky. "Well, look who's back. Come on and let me show you how to jump barrels," he said to Will.

Becky tugged on Will's sleeve. "Let's just skate."

"Watch this, farm boy," Doc shouted, pushing off. He circled, heading straight for the barrels. He crouched and then sprang high into the air with his arms extended, soaring like a bird of prey.

"He looks like an old heron pickin' out a fish," a toothless woman gasped. "Why, he even lands like one."

Doc landed in a squat, keeping his balance. He took a bow, grinning at the Krouses.

Pa Wallace heard applause from the direction of the pond and stopped playing. Buck had been watching Doc work the crowd the whole evening, wondering who Doc would get to first.

"Come on, farm boy, I'll start you with only one barrel," Doc said.

Pansy clenched her fingers as she watched Doc. Since they arrived, he'd barely spoken to her and she noticed him from time to time watching for Becky to show up. When he pulled up next to Becky and Will the second time, Pansy cornered him. "Come on," she said, reaching for his hand. "Let's get a drink."

"Good idea," Doc said. "It's probably best you pack it in, Krouse. You're better with your fists than your brains." Doc took Pansy by her hand.

"Get back here, blow hard," Will shouted.

Becky turned him. "Will, you've had too much to drink."

Doc grabbed a straw broom laying at the edge of the ice and skated back out to the barrels. "I'll even clean the ice for you, farm boy," he yelled.

More clouds had blown in and a heavier snow began to fall. Doc broke off a handful of straws from the old broom and dropped them in front of the lead barrel. The snow covered them as they landed.

Will started circling. He knew he had a couple of dozen bystanders watching him skate past the barrels a second time. He knew that he had to do this jump, even if it killed him. He circled a third time.

"C'mon, Will, teach him a lesson," came a yell.

Will lowered his head and sped straight for the barrels. Approaching the lead barrel, one of his legs shot out from under him straight up into the air. The other caught the top rim of the first barrel. He felt his body somersault, then land hard in between the barrels.

Standing at the edge of the pond, Buck Wallace jumped out of the way as a barrel came skidding across the ice. A fat kid took the blow, falling flat on his back.

Doc chuckled.

"Oh, no," Becky gasped as she skated over to Will.

"That'll teach you to push me around," Doc muttered as he skated off. "Hope you broke some bones, then that bitch of yours will be begging for the ol' Doc, won't she?"

Buck came up and pulled Becky back from Will. "What hurts?" he asked.

"My knee, I think it's broke."

"Try moving your foot," Buck said.

"Oooh, my shoulder ..."

Buck grabbed Will's arm and gave it a strong yank.

"Stop, Buck," Will yelled.

"That shoulder's fixed now," Buck said. "You dislocated it, that's all." He stared down at Will's motionless body. "I believe he's done passed out, Becky."

"Will, Will, talk to me." Becky rubbed his face.

"What happened?" Will asked.

Becky dabbed some snow on Will's forehead. "Is his

leg broke, Buck?"

"Nah, Becky, he just twisted it," Buck said.

"Thank God." She pushed Will's hair away from his eyes.

"C'mon, a couple of you boys help me get him off the ice," Buck said, directing one on either side of Will. Buck took his legs while the other two grabbed his arms.

"Put me down," Will said.

"Quiet, dear," Becky said.

"Here, let's put him over here by the fire," Buck said. "Slide that log under his leg ... no, this one."

"What happened?" Will asked.

"You twisted your ankle and I had to pull your shoulder back in place. You'll mend," Buck said.

"Where's Doc?" Pansy asked.

"I heard someone say he went to fetch his black bag," a woman in the crowd spoke up.

"Somebody get Will a drink," Buck said.

"He doesn't need any more," Becky said.

"Yes I do," Will said.

Buck bent down to get a closer look at Will's skate. "What's this?" He pulled a piece of straw from the front of the blade and held it out for Will to see.

Will and Becky, pulling away in the sleigh, could hear the voices of the hangers-on.

"I'm glad you're letting me handle the Belgians, Will," Becky said, guiding their sleigh over the snowy path home.

"Seems to me that you just jumped up and took the reins."

Will and Becky pretended to enjoy the snow covered countryside as they headed home, but all Will could think about was the time at Honey Boy's that Doc took a swing at him. Now here he was tonight, grabbing at Becky. Then there was the straw. He didn't mention to Becky what Pansy told him when they first arrived. "Watch out, Will," was all she would say.

Becky was trying to figure out what had gotten into Doc. He'd always flirted with her, but tonight he crossed a line. Becky sensed the aloofness in Pansy when they spoke. But Pansy knew, of course, it wasn't good enough for Doc to just pretend anymore.

Becky broke the silence, rubbing her nose against Will's. "I love you."

Will wrapped the blanket around their shoulders and they snuggled together. Becky felt his hand touch her thigh.

"Stop that, Will."

Will rested his chin on her shoulder. "I'm just sore, not sick. You keep those pretty little hands of yours on the reins."

"These hands are going to take care of that shoulder of yours," Becky said.

Once the horses were unhitched and in the barn, Will limped into the house. He was wet and frozen. In the kitchen, he stripped down to his long johns. Becky was already in one petticoat and her camisole. They sat and steamed in front of the woodburning stove. Becky looked at him, sitting up straight, his eyes closed. She got up, walked behind the chair, and began massaging his shoulder.

"What's that smell?" Will asked.

"Sloan's liniment."

"Ain't that horse liniment?"

"No," she laughed.

Will leaned his head back and looked up at her. "I can feel my toes again."

She bent down with her face close to his. "If you only would have listened to me."

He cracked his knuckles. "And let him get away with his goading?"

"Will, Earl scares me."

CHAPTER 4

Pansy was half asleep, her mind playing tricks on her as she lay in bed. It seemed that directly in front of her, a few feet away, was Doc, making her watch him as he undressed Becky.

Pansy bolted upright, disoriented. She was not in her own bed, she was in Doc's. She remembered he'd asked her to wait for him there. He hadn't come back.

She wiped the perspiration from her forehead with the sleeve of her nightgown. It was raining; maybe the sound of it woke her.

The nightmare was so powerful she couldn't shake it off. She got out of bed and looked at herself in the moonlit mirror. She felt sick, dirty. She held out her hands, covering her reflection, then wiped the tears from her eyes. She felt the fine lines in their corners.

In the dark, she groped her way to the dresser. She knew by touch where to find the big box of matches she always kept there. She lit a candle and looked at the clock: 1:00 am. She reached into her handbag on the nightstand and took a long drink out of a small silver flask. Where was Doc?

Doc waited until Wendell was out of sight, turned around and went back into Honey Boy's.

The place was now empty, except for one of the old-timers sound asleep at the end of the bar. Doc shut the door behind him and walked over to where he had been sitting.

Honey Boy was straightening the liquor shelves. "I thought you called it a night," he said over his shoulder.

"Changed my mind." Doc took off his derby and flipped it on the stool next to him.

Honey Boy reached for a bottle of Canadian whiskey and held it up for approval. Doc motioned him over. He marked the label with his fingernail before passing it across the bar. "She's all yours, Doc."

Doc filled his glass half-full and raised it to his lips. The old-timer started snoring. Doc paused and set the glass down. Honey Boy made his way to the end of the bar and shook the man's arm. He raised his head, one eye opened.

"Time to go," Honey Boy said.

The man braced himself against the bar as he slid off his stool. He looked down at his feet, deliberately placing one boot in front of the other as he stumbled out. Doc got up to lock the door.

Doc slid back on his stool. He tossed down his whiskey and refilled his glass. Wendell's bullshitting seemed endless. He would be glad when the campaign was finally over. His night was wasted, barely listening but nodding all the while Wendell rambled on. You couldn't get drunk enough after a night like his.

But Doc was impatient. When the Sheriff's office became vacant and Wendell first said he wanted the job, Doc was thrilled. He knew Wendell and he knew he could persuade him to do whatever Doc thought was best. The sheriff's office would also give Wendell connections with people Doc might like to know. What Doc hadn't counted on was Wendell's lack of independence. He couldn't campaign without his friends' continual support and loyalty. Getting Wendell elected, however, was costing Doc time and money. He was wearing thin of the whole process.

Doc ran his finger around the edge of his glass. A faint giggling came from upstairs, one of Honey Boy's girls. It reminded him of the night he skated with Becky at the Hollow. Will was nothing but a miserable-ass farmer; he was a doctor. He swirled his whiskey and dumped it down, then reached into his vest pocket and pulled out a cigar. "Got a match, Honey Boy?"

Honey Boy slid a box of matches down the bar and went back to wiping glasses. He could tell Doc had a woman on his mind. Honey Boy knew most of Doc's women. He even shared some of them.

Doc dipped the end of his stogie into the whiskey, licked his lips, then took a deep draw. He tilted his head back and watched the smoke rings shoot out. A different roll of the dice, and he'd have been the one with Becky – without those urchins of hers. Will was nothing without her. Doc reached into his pants pocket and pulled out a wad of crumpled bills. He peeled off two and threw them on the bar. "That should cover it, Honey Boy."

He grabbed the bottle and headed out the door. A little squall blew in his face. He pushed his derby down tight, and turned up the collar of his coat. "I'm not through with her sweet ass yet," he said, and started towards home.

Will stood in the doorway of the bedroom, his arms folded across his chest. He squinted at Becky. "I hate to say I told you so."

Becky sniffled and then blew her nose.

"I knew it was too cold to go to a skating party." Will pulled a chair next to the bed and sat down.

"Anyway we had fun," Becky said as she leaned back against her pillow.

"Kids are all down," Will said.

"Did they wash?"

"Yes."

"Brush?"

"Yes."

"Say their prayers?"

"Yes, yes, everything, Becky."

She reached out. "What's that you have in your hand?"

"That's my surprise for you tonight," he said, holding up a book. "Finished with your tea?"

Will lifted the lid off the teapot and eyed Becky. "Atta girl."

She wiped her nose and pulled the quilt up under her chin. Will sat gazing at his wife.

She looked over at him. "Something wrong?"

He shook his head and chuckled. "You look like a little girl laying there in that night cap."

"Then read me a fairy tale."

"What would you like to hear?" Will asked as he stroked her cheek.

She curled her bottom lip and thought for a moment.

"I'm between *Hansel and Gretel* and *Little Red Riding Hood.*"

"Then *Little Red Riding Hood* it is." He paused. "English or German?"

Becky started to laugh when the coughing started. "English," she choked out.

Will reached for the washcloth on the bedside table, and dipped it in the basin. He wrung it out and laid it across her forehead.

Becky closed her eyes and placed her hand on Will's leg. He opened the book and began, "Once upon a time..."

"Will?" Becky interrupted.

"What?"

"You look uncomfortable in that chair."

"Make a little room for me," he said as he crawled next to her. "Here, raise your head." He fluffed her pillow, then propped himself up against his own. "That's much better," he said, situating himself.

"I haven't invited the big bad wolf to bed, have I?"

"Maybe." He bared his teeth. "You kind of look like grandmother in that night cap."

"I thought you said I looked like a little girl," she giggled.

"In the eyes of this old wolf you do."

Becky snuggled next to him. "Just read to me Will."

He had only read a couple of pages when he looked

over and saw her eyes were closed. Will set the book aside and kissed her on the head. "Sweet dreams." Will leaned over, cupped his hand and blew out the lamp. Half asleep, she rolled towards him and put her leg over his. He lay his hand on her chest and felt that deep vibration he wasn't able to find in little Addie. He lay awake listening to her irregular breathing.

He changed his thoughts to better times. It was graduation day at the high school. Will knew that Becky was going away to college and he didn't know how to think about that. *The two of them, without prearrangement, walked away from the school down towards the covered bridge. It was a hot day so he suggested they sit by the creek in the shadow of the bridge. It was a favorite spot of his, a place to get away to.*

The rays of the noon sun pierced several cracked shingles atop the covered bridge and through the narrow slits between the floor planks, illuminating the rippling water beneath in ever-changing kaleidoscopic patterns. A collage of hand-carved initials and dates covered the beams and wallboards inside the bridge. Will did not show her, among the others, the rough heart around the initials W.K. + R.K. that he had put there one solitary afternoon.

He remembered sitting on the bank, wet and shivering a little, his pants pulled on over his wet legs, as he watched Becky below the bridge, standing in water waist deep and then starting up towards him. Beads of water dripped from her long hair down over her bare breasts. He couldn't breathe.

Buck left his buggy out behind a building and rattled the locked door open. The room was small. He inhaled. She always smelled good. He slouched down in a chair and waited. He heard the front door. That must be her. He hid behind the door as she opened it.

Hattie stepped in, her arms full of packages.

Buck slid behind his sister, reaching around and groping her breasts.

"Buck, let go."

"How'd ya know it was me?"

"Please." Hattie tried to break free from his grip.

Buck kissed her neck and tightened his hold. "How'd ya know?" he repeated.

Hattie looked around the room, fixing her eyes on the iron poker by the fireplace.

Like an animal who smells danger, Buck followed his sister's gaze. "Huh-uh, you little bitch."

"I weren't thinkin' anything," she said.

"I bet." His right hand was now inside her dress, pulling her closer to his body. "I'm waitin'," he said.

She stopped fighting him. "For what?"

His breath was in her ear. "For the last time, how'd

ya know it was me?"

"Buck, I need to get to work."

"That's what you call it?"

She felt his other hand pulling up her dress. "Be nice. I'll even buy you a Canadian whiskey at Honey Boy's."

He pulled back. "I ain't finished with you."

She knew. The first time, he brought her little things to do it. She was twelve. Now, she found herself buying him off not to do it.

"It better be Canadian," he said.

She turned and rubbed his unshaven cheek. "It will be. I promise."

They drove to Honey Boy's without conversation.

Buck pulled the rig up in front of the building. Hattie felt the warm air hit her body as Buck pushed open the door to Honey Boy's. The door flew back, hitting the heel of her hand.

"Thanks alot, Buck."

The outside air rushed in.

"Honey Boy, grab me a bottle of that Canadian," Buck said, pointing to the top shelf.

Honey Boy was surprised to see them together. He looked past Buck. "Hattie, you okay?"

"The twins around?" she asked.

Honey Boy's eyes cut toward the stairway.

"Give Buck whatever he wants," she said. "He gave

me a ride here."

"Ain't you gonna have a drink with your big brother?" Buck asked.

Hattie turned and saw Doc, Wendell, and Will. Wendell waved his hands as he spoke. Doc fussed with his spectacles. Will wore a blank look.

Hattie wanted them to notice her. Then, the odds of Buck causing trouble would be reduced.

"Am I buttin' in?" she asked as she bumped into their table.

Will tipped his hat. Wendell rattled on.

Doc hooked his spectacles back over his ears. "Well, look who we have here, boys, Miss Hattie Wallace. Pull up a chair."

"I'll pass, Doc," Hattie said.

Will's glass was still full. Her eyes darted to where Wendell and Doc were sitting. They had been there a while. Peanut shells were scattered on the table in front of them. Will looked troubled.

She started up the stairs, then heard the words "My campaign." So Wendell was trying to shake out some more cash for his Sheriff's race.

Doc motioned for Will to drink up, then raising his own glass, said, "Through the lips, over the gums, look out belly, here she comes. Here's to Penn County's next sheriff."

Hattie paused at the top of the stairs, then vanished. Upstairs, she knew, she could disappear into a different world. The twins were queens of the world upstairs and Hattie fit in there nicely.

She hadn't even looked back for Buck. She didn't care if he'd gone or not. She could also make disappear the people who most troubled her — Buck, Pa, and the men who paid her calls — her "beaus." Still, they all thought she was available, that they could do whatever they liked to her. She was sure she brought out the worst in them.

Doc noticed that Will's hand had stopped shaking. He picked up the bottle to refill Will's glass. Will placed his hand over it.

"Let bygones be bygones, Will." Doc grabbed the bottle and Will's glass, spilling the glass over as he poured.

"Doc's right, Will, ease up," Wendell said.

There was a time when Will could out skate Doc and out drink Wendell. That was before he'd married. He lifted his glass and downed the whiskey.

"That's better," Doc said.

Will nodded. "Maybe I'll get a good night's sleep."

Doc reached into his vest pocket and pulled out three cigars.

Bygones be bygones — in a pig's ass. Krouse would be getting his. Ol' Doc was going see to that.

CHAPTER 5

Will had already turned the cows out to pasture by the time Becky woke up. He came upstairs to change and she was lying in a little ball under the quilt. "Will Krouse, do you always have to be up before the chickens?" she asked.

"You won't be going with me over to your ma's place?"

"Why are you going to Mother's?"

"I promised I'd help with those porch boards, remember?" Will sat down on the edge of the bed and put on a pair of clean socks.

"Why don't you wait until the boys come home from

school, then they can help." Becky started coughing.

Will waited until she stopped.

"It'll be too late. It's an all-day job. Besides, Professor Knobbs will be there to help me."

Professor Clarence Knobbs and his wife, Cora, moved to Indiana a short time after Becky graduated from Pennsylvania College where Clarence taught agriculture. Becky was his prize student and became the daughter the Knobbs' never had.

During her second year, Becky left her dormitory and moved in with the Knobbs. All she talked about was her family back in Indiana, and a boy named Will Krouse. When she came home to him, it was Will's idea to cut out forty acres of his choice land and sell it to the Knobbses so they could be nearby. In return, the retired Professor taught Will the newest technology in farming and raising cattle.

Will went downstairs to check his tool chest. Becky followed him and standing on her toes, put her arms around his neck. He gave her a kiss and slid his hand down her back. "I could be convinced to stay," he said. "The boys ain't up yet."

She turned and waved her hand. "Oh go on, get."

In the barn, Will was surprised to see that Aaron had remembered to brush the mare's mane the night before. It was a good thing — Aaron taking on responsibility. Will needed as much help as he could get.

Will hitched the mare to the buggy and headed out on the road to Grandma Kepler's.

There are wet spring days in the Midwest when, if you walk a hundred yards with the doors to your senses open, you'll feel dizzy at the explosion of life — plant, animal, insect — when you'll know how powerful life is, and how very, very hard some men have had to work to bring darkness out of this glorious energy.

Where does time go? You look around you at the road, and the green grass; you look at the birds, and nothing has changed, but you've changed. Could have been yesterday Becky and he were getting married. Unlike most women, Becky didn't complain about aches and pains, not even after giving birth to all those kids — and in spite of the fact that she and her sister were both born with weak lungs, damn it. Will was as strong as a horse but he wasn't feeling any younger.

He could picture her, standing next to him in her white wedding gown that her mother made. You didn't get a lot of years on this earth, but you could remember the best parts as if they were yesterday. They never left you.

Then Will stopped thinking and began paying attention to the little washouts in the road, the occasional sign of winter damage — a fallen tree, a damaged roof on an outbuilding.

He'd been hearing something for a minute before he stopped the buggy and listened. It was a cow bawling out in the Smith's pasture. He got down, unhitched the mare and ran in the direction of the sound.

Over a little crest, he saw a Holstein. She was ready to drop her calf and was having trouble doing it.

Will bent over her. "Easy, girl. What are you doing out here?"

He pulled her tail, getting her in place, then took off his jacket and set it down on a dry piece of fieldstone. He rolled up his sleeves.

It wasn't long before the wobbly-legged calf was standing on its feet next to its ma. That's when the man ambled over the hill.

"Will Krouse?"

"It looks like you just increased your herd, Mr. Smith."

"I've been looking all over for her."

"You want me to help you get them back to the barn?"

"No, I brought my bell cow along. I'm in your debt, Will. How's the Mrs.? We miss seeing her at church."

"She's pretty busy," Will said.

"I been hearing about that bull of Aaron's. I'd like to come by to see it..."

"Our door's always open," Will said.

He went back to the wagon, found some rags under the tool chest, and wiped his hands.

There used to be mornings like this one, he remembered, when there were no worries, no obligations, when he felt some kind of freedom.

Will pulled his wagon to the side of Grandma's house and walked around to the front steps. The first time he came out to the Kepler place was with his father as a young boy. That was over twenty years ago. He, Callie, and Becky would play outside in the rain, the porch roof covering them almost all the way around the house. The roof hadn't prevented those planks from rotting.

Will climbed the steps to where Grandma stood. Her gray hair was always kept pulled neatly into a bun. She wrapped her arms around him and kissed his cheek. "How's Becky and the children?"

He forced a smile. "She's still trying to shake that cold she caught at the Hollow."

Grandma patted his shoulder and opened the door. Will followed.

The aroma of blueberry muffins filled the kitchen. Grandma Kepler pulled them out of the oven and set them on top of the stove. She laid her pot holder on the cupboard.

"Is there any coffee left?" Will asked.

Grandma smiled and pointed. She'd already set a place at the table for him. Will sat down. He took a drink of coffee, swished it around in his mouth and took in a deep breath trying to cool his tongue. A cup and a half later, he looked down at his plate. The muffin was barely touched. He'd taken a small bite out of politeness.

Grandma sat watching him.

He needed to break the silence. "I'm sure glad you taught your daughters how to cook, Grandma." He paused.

"Callie was a wonderful cook, and so's our Becky."

"Grandma," Will said, "I was wondering, when did you first realize Callie had consumption?"

Pansy jumped when she heard a crash coming from Doc's office.

She got up from her desk and stood at the door. "Doctor? Is anything wrong?" She knocked. "May I come in?"

The door yanked open.

"What is it, Pansy?"

Her eyes shifted about his office. Laying on the floor was a broken picture frame, its glass scattered.

"Oh, I'll clean that up," Pansy said.

"Suit yourself," Doc said.

She took the broom and dustpan from the closet and began sweeping up, dumping the broken pieces in the wastebasket. She laid the photograph on his desk. It was her favorite picture of Earl's father and mother. There was a dent in the plaster where the frame had hit.

"I'll replace it for you, Doc."

"Don't bother."

"What's wrong?"

"All this doctoring is smothering me."

She remained silent.

He continued. "Everyone else is doing what they want, except me — even you. Take Wendell, for example. He's quitting the railroad where three generations of his family have worked so he can be sheriff. Even the Garner whores are getting jobs." He rested his head between his hands.

Pansy laid her hand on his arm. "What would make you happy?"

"Something different."

"Don't you want to practice medicine any more?"

"Get out," he said, brushing her hand away.

"I'm sorry, Doc, go on."

"There's nothing more to say."

"What would you like to do?"

"I've done plenty for Wendell. The least he can do is get me an appointment out at Long Pointe."

"Long Pointe?"

"That's right. There's going to be an opening on the board."

"What would you do there, Doc?"

"Not all this doctoring I'm doing here in Hampton day in and day out," Doc said. He was getting tired of hearing about the Krouses. "I'd even take you with me."

"What would I be doing? Would you close this office?"

"You'd do what I want you to do," Doc said. Should he at least pay Becky a professional visit?

The bell on Pansy's desk rang.

"That's Mrs. Walters ... your appointment," Pansy said. She kissed Doc's cheek, walked over to his desk and picked up the photograph.

"Tear it up," Doc said.

Pansy looked over her shoulder at him.

"Tear it up," he repeated.

She looked down as she began ripping it in pieces above the wastebasket.

"Bring Mrs. Walters in, Pansy."

A light drizzle came down on the roof of the Hoops Boarding House. Prudy sat on a wooden bench gazing out the window of their upstairs bedroom.

Ruby was straightening out some things in an old

trunk they took with them when they left Carbon Center. "Hey Prudy, remember this?" she asked, holding up a cracked ceramic pot.

"Do I," Prudy said.

"Come on, honey, sit by the window with me and watch the rain." Prudy stood up and reached for her sister's hand. "It's funny, you pullin' out that old crockpot. I was just thinkin' about home myself."

"What about?" Ruby asked as she sat down beside her sister.

"Do you think Ma ever knew we stole money from this?"

"We didn't steal, Prudy. Why would you say a thing like that?"

"Well, we didn't always put in all the money we earned."

"That's different. We certainly didn't take it once it was in."

As if there were a direct shortcut through time, Ruby remembered two young girls inside a tar paper shanty, as they kneeled facing one another, their hands extended in front of them. Prudy's face then looked exactly the way it did now and Ruby couldn't take her eyes off her — knowing, as only twins could — what she herself looked like by looking at her double.

Ruby almost believed that if she turned her head she

would see the woman with dark eyes, holding a dollar bill over a cracked pot, this same cracked pot that now sat between them. Ruby remembered the feeling of that time. She could almost smell the ashes in the iron stove resting on a square sheet of tin and see the empty coal bucket. She could see the old rags and paper stuffed into the unpainted wallboards. She knew the feel of having her dress tighten across her breasts and hips every time she put it on, though she was thin then as now. Don't look in the corners, she thought. Don't look at the single bed in one corner, the bunk bed in another. Pay no mind to the forgotten miner's hat under the bed, the empty brown half pints, the corks kicked into the corners. Don't look at the woman with the dollar bill. She had a nasty bruise under her eye and a cut lip. There were bruises on her arms as well. If she looked away, Ruby thought, it would all come back and she might be caught in the past. If she looked at the woman, the man who she brought home here, the man with the hard hands, might walk back in the door.

Was she remembering Carbon Center just one day, Ruby wondered — maybe the day they received the eviction notice? Or was that how it was every day before they ran away?

Prudy snapped her fingers in front of Ruby's face.

"I'm sorry, Prudy, I must have drifted off.

"Wendell wants you and me to get out of the flat-backin' business," Ruby said. "He's going to get us some real jobs when he's sheriff."

"Sounds like love to me," Prudy said.

Ruby pressed her lips together. "But there's some things that I don't find exactly ... what's the word I'm lookin' for?"

"Admirable?" Prudy said.

"That's it," Ruby said. "I don't think Doc's a good influence on Wendell."

"That's nice to know since I'm usually the one layin' down with Doc."

Ruby shook her head. "That don't count. That's for money, Sis."

"And you're not takin' any money from Wendell?"

"Hell yes, I am. Why shouldn't I? Isn't everybody just usin' each other anyway?"

"Explain that to me."

"Figure it out yourself," Ruby said.

"You said everybody; that includes me."

"It don't always have to be bad. You and me keep each other's spirits up, you know, by talkin' to each other, tellin' our deepest thoughts."

"Don't you trust Wendell?" Prudy asked.

"I don't know how far he'll go to get what he wants."

"You mean like runnin' for sheriff?"

"More like what he has to do to win," Ruby said.

Even with Aaron's help, Will was hard pressed to keep the farm running. Becky was doing what she could but she was tired a lot of the time. It couldn't go on.

With the boys gone, Will drove into town.

Honey Boy looked at the clock when Will came in. It was still early. He shrugged but said nothing. He set down a shot at Will's favorite place. Ten minutes later, Will was tapping the bar.

He looked up at Honey Boy, then back at the empty glass in front of him, turning the glass with his thumb and forefinger.

Honey Boy leaned forward across the bar. "Don't get me wrong, I enjoy your company, son. But I ain't never seen whiskey cure much of anything."

Will was silent. He had been trying all day to remember when he first knew that Becky had consumption. What about the others? Was it common knowledge — something they all talked about behind his back? He could still see the look on Grandma Kepler's face the day he asked her about Callie's sickness. She didn't have to say a word, her eyes told it all.

Now Becky was pregnant.

Will raised the glass to his mouth and emptied it. Honey Boy refilled it a third time.

Prudy came from upstairs and saw Will. She took a seat next to him and laid her hand on his. "You got any coffee made, Honey Boy?"

"Yep."

Honey Boy waited for Will to say something, but Prudy had already picked up his whiskey glass, wrapped her arm around his and was leading him over to the table. The old warrior was glad that Prudy showed up when she did.

"So how's that family of yours, Will?" Prudy asked. She smiled at Honey Boy as he set two cups in the middle of the table and walked back to the bar.

Will breathed in the smell of lilac. It was a smell he associated with the twins as far back as he could remember.

"Will?" Prudy reached across the table, taking hold of his hand.

She noticed the dark circles under his eyes.

"Becky's bad sick, ain't she?"

Will tossed down the remainder of the whiskey, then pulled one of the cups in front of him. "Prudy, Becky's not going to ..."

Prudy squeezed his hand. "You know, Will, it's not up to us to know our fate."

"She's going to have another child."

Prudy swallowed. "Does her ma know?"

"Not yet," Will said. "She says she's going to tell her at the church picnic next Sunday."

"Will, does Becky know how sick she is?"

"She talks of Callie."

He pushed his chair away from the table. "I'll be on my way."

"If there's anything Ruby and I can do, Will ..."

"You're good girls, Prudy," Will said. "Tell Ruby whatever you want, but keep it to yourselves."

Honey Boy walked over to the table and refilled Prudy's coffee cup.

"That boy has troubles," he said.

"More than you can imagine," Prudy said.

The warm spring air carried the sounds of the Krouse household as they readied themselves for Sunday morning services at the Free Methodist Church.

With the children finally ready, Becky hurried them out the front door. Will was in the wagon waiting for them.

There were beautiful red maples along the road and birds everywhere. To Becky, who'd hardly strayed from the house in a month, it all seemed wonderful.

The church was full. It was because of the spring picnic being held after the services.

Will spotted Aaron and Jacob waving to get his attention. "It looks like your mother and Professor Knobbs saved us a seat in front of them."

"Oh, good," Becky said.

Will, Becky and the children squeezed in the pew.

Then, for Will, there was a blur of talk, mixed with song. His thoughts were on Becky, who, though pregnant, seemed to him to be slipping away from him.

After the services, the men started setting up tables as the women got the food ready. They carried plates of fried chicken, homemade pies, and their favorite dishes.

Grandma Kepler tied on her starched white apron. "Let's get these men fed." She glanced over at Becky who started coughing.

"That ol' cold still hangin' on?" Grandma asked.

Before she could answer, Samuel broke in.

"Ma, I want to eat with the men."

"You and Addie will eat with your Grandma and me after we feed all the men."

Samuel looked down at the grass, sulking. "Aaron gets to eat with them."

Becky arranged another place setting, then paused and glared at Samuel. "Please quit arguing with me."

Grandma Kepler took Samuel's hand. "Come on, child, you sit next to your old Granny and hold my fan."

Samuel took the fan, spreading it out like a small accordion.

"Mother, you sure you want him to have that?"

"He ain't gonna hurt it. Are you, honey?"

Samuel fanned himself. "No, Grandma."

Grandma Kepler patted his head. "Look at all those freckles on his face."

"They'll fade away ... well at least most of them. The other boys had them and so did Will when he was little. Remember?"

"Otto used to tease him somethin' awful. I can still hear him: 'Will, do you have change for a freckle?'"

Becky lowered her head. "I miss Father."

Grandma Kepler wiped the corners of her eyes. "We all do, dear, but look at what a wonderful family you've been blessed with."

Grandma caught the look on her daughter's face. "You've got somethin' on your mind child?"

"When I was little, I never understood why the men and older boys ate first. Now I do." Becky put her hands on her hips. "It's to get them out from under our feet."

Grandma laughed. "Let's get them fed."

Becky seemed tireless. She had to demonstrate her health, her good spirits in front of all these people, especially her mother. If she didn't appear healthy, she thought, she might really get sick. Grandma Kepler waved the white flag first.

"I'm tired, Becky. Let's sit down and talk," Grandma said. She took Becky's hand, leading her over to a bench shaded by a big tree that grew against the cemetery fence. She slipped her swollen feet out of her shoes. "Look, there's a bluebird buildin' a nest in that fence pole."

"Where?"

Grandma pointed. "See? Follow the gate down."

"Yes, I see it now."

"I'll bet she's ready to lay her eggs."

"Mother, I'm going to have a baby," Becky said. She started crying.

Grandma placed her hands on Becky's stomach. "Just think, a new life. Now, now, honey, there's no reason to cry. Will must be excited."

"That's what worries me the most. Will's not himself lately."

"I imagine with it being spring and all, he's got the farm on his mind and the boys aren't really old enough to be of much help."

"It's not just that, he's worried about my cough. I've had it over four months now."

"I worry about you too, Becky. You might have walking pneumonia and if you do, you'll need bed rest or you'll lose that baby."

"Who's going to cook and clean?"

"I'll ask Molly Prater if there's a young lady in the

church that could help out."

"Mother, you know she's expecting herself."

"That doesn't make her helpless, honey."

"I can't stay in bed and let everyone wait on me."

"Everything will work out." Grandma gave Becky a squeeze. "I suppose Will would like another boy."

"He just wants it to be healthy."

Becky lifted the end of her apron and wiped her eyes. "Momma, I don't know whether to be happy or sad."

Grandma Kepler knew one thing for certain. Whenever she called her Momma, it meant her Becky was scared.

CHAPTER 6

It was a perfect day for the Penn County Fair and the clear blue sky had brought a crowd; and for Aaron's bull, Durham, a blue ribbon. Not content with one prize, the boy convinced his pa to let him enter the greased pig contest.

Wendell's campaign speech was supposed to begin at three o'clock. Will felt obliged to make an appearance, taking Aaron with him. Afterwards, the two headed home.

Will woke up as Aaron turned into the drive. The moment his eyes opened, Aaron handed him the reins and ran inside, still caked in mud to show his mother the prize he'd won. Will put the horse in the barn, fed him, and found a place for the pig in a stall they sometimes used for calves.

When he went inside, Aaron was in the kitchen stripped to his underwear, washing himself in the sink. Will made his way upstairs.

Becky was in bed. She smiled. "What a beautiful ribbon, Will."

"He's pretty proud," Will said.

"What's it say?" Samuel asked.

"First place — what do you think a blue ribbon says," Jacob said.

"Be nice, Jacob," Becky said.

Will checked on little Addie and re-tucked her in before Aaron bounded back into the bedroom.

"Will, now that you're both here," Becky said, "what's this I hear about winning a pig?"

"His name is Ham," Aaron said.

"He's in the barn," Will said. He shrugged.

"This is a runt pig or..."

"How'd you win him?" Jacob asked.

"Greased pig contest," Aaron said.

"I want a pig too," Samuel said.

"Can I go see it, Ma? Can I?" Jacob asked.

"All right, but take Samuel with you."

"Last one to the barn is a pig," Jacob said.

"Jacob, Samuel, don't be running down those stairs." Becky eyed Will.

"I better go with them," he said as he turned to follow the boys.

The back door banged shut. Aaron put his arms around his mother.

"Too late, Ma. Do you want me to tell you about the pea in the shell game?"

"You and your father weren't gambling, were you?"

"Heck no, that's not gambling. Pa told me how most everyone loses."

Becky patted her son's arm. Aaron was glad to see her smiling.

"Then Pa took me over to Mr. Gates's tent."

"And what went on there?"

"Oh, nothing, just a bunch of men smoking and drinking."

"Sounds like you two had a good time."

"It would've been a lot better if you were with us," Aaron said.

"I'll be with you at next year's fair. We'll all go together," she said.

"Do you promise, Ma?"

Becky held out her arms. Aaron leaned in and she hugged him tight. "I promise. Now go and show your brothers ..."

"Ham?" Aaron said.

"Yes, Ham."

The next evening, Will rode into town to attend a Grange meeting. Will stood looking over the crowd when Wendell walked up.

"What the hell is this all about?" Wendell asked.

"Sorry, Wendell, I don't know what you're talking about," Will said.

"Well just take a look," Wendell pointed.

"I'll be damn, she did show up," Will said.

"You know her?" Wendell asked.

"No, but the professor told me about her," Will said.

"I was goin' to give a campaign talk tonight," Wendell said.

"Maybe you should start with her," Will said.

"Doc, Doc, come here," Wendell said.

"Settle down, Wendell, I already heard about Miss Hanna Ames," Doc said.

"Damn it, she's not even a vote," Wendell said.

"No, but she's sure a looker," Doc said.

"But ..." Wendell said.

"Shhh." Doc looked over to the podium.

"Good evening, gentlemen, I'm Hanna Ames, Penn County's new veterinarian. I look forward to working with you all and I'm sure that I can learn from your experiences."

With her blonde pigtails and school girl dress, she could have easily passed for sixteen, but her figure gave her away. Examining her fine features, she could just as easily been standing on a Broadway stage instead of in a Grange hall.

"Doctor Slayer informed me that ..." Hanna scanned the group of farmers when her eyes met those of Will Krouse. Will waited for her next words. They didn't come. Instead, she smiled at him, batting her eyes.

"Wendell Gates, Missy, or Sheriff Gates," Will called out.

Hanna took a deep breath. "Thank you, sir. Yes, Doctor Slayer informed me that Sheriff Gates has a few words to share with you tonight, so if it's agreeable with you folks, I'll save what I had for another time," Hanna said.

"Let's give our new vet a hardy round of applause," Wendell said.

About an hour later, the meeting wrapped up. Will woke out of some deep dream that had to do with the spring under the rocks. The cow was giving birth again, but Will couldn't find it. He was trying to make some sense out of it when he heard Wendell announce that drinks were on him at Honey Boy's.

On his way out, Wendell spotted Will. "You comin'

with us?"

"No, Wendell, I'm heading home."

Wendell stopped for a second and watched Will walk away. He appeared a little worn, Wendell noticed. He saw Doc looking too.

"He's about as useful as teats on a bull," Doc grinned. "But he is a vote."

Honey Boy noticed some of the regulars trickling in. If someone had told him that there was a political meeting tonight and his customers would be late, he'd have forgotten immediately. Honey Boy was a barkeep at the moment. He only cared about getting everyone served.

Wendell paused just inside the door of the crowded saloon and stretched up on his toes. He noticed Ruby and Prudy at the table in the corner.

Wendell tapped Doc's shoulder and pointed. "There's the girls."

Wendell put his fist over his mouth, muffling a belch, then grabbed a chair. "You girls been here long?"

"First drink, Sheriff," Ruby said.

Wendell smiled at her.

"Well, that's what folks are callin' you," Ruby said.

Honey Boy set down another round of whiskeys.

"Was Will with you fellas?" Ruby said.

"He was, now he ain't," Doc said.

"Is he comin' back?" Prudy asked.

"No, he had to go home to his precious wife," Doc said.

"Probably what you would like to be doing, eh Doc?" Prudy giggled.

Ruby kicked her sister under the table.

"You little ..." Doc said.

"Easy, Doc," Wendell interrupted.

"Let's not get into a name callin' contest so early in the evenin'," Prudy said. "Besides, it ain't exactly a secret you still have an eye for Becky. Heck, I'll bet you wish it was Will who was sick."

"That's enough, Sis. Let's talk about something else."

"Hell, let her talk, nobody listens to her anyway." Doc glared at Prudy. "Now that I think of it, maybe Will is a little sick ... in the head."

"What are you talking about?" Ruby asked.

"I hear he's not sleeping too good these days. He's been wandering around a lot," Doc said.

"Who told you that?" Ruby asked.

"He told me himself."

"I don't believe you," Ruby said.

"Which is it you don't believe, that he didn't tell me, or that he can't sleep?"

"Even if he did tell you, I'm sure he didn't want you

to blab it to the world," Ruby said. "Don't you doctors have some sort of rules about keepin' your trap shut?"

Prudy downed her glass of whiskey. She wet her lips and leaned toward Wendell. "Doc's always been jealous of Will. He thought Becky might change her mind once she went away to college. Well, he was wrong."

Prudy turned to Doc. "Did you think Becky'd end up marryin' you just because you became a doctor?" she asked.

Doc looked up at her. "What?"

"Becky's always been in love with Will," Prudy said. "The only way you'd ever have a chance with her would be if Will was dead."

"Good Lord, don't talk like that, Sis," Ruby said.

"Dead, huh?" Doc said.

Didn't the whores ever shut up? Should Will be killed? No, that would be too good for him. Torture would be better. Wasn't that what he'd done to me over the last ten years? Becky should have been mine. The crazy bastard should be locked up.

"Wake up, Doc," Honey Boy said, leaning over Doc's shoulder, lowering the tray of whiskeys.

Doc jerked back in his chair and wiped the beads of sweat off his forehead.

"Hey Wendell, how's my appointment out at Long Pointe coming along?" Doc asked.

Will went to bed early but woke up at two in the morning and lay in bed, wide awake for hours thinking and listening to Becky's breathing. Not long after four, he got out of bed. He did the chores, not rushing, and when he heard the voices of the kids and Becky in the kitchen, he had already hitched up the Belgians. He went straight to the field without coffee.

By noon he had managed to half dislodge a huge fieldstone not far from where his father was buried. Now he was feeling too hungry to go on digging in the heat of the day. He went back to the barn.

He unyoked the Belgians and, without thinking, hitched the horse to the buggy. He had no plans, no obligations. In fact, there was a great deal to be done here, and Becky needed all sorts of attention.

Walking to the house, he persuaded himself that he had things all backwards. He was tired and hungry. He wasn't thinking clearly, and if he'd hitched up the horse, he must have a reason to be going somewhere.

"Good afternoon," he said, coming through the door. There wasn't a sound. Becky must be napping. The boys? ... who knew? Will found a leftover drumstick and a couple of slices of stale bread.

Wire, he thought. I need a new roll of wire. Maybe I ought to stop by Grandma's, see how everything is.

When Will arrived, he lingered, barely leaving the kitchen doorway while he talked and drank a cup of coffee. Will waited for Grandma to bring up Becky. She didn't. There was no point in it.

Will rode into town then, and went by the general store. He picked up the smallest spool of wire possible and a paper bag of wire nails. He bought a newspaper. Passing Doc's, he noticed Hayward Kurtz's rig there. Will scratched his head, trying to figure it out. He drifted down to Honey Boy's early. There was very little he could make sense of these days.

Three or four whiskeys later, Will settled up and took a back road home. It was nighttime, so he put his mare in a slow gait along the old road, which was full of ruts and washouts.

Doc passed Will in the moonlight. Talk about intuition. Not two nights ago, he'd told someone that Will was wandering a lot. Now, lo and behold, here he was riding down a road far from home, hours after sunset. Will was crazy all right.

Halfway out, Will brought the mare to a rest. What a thing that would be, Will thought. To escape, to leave the past behind. But some people, maybe all people, seemed to be followed by trouble they couldn't shake off. Wendell could trick himself out like a regular politician, but he was just a railroader at heart. The twins hadn't been able to leave Carbon Center behind either. They could lose the gloominess of their childhoods, and yet Carbon Center was in everything they did. And Will was just one of the Krouses, a farmer.

Sometimes it seemed like fate was contagious. Will was about Aaron's age when his mother died. He could scarcely remember his own childhood. It had all toppled one day when his grandfather came downstairs from the bedroom, his eyes bright red, and took Will aside to tell him that his Ma had gone to be with his Pa. Will, thinking about his children and fearful of the worst, imagined it happening again. As if there was some sort of curse on the family.

CHAPTER 7

At some point, hard as it seems, most of us will have to think the unthinkable. How to face life after tragedy. We will sit in a room waiting for someone to die, knowing that whatever happens we still have to fix supper for the kids. And we will wonder if there is enough milk. Many of us will wait in dread for news to arrive — news that will break our hearts — but in the meantime, we need to shave and get dressed and go to work.

Without self-consciousness, Will started to think about how to raise his kids by himself. What he knew for certain was that there would have to be women involved, somehow. His own Grandma was very good to him after his mother died but she wasn't enough.

Will started taking Aaron along with him on his trips to Grandma's. He also drove into town and brought Mildred to his place for a visit. He offered the use of his wagon to the twins.

Honey Boy felt Hattie come through the door that night. He was relieved to see her. She looked spry as always — a little too spry. There was trouble on her mind. She was pretty, but all the girls who worked for Honey Boy were pretty. She wasn't the brightest or funniest. The twins were that. If only he hadn't been forty years older than she was. What interested him most about Hattie was that she was all mystery. One could never really tell what she was thinking.

"Hattie, I need a word with you," Honey Boy said.

He went up the stairs and stopped at the cubbyhole where he kept his desk.

"Did I do something?" Hattie asked.

"This ain't directly about you," Honey Boy said. "Your pa and brother came by to say they're raising their prices."

"Are they gone?" Her voice was almost inaudible.

"Yep," Honey Boy said. "They was roarin' drunk and said they was gonna look you up." He paused. "I told 'em that I wouldn't pay any more than I am. After all, fair's fair."

"I don't know anything about their business deals," Hattie said.

"I've always been good to you and your little sister, ain't I?"

"Yes, you've been real good to us."

"Then you sure you want to quit working upstairs?"

"I want to try. Stella's got her a pretty good job out at Long Pointe..."

"I caught wind that Doc's still visitin' you. But it seems I ain't seen none of that."

Hattie hesitated. "I weren't goin' to take care of him, but he said he'd pay me extra. I didn't mean to go behind your back."

"Then what's this I hear about Hayward Kurtz?"

"I swear, Honey Boy, it's just those two. Doc for the money and Hayward's made me some promises."

"What kind of promises?"

"He told me he would watch out for Stella at Long Pointe."

"That don't sound like Kurtz to me."

"Well ... he said he could cause Stella a lot of shit out at that crazy house if I didn't fuck him."

"That sounds more like the bastard I know."

"Honey Boy, I intended on giving you your share. Here, take this." She took a coin purse from her pocket.

"Put that away, Hattie, you don't owe me nothin'. You're family. I told you, you got a home here any time. You may want to stay here tonight with Buck and your Pa on the prowl."

Hattie lowered her eyes. "Thanks, Honey Boy."

Honey Boy cocked his ear toward the staircase and pulled himself to his feet. "Let's go get them customers watered, Hattie."

Doc yawned and poured himself another drink. It must have gotten late. He'd needed his solitude and stayed away from Honey Boy's that night.

He dozed a little and then realized he had been hearing a pecking sound on the outside door. He pulled his jacket from the coat hook and slipped it on as he walked up front.

"Open up, it's raining."

He squinted, trying to peer through the leaded glass. No sooner had he lifted the latch than Hattie barged in.

"What the hell you think you're doing here? It's almost midnight," Doc said.

"It's only ten o'clock," Hattie said.

Water dripped all over the floor as she took off her hat. She was breathing heavily. "Aren't you goin' to help me with my wrap?"

"I'm not going to do anything until you tell me why

you're here at this time of night."

"I have to talk to you," she said, shoving her coat at him.

"Are you sick?"

"No, I'm pregnant."

Doc walked into his back office and sat down at his desk.

"Sit." He leaned back in his chair, staring at her over his spectacles. "And whose is it?"

"Yours."

He laughed. "You must be a little addle-brained. Then, of course, maybe you're just outright crazy. Besides, how would you know whose it is, Hattie? You're a whore."

"It's yours all right." Hattie shifted in her seat. "Then again, it could be Kurtz's. But it ain't."

"Who else is on the list?"

"Nobody," she said.

"Does Kurtz know?"

"No."

"You shouldn't have this baby."

"I knew you'd say that, you bein' a doctor and all. I even thought that maybe you'd fix it so I wouldn't be pregnant. But I wouldn't ask you, you bein' the father."

"So that's what this is all about?" Doc asked.

She hadn't really planned this conversation and realized she didn't have all the answers. "I don't know what to do," she said.

He was moved, her thinking of him in a time of need. He got up and stepped out from behind the desk. She leaned toward him. "I'm sure we can work something out," he said, feeling her breast. "Why don't you stay a while?" He was already undoing the buttons on the back of her dress. "...Since you made the trip."

She started to pull away.

"I have cash," he said.

It was after midnight when Hattie finally left on foot. He'd insisted. Once she was gone, Doc went to the file cabinet that held all the patients' records. Kurtz was a patient Doc inherited from his father. He'd looked at his record once, when Kurtz came in with an infection. He vaguely remembered his father mentioning something.

The records went back decades on yellowing paper, his father's old-fashioned handwriting, full of curlicues. He could still read the old man's notes: *Orchitis — Bilateral Infection of Testicles > Sterility.*

There were some additional comments written on the back of one of the papers: *Patient advised to bed rest / Patient ignored Dr's orders.*

"That's Kurtz, all right," Doc said.

Pulling the rest of the file out, he carried it over to the desk. His half-smoked cigar sat in the ashtray. Doc thought for a moment as he laid the papers down and tapped the dead ash off the stub. He clenched the stogie between his teeth. Ripping the papers into small pieces, he pulled a matchstick from the desk drawer and struck it with his thumbnail. The flame burned brighter with every puff until the cigar glowed. He tossed the papers into the ashtray and touched the match to them. Kurtz's affliction shot up in flames, then crumbled to ashes.

Doc opened one of the side drawers in his desk and felt around for the half pint bottle he kept there. He leaned back, uncorked the bottle and took a long pull. He swallowed, then wiped at some that dribbled on his chin.

His eyes opened briefly, as the empty bottle dropped from his hand onto the hardwood floor.

Hattie woke up the next morning, still in her petticoats. Like other recent mornings, it was the sickness that woke her. She threw on a robe and ran to the outhouse and vomited and then rested and threw up again. She hadn't had much to eat for several days and it was a futile exercise. Except that when she was done, she felt she had gotten a little of Doc out of her system.

She went back in, washed her face and sat on the bed until she was better. She drew all the blinds in her room. She took off her robe, then her petticoats. She still felt exposed, so she put the robe on again and dragged a chair over to the mirror on the wall. It wasn't a very big mirror and it had been hung too high for Hattie who wasn't much over five feet tall. She stood on the chair and examined herself. This wasn't how she imagined she'd feel. Other women had baby after baby, and each one was a joy, and a blessing, and hope for the future. Hattie was filled with sadness at the thought of this potential new life.

She rested another half hour and then got up, rummaged through a drawer and found paper, pen and ink. She didn't like to write letters. It didn't come easily to her. Nevertheless, she needed to write Stella. She didn't mention Kurtz or Doc. She just said she was pregnant and that the father didn't want her to keep the child but that she thought she might. Hattie jotted a P.S.: *Don't worry about me, Sis. I got my lucky two-headed match.*

She knew what Stella would say. Stella had made peace with her place in the world. Stella would tell her that nobody Hattie was likely to sleep with — not Doc, Kurtz, or anyone acceptable — was likely to marry a girl from Beaver Hollow. She picked up the match box she lifted from Doc's office and read out loud, "Gas Light Club, Chicago. Dancing girls, come visit them."

An hour or so later, Doc rode back into town. He left his horse at the stable and walked to Honey Boy's without stopping to wash up. There was a crowd there, spilling over from the victory party.

Prudy stepped in front of Doc as he came in the door. "Why haven't you been to see Becky? You know she needs a doctor."

"To be honest, I think of her all the time," Doc said. "But I'm not God you know. I'm just a simple country doctor. Now get your ass out of my way."

Prudy stormed off.

"Over here, Doc," Wendell waved.

Doc made his way over to Wendell's table.

"How about something to eat?" Wendell asked.

"What's that on your plate?" Doc asked.

"Pork loin."

Wendell motioned to Honey Boy and pointed to his plate. "Bring Doc the same," Wendell said.

"Comin' up," Honey Boy said.

"So does victory taste sweet, Wendell?"

Honey Boy set a plate in front of Doc and went back to the bar.

"Sometimes I wonder what this is all about, Doc."

"It's about you and me having this good dinner together."

"And that's it?"

Doc started cutting the pork loin into small squares. He had Wendell in his pocket. What else was there for him to say?

Wendell slid his empty plate to the center of the table. "I got you that board appointment, Doc."

"Thanks, Sheriff. Guess you were saving the good news for last, huh?"

Sheriff Gates already disliked his new job.

On the second floor of the ivy-covered institution, Doctor Steinberg stood beside the model of a human skeleton. In his thick hand was a wooden pointer, its rubber tip resting on the skeleton's lower vertebra. He looked toward the only female student in the classroom of twenty. She had her hand raised. The rosy-cheeked professor peered over his spectacles acknowledging her, his expression stoic. The other students looked toward the model that dangled from its metal rod. Sitting at a desk in the back of the classroom, a young man in a starched white collar and bow tie looked down at a page in his medical book. On a paper tucked discreetly inside was an entry from his diary: Friday, March 13th, 1905. Doctor Slayer Jr. examined Becky Kepler today. He used his new office procedure. Instead of Miss Kepler disrobing behind the examining room curtain, she took her clothes off one piece at a time as I looked on – just like she did when I watched her through my peep hole in father's office. I was thirteen. It felt so good back then, but it will feel so much better with her watching me. I promise.

Will looked at his Belgians. Their manes were tangled and caked with mud. Bare corn cobs were strewn about the barn. The blades on his own windmill stood frozen despite the strong breeze coming out of the south. He had promised to help Professor Knobbs with Grandma's windmill. It was an excuse to get away. Becky needed someone with her all the time now. Mildred volunteered, so Will rode off. When he arrived, he and the Professor took the new part out of the box and replaced a broken cog on a main wheel.

With no excuse for staying, Will walked into the kitchen to tell Grandma goodbye. It smelled the way his own kitchen smelled when Becky was able to cook. He had nothing to chat about. None of them did.

Riding home, Will knew he could count on Grandma Kepler. Crossing Sugar Creek on his horse, he felt a lump in his throat and swallowed, then licked his dry lips. He stopped to sit under the old willow at the foot of the covered bridge.

His life was crumbling all around him. He couldn't sort things out. Becky had consumption. All the signs were there, coughing up blood and labored breathing. He didn't even notice the tears gathering in his hands.

The water swirled beneath the bridge. He watched a small tree branch caught up in the water's circular motion. The current wouldn't release it, nor would the small twig go under. He lowered his head and ran his fingers through his hair. If only he knew the answer. His family depended on him, but no one could help him. He came to the same conclusion each time. He would have to take his family to Grandma Kepler's place. He was losing them and his farm. He knew he had to pull himself together, but how?

The lace curtains blew back when Mildred raised the bedroom window.

"I'd be able to come more often if you were staying at your mother's place." She wiped her hands on the dishtowel she was holding and turned to Becky. "Are you asleep, dear?"

"No, I'm just resting my eyes," Becky said.

Mildred sat down in the rocker next to the bed. "Can I get you something?"

Becky began coughing. Mildred poured a glass of water from the pitcher and handed it to her. Becky took a sip. She was having trouble talking today.

"I've been wanting to ask you, Mildred ...," she said. "It's a secret."

Mildred swiped her finger in an 'X' over her breast. "Cross my heart."

"If I die, I'd like for you to raise my baby."

"Becky, stop that kind of talk," Mildred said.

"Please listen, Mildred. Will can't keep this place going and raise the children by himself. He's worried sick."

"You're not going to die," Mildred said, not wanting to discuss what she couldn't imagine.

Becky froze her with a stare.

"What does Will want?" Mildred asked.

"He thinks the same as you do, that I should go to my mother's and take them with me. I still think it's too much for them. My ma is getting old."

"Why me?"

"You always wanted a baby. Don't you still feel the same way?" Becky asked.

"You know I do, but ..."

Mildred felt it was disloyal to talk like this. She would have been the first to say that she was being superstitious, but she was afraid that making plans for Becky dying would doom her friend.

Becky rummaged under the covers and pulled out an envelope. "These are my wishes," she said. "All written down. You hang on to this. It's even been witnessed. Keep it safe; keep it secret."

"Becky, how can I?"

"Promise that you won't even tell Wendell. Put the envelope in your purse before you get it all wet."

Mildred dabbed her eyes. "You're a much stronger

person than me."

"I'm not, Millie. But I know what my family needs."

"What if me and Wendell don't stay together?"

"Then you go to my mother's and you help each other out." Becky had said her peace. She started coughing. When she heard the door open downstairs, she tried to quiet herself. It wasn't necessary; the man coming upstairs was determined not to hear.

"Anyone home?" Will shouted as he walked up the stairs, pausing in the doorway.

"We're upstairs, Will," Becky said.

Will came into the room. "Mildred, you're staying for supper, aren't you?"

"No, but you and the children's plates are keeping warm on top of the stove. All I need is a ride back home," Mildred said.

"Aaron will carry you back. You go ahead and get your things together while I hunt down Aaron and his brothers. Where's Addie?"

"Sound asleep," Mildred said.

"I appreciate you cooking for us, Mildred," Will said.

Mildred kissed Becky's cheek.

Becky lay back against her pillow and closed her eyes. Within a couple of minutes, she was fast asleep.

Mildred watched the quilt rise and fall in rhythm with her breath. Before she walked down the stairs, she checked to make sure the envelope was still in her handbag. Her hands trembled as she latched it.

CHAPTER 8

Throughout the night, Becky tossed and turned. She didn't hear the usual sounds of the crickets and the occasional bobwhite calling out for his mate, only Will's footsteps as he paced the floor. On his feet, he was half asleep but his body, mind, and spirit quarreled, one pointing him one way, one pointing him another.

Becky worried about their children and the unborn baby that made her aware of its presence with an occasional kick.

She must have fallen asleep towards morning, because it seemed in no time that the sun was up. She wiped the sleep and the traces of tears from her eyes.

Something woke her. She heard faint voices coming from the bottom of the staircase.

"Go on up, girls, she'll be happy to see you."

"You sure, Will?" Ruby asked.

"Positive."

Will rubbed the coarse stubble on his chin and opened his mouth as if to speak.

Prudy gave him a hug. "Are you all right?" she asked.

"I'm fine."

"It's quiet. Are the kids asleep?" Ruby asked.

"They're over at Grandma's."

"Who's there, Will?" Becky's voice came from upstairs.

"Go on up," Will said, "before she comes down."

Ruby reached up to push Will's hair out his eyes. "You do whatever you need to do. Prudy and me are gonna sit with Becky for a while."

Will's hand shook as he patted her shoulder. "I'll be out in the barn."

The twins made their way upstairs to the bedroom. They popped in through the open door. They plumped pillows, found a vase, stuck in some wildflowers they'd picked along the way, chattered, made jokes, trying to make Becky comfortable.

She was perspiring. Prudy blotted her forehead with

a damp cloth.

"Has Doc Slayer been here yet?" Prudy asked.

"No. Will wants him to, but ..." Becky hesitated. "I'm sure I know what's ailing me. So is Will."

"Oh, Becky," Prudy said.

"I worry about my family and pray that I'll live to see my baby," Becky said.

"Don't talk that way," Prudy said.

"Let her have her say, Sis," Ruby said.

"Did you girls get a good look at Will?"

"Yes," they answered.

"It's not like Will to give up. He doesn't even comb his hair."

"He ..." Ruby started.

Becky interrupted. "He's worried himself sick. He can't sleep nights and walks the floor. He's giving up, not only on me, but on himself."

Ruby turned the cool washcloth over, placing it on Becky's forehead. "Becky honey, you're his whole life."

"Will's always been there for everyone else," Becky said.

"Becky, not everyone that gets consumption dies," Ruby said.

"She's right. Our Momma didn't," Prudy said.

"No, maybe not everyone — just ..." Becky sobbed.

"Don't you go givin' up, Becky," Ruby said.

"I can't ... my baby. It's due in a couple months. Will wants us to go to my mother's."

"What do you want?" Ruby asked.

"I want you girls to talk to Will before he has a complete breakdown."

"What could we say?" Prudy asked.

"For starters, tell him he looks like hell."

"Becky," Prudy said.

"You know how men are. Sometimes they just need to get their feelings out, but they don't know how. Maybe you girls can take a little extra time to listen to him when he stops in at Honey Boy's," Becky said. "I know Will still likes to take a drink with the old bunch every now and then."

Ruby nodded. "You can ..."

"Count on us," Prudy finished.

Becky held out her arms as they both climbed up on the bed to give her a hug. The door closed downstairs and the girls seized the opportunity to take their leave. Becky lay alone. She couldn't remember what it felt like to feel strong. From downstairs, she could hear their voices.

"Will Krouse, you look like hell," Ruby said.

"Comb your hair and get a shave," Prudy added.

Becky convinced Will to keep Aaron home from school for the next few days. The boy was good company for him.

Aaron was helping Will carry the cans of fresh milk to the milk house to be cooled when he spotted a buggy pulling up. He shouted for his pa. Will put his hand over his eyes to shade the morning sun. It was Cecil.

They walked over to the buggy.

Cecil smiled and reached out to tousle Aaron's hair. "He's twice the size since I last saw him, Will."

"I was ten then, Uncle Cecil," Aaron said. "You ain't been out here since last summer."

"What brings you by, Cecil?"

"Since when do I need an excuse to see my little brother and his family?" Cecil asked.

"Have you had breakfast yet?" Will asked.

"Yep, it's almost eight o'clock," Cecil said, glancing up at the angle of the sun. He looked at Aaron, then turned to Will. "I was hoping maybe you and me could talk in private."

Will looked at Aaron. Something filled him with misgivings. "You put the rest of the cows out to pasture, Aaron," he said.

The boy hesitated.

"Go on now," Will said.

Aaron walked away. If he was doing a man's chores, why shouldn't he be able to sit in on the men's business?

"You want to go up to the house and talk?" Will

asked.

"No, no, let's just stay outside."

Will led Cecil over to the milk house and they sat down on a bench.

"Will, there's a lot of talk that Becky's pretty sick and that you've not been takin' too good care of yourself."

Will looked away, then jammed his hands in his over-all pockets.

"Here's the long and short of it," Cecil said. "You know Minnie would be more than happy to look after your little Adeline and your boys could help out around my place. My boys and me will take care of your herd. It looks like Aaron's already a big help to you. Does he run a team yet?"

Will didn't answer.

"What do you say?" Cecil slapped him on the arm.

Will glanced at his brother. "You caught me off guard, Cecil."

"Be honest with yourself, Will, you can't take care of Addie and Samuel without Becky. Jacob's still too young himself to be any real help. Then take Becky, from what I hear, she needs doctoring. Ain't that so? You're going to have to make some decisions here, Will. Besides, if you can't depend on your big brother, then who can you depend on?"

Will shook his head. In the past, his big brother's

help had usually been to his big brother's advantage. "I want to keep my family together."

"They will be. I got plenty of room at my place. My sons are pretty near full-grown. They both do a man's work. You just see that Becky gets taken care of and let me worry about the rest."

"I don't know, Cecil. We've pretty much decided that Becky and the kids are going over to Grandma Kepler's place," Will said.

"She's no spring chicken, Will," Cecil said. "And Grandma doesn't need that put on her."

"Mildred Gates is going to stay with her too," Will said.

"Have it your way, Will," Cecil said. "My door's always open. But the other part of the equation is that you can't run this place alone so long as Becky is ... so long as she's sick. You're going to need some help and ain't that what family's for?"

"And don't think that I don't appreciate it," Will said. He tilted his head back and gazed at the gray clouds moving in from the west. He didn't expect the other shoe to drop so quickly. When he looked back at Cecil, he had already pulled a thick bundle of papers out of his pocket.

"One other thing. My attorney told me that I'm going to need your Power of Attorney to manage your farm ... you know, to buy and sell the milk and the crops. Naturally, I'll keep your records separate from mine, but I'll get back to you on all the details. You look these over." He laid the papers on the bench next to Will and got up.

Will watched Cecil pull away. When had he agreed to give everything to Cecil? Would Cecil do him wrong?

"Pa, I don't want to go to Uncle Cecil's and Aunt Minnie's."

Will turned. Aaron was at the corner of the milk house, the boy had been waiting for his uncle to leave.

Will put his arm around him. "Let's move these milk cans inside, son."

When the day came, Will had just enough of his wits about him that he knew how to prepare for it.

He gazed at the orange glow of the morning sun creeping over the edge of the field. It wasn't the same sunrise he had always looked forward to in the past. He turned away from the window and paced the kitchen floor.

Lord, what's become of me? he asked himself. His whole life, Cecil had never really been there for him, but what choice did he have now? Otto's fatal heart attack and Callie's final days raced through his mind. The twins once told him how scared they were when they said their goodbyes to their ma. They had no choice. Did you have to be young and foolish to resist the current?

Will walked to the back door and opened it just as the rooster began crowing. The familiar sound of a new day. But it was not an ordinary day. He breathed in the cool morning air and looked out over his fields. His body shivered. Something near the barn caught his attention. A red-tailed hawk roosted on his plow. Will waved his arms and the hawk soared upward, high into the sky, as if it knew something.

He turned just as Becky's arms reached around his chest.

"My, but don't you look handsome this morning." She rubbed his smooth cheeks and sniffed his neck. His hair was parted down the middle and slicked back. Before she could reach up to run her fingers through it, Will made a move for his comb.

Becky smiled. "You won't need that, dear."

The darkness around his eyes was even more prominent now.

"Are you going somewhere, dear?" Becky asked.

"After Doc Slayer leaves, I'm taking you and the children to your mother's."

Will rubbed her belly.

"She'll be able ..." He stopped himself, his voice unsteady.

The silence sounded like a death sentence. He had just told her he was surrendering.

"But Will ..."

"I'm going to tell Aaron and Jacob while they're doing their chores."

"I'm just so happy to see you so ..."

"Me too," he said.

Of all people, Doc thought as he read the note left tacked to his door sometime during the night. The Reverend Prater, bringing the message. He'd visited the Krouses the night before, forced Will down on his knees to pray, and got his permission. Will and Becky had finally agreed that they needed to know for sure.

It struck Doc as funny because, of all people who might have left the note, the pastor was the least likely to understand the real situation. The pastor didn't know what Doc had given up to come back to Hampton for Becky Kepler, or how much tolerance he'd shown Will, even when Will managed to provoke him. Nor would the pastor ever understand how much restraint Doc had shown in acknowledging that he did still desire Becky, after all of these years, these children, these mistakes. What were they all expecting of him, bringing him in during this - the last act?

Doc closed his eyes for a moment. "You may have been with Will all this time, but you were mine at the very end." His mouth watered as he envisioned her laying helpless in her nightgown. He reached into his vest pocket, making sure he had the small vial.

He brought his mare to a halt in front of the Krouse place. He spotted Will coming toward him, putting his watch back in his pocket.

"I thought you'd come sooner," Will said.

"You didn't give me much notice," Doc said. He'd learned a long time ago the professional manner of responding to hostility with calmness. He grabbed his black bag and followed Will up the porch steps.

Will opened the front door. "She's upstairs," he pointed. "I'll be down here in the parlor."

Doc took off his derby and started up the stairs. He stopped halfway and turned back toward the kitchen when Will was out of sight. Taking a cup, he poured himself some coffee from the pot on the stove, then quickly dumped the contents of the vial into the coffee pot. He walked back to the staircase.

"What took you so long?" a voice called down at him.

Mildred Gates stood at the top with her hands on her hips.

"Sounds like you should have sent word a few months ago," Doc mumbled as he paused beside her.

Mildred started to speak but her eyes welled up. Doc had the routine down pat. "You wait downstairs with Will," he said. "She needs as few distractions as possible."

Mildred pointed at the closed door, then noticed the cup in his hand. "Is that coffee?"

"No, water."

"Wouldn't you rather have some coffee, Doc?" Mildred asked. "I was just about to get Will some."

"No thanks, Millie, you go on and take care of Will. If I need you, I'll give a holler." He waited until she started down the stairs. "What would farmers do without their coffee?"

Halfway down, Mildred turned back when she heard the bedroom door close.

The curtains were drawn and Becky was lying in semidarkness. He wasn't sure she was awake. He could see the outline of her body beneath the covers. Will's child. A pity.

"Can you sit up for me, Becky?" Doc asked, pulling a chair next to the bed. His hands trembled a little as he opened his bag. He laid his stethoscope on the bedside table next to the pitcher, then slid a thermometer from its case and gave it a couple of shakes. "Open that pretty mouth of yours so I can slip this in." He pressed his finger hard on her bottom lip and put the thermometer in her mouth. She winced. Her lips were as full and lovely as ever. Doc faltered, looking deep into her eyes. He took the damp cloth and bathed her brow. His fingers brushed the sides of her breasts as he adjusted the covers around her. He noticed that her breasts had started to swell. They were curved and full and it was his medical opinion, that they were very enticing.

Becky caught his stare. He waited a moment and then removed the thermometer.

"Do I have a fever?" Becky uttered.

"Not much." He pulled the cover down and squeezed her breast. "These seem to be full of milk. It looks as though your nipples are leaking a little but don't worry, I'll rub some salve on them to keep them nice and soft."

"Stop that, you're hurting me," she said.

Doc poured some alcohol onto a piece of gauze and wiped the thin glass tube before placing it back in its case.

"Be still, Becky, I want to take your pulse." He took her arm and placed his finger on her thin wrist. "Hmmm," he murmured. "Your temperature is slightly higher than normal."

She scooted back further against her pillow. "Are you finished?" she asked.

"Don't be difficult, Becky," Doc said. "How labored is your breathing?"

"Very," she said.

"When you cough, is there ever any blood?" Doc asked, taking the vial from his bag.

She nodded.

"Open up." He placed a spoon between her lips. "Swallow," Doc said.

The liquid soothed her throat as it ran down.

"Are you feeling any discomfort in your chest or ribs when you breathe?"

"Sometimes," she said.

"How's your appetite?"

"Fair, I guess."

Becky watched him take the stethoscope from the table. She pulled the covers back up to her neck and sunk down in the bed.

"Come now," Doc said. "Let loose the covers, I have to listen to your heart and lungs. I am your doctor, Becky."

Shifting back up, she lowered the blanket.

"I need you to untie that pretty ribbon on your gown."

Her fingers fumbled for the bow. She closed her eyes and pulled the ends loose. Were her thoughts running away on her?

"Be still," Doc said. He lowered her gown off her shoulders, placing the stethoscope between her breasts.

She flinched as the cold metal touched her skin.

"You know, Becky, this isn't the first time I've looked at these sexy tits," Doc said. "Thanks to good ol' dad and a small peephole in his office. Of course they were smaller then, but at thirteen what could you expect? I wanted to play with them that day and ever since."

She was now caught up in a nightmare. One in which she couldn't scream out. Her body was petrified. Trapped in darkness, she could hear Doc's words, but she couldn't see him. She was helpless.

"See, it's all your fault, with your tempting, teasing, and tormenting ... all these years." Doc pulled the covers down further.

She felt his mouth on her breast, his hands exploring her body. His voice echoed. "Your doctor is going to give you a good fuck. Ain't that what you been waiting for?"

He held onto her chin and nodded her head.

"Okay dear, but be patient. We have to play first."

Tears welled in Becky's eyes. Please, oh, please, let this end.

"Look dear, tears of joy from those beautiful eyes of yours. Can you feel the wetness on your warm thighs?"

Doc pushed her legs apart. "Time's up," he said as he unbuttoned the fly of his trousers. "Here's what you've been wanting, bitch."

The bedroom filled with Becky's screams. Doc's manhood went limp as her shrill cry rang into his ears. He reached down trying desperately to bring his hardness back. He failed.

Mildred heard the first scream. The bowl of snap green beans flew from her lap. Will was jarred awake by Becky's second scream. He was groggy and scared at the same time. He felt Mildred slapping his face while she grabbed his shirt collar, shaking him.

"Will, what's wrong with you? Get up," she screamed.

He pushed her aside and ran upstairs, skipping every other step.

He grabbed the doorknob and pushed. His hand slipped off the locked door. He stepped back and kicked the door in. His eyes seemed to take in everything at the same time. Becky lay passed out and half-naked on the bed. Doc was straddling her when Will's knuckles smashed his nose, knocking off his spectacles. First came the sound of the crack, sounding like a chicken leg being snapped from its thigh, then Doc's blood splattering on Will's face.

"You no good bastard." Will hit him again and again.

Doc crossed his arms over his face, bawling out in rhythm with the blows. Will held him up, beating Doc unconscious before letting him fall. A loud cry rang out as Will's boot landed on Doc's side.

"You're going to kill him, Will," Mildred yelled.

"Yes I am going to kill the son-of-a-bitch."

"No, Will, don't do it." She came up behind him and threw her arms around his neck. Her feet lifted off the floor as he bent over to grab Doc. "Stop it, Will," she screamed in his ear.

Becky came to at Doc's first cry. She was still exposed. Her mouth hung open, her hands over her breasts.

It all happened in less than a few minutes. But in that short time, the course of their lives — all of their lives — had changed.

Doc pushed himself up from the floor. He was covered in his own blood. He stumbled to his feet, grabbing a pillowcase to wipe his face. Will watched his every move. He wanted to go after him again as much as he wanted to hold Becky, but he was paralyzed.

Doc stumbled to the doorway and, holding the rail, moved to the stairs. He started down them, the sound of his feet irregular and jarring as if a heavy trunk were falling downstairs. Something snapped in Will's head. He started to go after Doc. Mildred threw herself in front of him as the front door slammed. By the time Will pulled free and got downstairs he could hear the galloping of Doc's horse.

CHAPTER 9

For all of the arrogant presumption of his father, all of his desire to control, it seemed as though his hand was reaching up from the grave still trying to make Doc something he wasn't. Earl Jr. had to concede one good thing had come from it. The old man had installed Pansy as his devoted assistant in an apartment upstairs from his office.

He bellowed for her as he dismounted from his horse.

She found him sitting in his swivel chair, blood all down the front of him, a small mirror propped on his desk. He was snapping the cartilage back into place. She stood in the doorway and watched him. He was in too much pain to know what he was doing. He apparently succeeded because he grunted and slumped back in the chair half-conscious.

She went to the sink, pumped some water into a shallow pan, gathered cloths, cotton, alcohol and tape and went back into his office. She made the best she could of him.

Within a couple of hours — Pansy knew better than to intercede — he was on his feet again. He looked like one of the walking dead, both his eyes were beginning to blacken and though she'd done everything possible to make her bandaging look dignified, the tape over Doc's swollen nose looked like a bridle. His face looked like a raccoon's.

Wendell jumped out of his seat when Doc burst through the door of the Sheriff's office.

"What the hell happened to your nose?" Wendell asked.

"Forget my nose. I want that son-of-a-bitch arrested," Doc yelled. He demanded a warrant for assault, telling Wendell that Will was crazy.

In the cooler part of Doc's mind — the part that was always just a little above the fray, studying people, analyzing the situation, figuring out what had to be done — he knew that this was the only simple way out. The notion that the doctor might be in bed with a pregnant dying woman was unbelievable on the face of it. Nobody would give the idea any credence.

Wendell got on the phone, trying to find Judge Beamer without success. Judge Beamer would have to issue the warrant. Then the two of them repaired to Honey Boy's.

When Wendell arrived home that night, late, there was a light in the parlor. He saw Mildred peeking through the curtains.

He opened the door. He knew why Mildred had come home.

She glanced up at him from her rocking chair as he walked in the room. He sat down and waited for her to speak.

"I guess you already talked to Doc today," she said.

"Why's that?"

"Weren't you at Honey Boy's?"

"I spent the whole evening *listenin'* to him," he said.

"And what did he tell you?"

"He told me what happened," Wendell said.

"He told you his version," she said.

Wendell loosened the laces on one of his boots.

"All right, I heard Doc's version. I bet I heard it now six or seven times." Judge Beamer had come into Honey Boy's and he'd heard it again. "What's your version?" he

asked.

"Tell me what he said."

"No, Millie," Wendell said, starting on the other boot. "No hints."

He pulled one boot off and sighed when the other boot hit the floor.

Mildred took off her glasses. Not until then did Wendell realize how angry she was.

"Will and I were downstairs. And the next thing I know, Becky's screaming." Mildred continued, "She didn't scream for nothing. Besides, why would he lock the door? That should tell you something."

"The problem is, Millie, you didn't see anything. You said you were downstairs when you heard all the commotion."

"Yes, then I ran upstairs after Will. And by the time I reached the landing, the door was hanging off its hinges. Doc was still on the floor."

"Will hit him, right?"

"He hit him all right."

"And then what?"

"Doc took off back to town. Once Becky calmed down, she told me exactly what happened."

"What did Will say?"

"He went out to the field. We were afraid he might go after Doc, but he didn't. He came back late in the afternoon."

"Why'd you come home?" Wendell asked.

"I needed to talk with you. I figured that Doc would run to you."

"He did, and told me a different story," Wendell said.

"He's a liar," she said.

"Doc says Will's out of his mind. He accused Doc of withholding treatment from Becky, when every sane person knows there's nothing that can be done for consumption."

"Will's just as sane as you and me," Mildred said.

"Maybe it's jealousy then," Wendell said.

"Will jealous of Doc? Come on, Wendell, you can come up with something better than that. You know as well as I do, Doc's always been green with envy when it comes to Will. He's never accepted that Becky chose Will over him."

"Maybe Will's envious that Earl's a doctor," Wendell said.

"About as envious as you are, Wendell."

"I don't envy Doc."

"That's my point, neither does Will."

"I'm tired, Mildred. I need some sleep."

"Wait, I have to say this."

Wendell stared at her.

"Wendell, he was putting his hands on her. He was ... you know."

"Doc had his hands on Becky?" He paused for a moment, trying to picture it. Why would a man, with a husband in the house ...? "He's a doctor, Mildred. That's what doctors do; they put their hands on you to try to find out what's ailin' you."

She tightened her jaw. "It wasn't like that, Wendell."

"According to who?"

"According to Becky."

Wendell believed for a moment that there might be two sides to this. Doc would never ... "Mildred, for Pete's sake, she's pregnant and she's sick as a dog. Will's been actin' strange for months. Doc thinks he's crazy, a threat to the town."

"I tell you it didn't matter to him, Wendell. Doc wanted her and she's his, according to him."

"Doc says Will's a threat to his own family and he thinks he needs to be put away."

"What you don't understand, Wendell, is that Doc isn't always what he seems."

"The man does know a thing or two about insanity. He is on the board out at Long Pointe."

"Wendell, use your head. He's only on that board because you put him there in the first place."

"Well, it seems to me that he was just a doctor doctoring, in this case," Wendell said. "I don't know what Will thought he saw."

"Earl isn't like a real doctor. He never wanted to be one in the first place."

"What do you mean?"

"It's not important." Mildred shifted in her chair. "I'm sorry, I don't even know why I brought it up. It doesn't have anything to do with the Krouses."

"Dammit, Mildred, tell me what you know."

Mildred told him about the time that Doc invited her over to his house while his folks were away. It was the summer of their senior year at Hampton High. Doc told Mildred how beautiful she was and asked if he could sketch her. He explained how he always wanted to be an artist and even showed her some beautiful pictures that he had painted. He said that when his father found the paintings, he got a good strapping and Doc Sr. destroyed almost everything he had done.

"How come I never heard any of this? Doc and me have always been pals," Wendell said.

"Have you?" she asked.

"Why should I believe this story?"

"Because I have proof," she said.

"Proof that Doc liked to paint?"

"Proof that Earl might do anything with a woman."

"What are you talking about?

"Earl gave me the sketch."

"He gave you a picture he did of you?"

"If you don't believe me, I'll show it to you, Wendell."

"Get it," Wendell said. "Now."

She took a match and lit one of the oil lamps on the table. She took a key out of her sewing basket and went to the roll top desk where she kept her things. In the back of a drawer, rolled up in a box was a page out of a sketch pad. She unrolled it as she brought it back to the light and placed a paperweight and an inkwell on either edge to hold it flat.

Wendell was curious, but baffled. What possible difference could this make?

It didn't seem like much at first glance, a charcoal drawing on paper. There was no doubt that the picture was Mildred, as she was then. She was in the nude, with a ribbon drawn tightly around her ribs tied in a bow and the ends dangling down almost to her belly button. The artist had caught everything — the fact that one breast was slightly heavier, the shadow of the wrinkle in her belly, the mole at the top of her thigh, the lovely curve at the top of her hip going into her waist. He showed her seated, her legs slightly apart, her right wrist resting on top of her thigh and her left hand lifting her hair off of her neck. He'd caught a look in her eye, a wild, ready-for-anything look that Wendell remembered, that he hadn't seen for almost a decade. He didn't need to ask what had happened that day, after the sketch was done.

He moved the lamp a little closer. It wasn't just that Doc had had his wife, that he'd had apparently seen in her, during one afternoon, everything physical and sexual Wendell had taken a decade to learn. Doc had gone beyond that. There was some careful work around her mouth and between her legs. Wendell didn't have the words for it. He knew that, somehow, Doc had seen and drawn things in his wife's picture, things that have to do with desire, that men may see but never mention, never discuss.

Wendell took a deep breath. He rubbed his temples, circling them with his fingers.

"I'm sorry I had to show you," she said. "But Earl was doing something with Becky. And Will's not crazy."

Wendell yawned, his eyes half shut. He stepped forward, shifting his body.

What would Judge Beamer make of all of this? The laws were designed for crimes like murder and theft that were pretty cut and dry. Could they respond to the insight and wisdom of women?

"It's out of my hands, Mildred," he said. "Judge Beamer's already signed a warrant out for Will. It'll be delivered first thing in the morning. I'm gonna have to bring him in."

"And then what?" She moved farther away from

him.

Wendell looked at her. Why did he always end up disliking her? He went upstairs.

Her heart in her throat, Mildred did something she'd never done by night. She hitched up the horse to the buggy and drove out of town, heading for Grandma Kepler's.

Just after dawn the next morning, Mildred and Professor Knobbs pulled up to the Krouses' place. She'd spent most of the night tossing and turning. The Professor was at Grandma's before dawn and they'd sat in the kitchen and talked for hours. They'd decided what should be done. Will had to leave for a while. If he stayed in Penn County he'd be locked up. Who knew how long? Knobbs thought that if he had a little time he could set things straight, reason with people, and contact those with some influence.

They sent the kids out to play in the pasture while they sat in the kitchen drinking more coffee and trying to explain things to Will. He couldn't get it through his head that he was in trouble for protecting his wife. He couldn't believe that these two people, whom he trusted more than anyone, were saying what they were saying.

Will couldn't speak. He saw only shadows as he sat at the kitchen table, shaking. Becky was sobbing and he wanted to put his arm around her, but he couldn't move. Something about seeing Doc looking at her that way made him feel that he couldn't hold her — not right now.

"Will ..." Becky wiped her eyes. "I want you to go. I'll pack you a bag."

He told her he couldn't leave her. She told him she couldn't endure the thought of him in jail. One look at her and he knew she'd won.

"I'm sorry," Becky said. "You didn't have any choice."

The kids came in and Mildred asked Aaron to take her and the little ones down to Knobbs's farm. She needed their help gathering some firewood. Aaron got the hint. "I'll go hook up the rig," he said.

"You need time to think this whole thing over," Knobbs said.

Will remembered a time when the Professor talked about a family problem in the old country. Knobbs spoke to him as a man with experience.

It was still not yet noon and the bag had been packed. The Professor convinced everyone that Will should go, but he didn't know to where. Will was in trouble to be sure but Wendell could also be hurt by this as well — and Mildred too. She had, essentially, been witness to the crime. Certainly, she had ridden out to the Krouses' to warn Will because she knew that her husband would serve him with a warrant. They had to agree to a falsehood. Will told them he would know where he was going once he got there. About hitting Doctor Slayer? Nobody would know what happened, really — and the story would change, depending on who told it.

Will and Becky worked out a version of Knobbs's story, then sat down and told the kids. Aaron saddled the horse, taking extra care to put the best blanket on beneath the saddle. At the end of the drive, Will turned in his saddle and looked back at Becky and the children one last time. They were all out on the porch. No one waved. He led his horse down the road, looking at the reins in his hands.

Where was he supposed to go? Knobbs had given him a list of names of people in counties to the west and north, people who knew Knobbs, people he thought might help get him to Chicago. Chicago was a new and growing city. Will could lose himself easily there, according to Knobbs.

Chicago was one of the last places Will would think of going to. Crowds of people, buildings and houses on top of one another — that wouldn't do for a country boy.

He thought back to when he was a young boy and remembered the stories about an old Potawatomi shaman that lived near the swamp just beyond Beaver Hollow. Rumor had it the Indian was also a medicine man. They said he knew the landscape better than anyone, he knew secret places.

Will nudged his mare with his heels and headed for the Hollow.

He followed the road he knew away from town for a time, riding past the farms of folks he knew, but now wanted to avoid. In the heat of the early afternoon, it was likely no one would be outside. By late afternoon, he turned off onto an old hunting trail that ran for several yards through a thicket and then followed a dry creek bed, skirting the scattered shanties of Beaver Hollow.

The Indian's hut reminded Will of a beaver's lodge. He dismounted and laid the reins over his horse's head. "Anyone home?" he called out.

"Come in, Will Krouse," came a voice from inside.

Will stooped down and pushed aside the deer hide door. The inside of the hut was cluttered. Hanging on pegs were handmade tools and utensils. Cans full of trinkets were stacked in the corners. The old Indian patted the plank floor. "Sit."

"How do you know my name?" Will asked as he settled himself on one of the fur pelts.

"Don't you know mine?" the shaman asked.

Will remained quiet, waiting for his eyes to adjust to the darkness.

"You need powerful medicine. That's why you come here."

The Indian's words sounded strange, if not funny to Will. Here was a medicine man offering help, when another was hunting him down.

"Do you have tobacco?" the shaman asked.

Will felt his pockets. "No."

"Look in bag."

Will opened the bag that Becky had packed for him. He felt around inside and pulled out a square of tobacco.

The Indian grinned as Will handed it to him. He took out his knife and cut off a piece, then poked it into his toothless mouth and sucked on it. He kept his eyes fixed on Will, waiting for him to speak.

"I don't know what to do," Will said.

"You in trouble with the law?"

"I'm not sure. Maybe. Probably, yes. My wife is sick," Will said.

"My people always in trouble with your law." The Indian held out the cake of tobacco.

"No, keep it," Will said.

The Indian bowed his head and stretched his arms out in front of his body. He began to chant.

Will noticed the Indian's long braided cue at the back of his shaven head — a telltale sign of the Potawatomi. After several minutes, the shaman looked up.

"Tell me what you'll do, Will Krouse."

"I don't know."

"Some things hard to know," the Indian said as he opened a small pouch that was tied to his leggings. "Here."

"What is it?"

"The medicine you came to find."

"It looks like a stone," Will said.

"It is."

"What should I do with it?"

"Keep it with you. When you need help, rub it and ask Wiske' to protect you."

"Wiske'?"

The shaman pointed up toward the sky.

Will held the small stone in his palm. It was smooth and flat, almost perfectly round, with three lines etched into the center. A diagonal line intersected them.

"You sleep," the shaman said. "Over there." He pointed to a corner where there was a stack of pelts.

Will lay down thinking he could never sleep. Five minutes later, he was out cold.

When Will awoke, it was nighttime.

The old Indian sat watching him. "You sleep good, snore like bear."

"Don't you sleep?" Will asked.

"I can rest anytime, but the great spirits came to me." The shaman told Will to follow the path he'd come in on west, until he came to the railroad tracks. Then he was to wait for the train heading south. "When it slows down for deer, jump on. The next time it slows, jump off. You find camp there."

"What kind of camp?" Will asked.

"My people would say a village where men hunt, fish, and rest. Your people call it a hobo camp."

"They'll be looking for me," Will said.

The shaman eyed Will. If a white man couldn't trust his own law, did a brown skinned man stand a chance?

"Wiske' figure it out for you," the shaman said. "Do you have anything in your pockets?"

Will pulled out his gold pocket watch. "Just this."

"I'll keep it and your horse for you," the shaman said. "I know the trappers. If I hear news about your family, I will get message to you."

Will left the Indian's hut and tried to recall which direction he came from. He remembered the stone and pulled it out of his pocket, rubbed it, and then stuck it back in.

He started walking down the trapper's path. He'd gone about two miles when he came to the railroad tracks. It was still dark when Will heard the engine's whistle. As the train slowed, he ran up onto the track bed alongside one of the boxcars. He saw a hand reach out.

"Grab on," the voice said.

Will felt himself swept inside.

"Keep your hands up, mister," the voice said. Then he demanded to know if Will had a knife or any kind of weapon on him.

Will reached in his pocket and retrieved the stone, holding it in his open palm. "No nothing, just this," he said.

The man reached out, feeling for Will's hand. He picked out the stone and after a minute or so he spoke. "They call me Horse, but you my brother can call me Nekabush-shah."

Will left on a Thursday. Telephones or no, the entire town of Hampton and most everyone in Penn County had heard about his disappearance by Saturday.

One version had it that he had met up with some kind of accident, maybe even been killed. One thing was certain; no one from Hampton had ever just walked off without someone knowing something. Doc's story — which nobody knew what to make of — made it also seem possible that Will had fled town. Yet fleeing Hampton without clear cause was almost equally unimaginable.

Reverend Prater spoke from the pulpit that Sunday. "Before I conclude today's service, I'd like us all to bow our heads and say a prayer for the Will Krouse family."

It was autumn and the leaves were starting to turn. Reverend Prater had his arm around Molly's waist as they stood outside, waving goodbye to the last family to leave. Not a few of the parishioners, but several who had been close to old Doc Slayer let him know that he was over-stepping his duties. Best not to say anything, especially from the pulpit, while the situation was still unresolved.

The Reverend and Molly sat on a bench afterwards. Molly bowed her head with him: "Lord, Will Krouse is a good man and we pray that you'll look after him, wherever he is. Help him and help all of us to understand whatever trials and tribulations fall upon us. Amen."

The two men walked down a trail to where a dozen or so men lay at the edges of a small clearing. Horse turned to Will. "Everything you told me last night, forget. And your name is … Stoney."

"Howdy, Horse," an old-timer said.

One of the men was cooking something in a large kettle. The smell made Will's stomach growl.

"Who's your friend?" a tall man asked.

"I'm Stoney," Will said.

They all gave Will the once over.

"Well, where's your manners boys? Dish up Horse and Stoney some of that there rabbit stew," the old-timer said.

Stew ran down Will's chin as he spooned it into his mouth. One of the men handed him a canteen.

Another one snatched it back. "Ain't that the one with the white lightnin'?"

"Yes."

"Give him water. Let's not kill him right off," he laughed.

Another fellow handed him the other canteen. Will leaned his head back, gulping it down. Some of it spilled out, following the stew down his chin. Will stopped to look around. A dozen or so pairs of hard eyes on unshaven faces were fixed on him.

The man with the scar across his eye could see Will was a tenderfoot.

"So what brings you here, Stoney?" someone asked.

The men stood waiting.

"He's trying to forget things, not remember them," Horse said.

The old-timer sat down next to Will. "Hell, most of us are tryin' to forget somethin'." He held out his hand. "I'm Sidecar."

Others lined up to shake Will's hand and spout their nicknames: "Patches, Pine Toe, Corn Tassel ..."

The man with the scar shook Will's hand. "I'm Switchblade."

The campfire crackled and popped and cast shadows in the quiet of the dark. Will leaned against a tree listening to the symphony of snores when he jerked up at the presence of Nekabush-shah.

Nekabush-shah placed his finger to his lips. "Gimme the stone," he said.

Will held out the flat stone. Horse turned it over in Will's palm and pointed to the three lines.

"What do they mean?" Will asked.

"The shaman didn't say?" Horse asked.

"No."

"Our custom say you must ask. Like white man religion say you must ask to be baptized with water," Horse said.

"Tell me then," Will said.

Horse took out his hunting knife from his deer skin legging. Cutting his finger, he let his blood flow through the three etched lines. Nodding, he handed Will the knife. Will complied.

"Now, my brother, our blood runs together," Horse said. "These lines stand for me'me'juk, mishkoswIn, and e'wetode'nuk, or hope, strength, and wisdom. Legend says I must offer you something. I pick the gift from the tongue.

"It's about a Creole trapper, Louie Three, who took a young Ottawa squaw as his wife. When they were running their trap lines in Canada, she was attacked by the great bear and killed. Louie Three trapped his way down to Indiana and met a Potawatomi squaw. Louie Three's blood was half Potawatomi, so he traded for her. They trapped here in Beaver Hollow. The second winter, she fell through ice and drowned. Louie Three ended up in Southern Indiana and took a Shawnee squaw as his bride. The third winter, Louie Three caught his lower leg in the white man's steel trap. Before long, a snow blizzard came. Louie Three and his squaw entered a cave. Just as he finished removing his lower leg, there was a cave in, killing his squaw. He cannibalized his own leg while searching for a way out.

"It's a tche sen, or flat stone, Will. Remember, the Wiske' can be a trickster or a good spirit, one who provides life lessons and necessities of life."

"What became of Louie Three?" Will asked.

"What do you want to happen to him?" Horse asked.

Not a week passed before Becky and the kids moved to Grandma Kepler's. The Professor observed that Cecil seemed more inclined to believe the worst about his brother than anyone else did in town.

Mildred moved in, taking a small empty bedroom upstairs. Grandma set up a cot for herself in the parlor, giving Becky her own bed. She'd made the same arrangement when her first daughter, Callie, was dying. Mildred and Grandma would stay with the children all day. After Aaron and Jacob came home from school, Mildred would help cook.

Becky had started to fade ever more quickly. At times, she'd forget that Will was gone, or she'd ask out of the blue if anyone had gotten a telephone call from him.

Grandma had been talking about the story of Job. Becky had never much liked God's part in the story — making a deal with Satan to test a good man's faith. One night, Becky was testing her mother's religious beliefs.

Grandma said that the whole story was meant to test all folks' catechisms. Becky said that God looked very cruel in this story. Could we worship a God who allowed us to suffer so? Grandma replied that folks do suffer, but we had to look at the bright side; the beauty of the earth, she said, remembering the hymn, the beauty of its trees and its clouds, the joy of children, that God existed and was good.

Becky sometimes had dark thoughts about her grandparents and their neighbors, the first immigrants. Had they asked for too much, leaving the old country, taking possession of the most beautiful part of the earth — America? Were their descendents doomed, because they had it too good? She wasn't going to be able to sleep

146

with this on her mind.

Grandma Kepler stood steadfast. God lets us suffer for a time, she said — the way you have to let children make their own mistakes. God knows that there is a happy ending awaiting us. At least, she said, there is a happy ending for those who believe.

Becky still didn't like what the story of Job said about God. God stands so far off from Job, she said. He's like an absentee landlord.

Grandma wiped Becky's forehead, then wrung her hands on the washcloth. Without the idea of God, how could we live, child? she asked.

"How could you go on after what you've had to accept, Momma? What can be worse for a woman than to outlive her husband and then her children?"

Grandma went back to the Bible and quoted over the sufferings of Job, the loss of property and livestock, the loss of children, the illnesses. Which would have been the most intolerable? Job tolerated them all.

"A pigheaded man," her daughter said.

They sat there, then, in silence first thinking about themselves, then each thinking about Will. Grandma had had the worst of it clearly. Yet she still had faith.

"Do you feel like Job, sometimes?" Becky asked.

"Sometimes folks suffer somethin' terrible over bein' struck with sickness, or losin' all their property, or losin' a loved one. Suffering's different for everybody. I feel like we're all Job," she said. "All bein' pushed to our limit."

"I trust our Lord, Momma," Becky said.

"I know, I know you do, honey."

The candle had sputtered out a few minutes earlier. Grandma sat and held Becky's hand in the dark until she fell asleep.

CHAPTER 10

Wendell surprised even those who supported him – most of all the twins, making good on his promise to get them new jobs. Unlike most politicians, he worked as hard once in office as he had worked to get the job. But many hours of most days, he spent trying to find what happened to Will.

The road back from Beaver Hollow cut across a corner of Will and Becky's far pasture. There'd been heavy rain for a couple of days and the shortcut was wet so Wendell took the long way around which carried him to within sight of the Krouses' house. From a distance, Wendell could see Cecil patching a hole in the roof of the barn. It amazed him that Cecil had spent his whole life on a farm, yet still managed to look like a gentleman farmer, a city person in retirement.

Wendell stopped for a moment and looked down the road that passed the Krouses'. He tried to imagine what Will might have been thinking as he left that day, the day after his fight with Doc Slayer. If he'd ridden down the road towards town, he'd have passed three or four farmhouses close to the road. He'd have been likely to see someone he knew. He wouldn't have wanted that. But going the other direction you'd have to ride to the next county before you saw anyone.

Wendell headed down the road away from town, riding right by the hunting trail where Will had turned off. A mile or two later, he crossed the railroad tracks and then came to the road that defined the edge of the county. He turned north. There were all sorts of squatters out here. None of them would have remembered or would have told the truth even if they had seen Will.

He was about to give it all up when he remembered that there was an old Potawatomi medicine man who lived just a ways off the road. Wendell didn't pretend to understand the Indians. He'd been accused of being a half-breed himself because of his coloring but he wasn't interested, as people sometimes are, in claiming Indian blood. He did know, from reading the files, that Sheriff

Brochman had relied on the old medicine man, several times. He and Will had spied on the Indian when they were boys, yet Wendell had spoken to him only once. That was when he first worked for the railroad.

Not sure he remembered how to get there, Wendell doubled back, following the edge of a line of trees to the east until he came to the tracks. He followed them for a half mile until he found a foot trail that led to the hut.

The old Indian was outside. "I knew you would be coming to see me, Sheriff," he said.

"How'd you know I'm a sheriff?"

He pointed at Wendell's vest.

Wendell adjusted his hat and looked down at his star.

"I knew you as young Wendell Gates before I knew you as Sheriff Gates."

Wendell reached into his saddlebag and pulled out a pint of shine. "Here, I brought you some fire water."

"You have chewing tobacco?"

"No, but I have a cigar," Wendell said.

"You're a good sheriff."

The Indian took the lid off the jar and held it out. Wendell knew the customs. He took a sip.

"I came to ask you some questions," Wendell said as he lit the old Indian's cigar, then his own. "That your horse hobbled behind that cache over there?" Wendell pointed.

"It came to me a couple days ago," the Indian said.

"Where's its saddle?" Wendell asked.

"Indians ride bare back, Sheriff," the shaman answered.

Wendell took off his hat and ran his fingers through his thick black hair. The Indian puffed on his cigar.

There was something the sheriff couldn't quite put his finger on, but he knew the old Indian was lying to him. He walked over to the horse to get a closer look when he spotted a saddle beneath a canvas cover. He could barely make out the initials 'W.K.' branded on it.

After a few days, Will started tagging along with one or another of the hobos on short forays. Horse had moved on. Will didn't have much energy, yet he wanted to help. He felt restless, confused. Through the kindliness of the hobos — and some luck — Will had amassed a change of clothes and some blankets. He depended on the generosity of the others for food. So if rabbits were caught, Will would clean and skin them, but he'd sit for hours at a time studying the stone with the messages. Could it change his luck?

The men were good to him. They swapped yarns with each other for his benefit. They enjoyed Will's presence. One night Patches insisted on giving Will one of Sidecar's harmonicas.

Sidecar started blowing out *Dixie,* while Will just blew.

"Give me that, Stoney." One of the men took the harmonica back from him.

"Guess that answers that," Pine Toe said, tapping a stick in time with the music on his wooden leg. "The boy ain't musical."

The music stopped. The men that were sitting down, stood up. Will turned. There stood the shaman in a flock coat and red sash. He was eloquently topped off with a crimson turban.

"Can we sit, Will?" the shaman said.

Will motioned for him to sit down.

The shaman turned and walked into the thicket. Will followed.

"Your son, Sammy, has yaknoge' mskwe', blood poisioning," the shaman said. He took Will's arm as they sat down.

"I'm going home," Will said.

"First listen. In this pouch is Echinacea and other herbs. Your son need to drink charcoal powder with tea and nothing but juices of the fruits."

He took Will's hand and placed the leather pouch in his hand. "Do you still have the stone?" he asked.

Will's hand trembled as he held out the stone. The

shaman saw the dried blood.

"Ride fast, but cautious, my brother," the shaman said as he pointed over to Will's mare.

Even as Will rode off, he struggled with what was the right thing to do. All of us, from time to time, are faced with these exact thoughts. Our answers usually come as friendly advice, or perhaps a sign. Will's came as both.

Coming his way, a man riding bareback raised his arm, palm out, as he came to a halt. Will remained silent as he kept his eye on the smooth faced half-breed mounted on the pinto pony. Will reached into his pocket and held out his stone. The man stared back at Will with hard eyes.

"Where you get this?" he asked.

"From a shaman," Will said as the man placed the stone back into Will's outstretched hand.

"There's a posse of men camped about a half hour back. They look for you," the half-breed said. "Those men looked dangerous. They are going to where your wife is. I listened in where they were camped."

Will repeated his conversation with the shaman.

"Give me the pouch, I know where the Kepler place is," the half-breed said.

A couple of the men sleeping around the campfire looked

up as the roan and its rider raced down the road past them.

"What the hell ... mount up men, it's him. Damn it, forget the fire. Get up." The man kicked one of his still sleeping deputies.

The twelve men from Keeatuck that Doc Slayer had paid to bring Will in tore down the road. Soft clay kicked up in the hind rider's faces. The morning sun shone on the red clay road making the tracks of the fugitive easier to follow. The fugitive pulled his horse to a halt when he heard the gun shots.

"Get off that horse with your hands up high, you son-of-a-bitch," the Keeatuck sheriff yelled.

"It's him all right, Sheriff," one of the deputies said, pointing to the initials 'W.K.' branded in the rider's saddle.

"Turn around, Krouse," the sheriff said. He turned to one of his men. "Hand me some rope."

When Mildred opened the door, a dark skinned man with long hair handed her the small bag.

"It's for Sammy." He repeated the shaman's instructions to her. "Will's message for his wife inside pouch."

"Where's Will?" Mildred asked.

The half-breed hopped on the pinto and galloped off.

Will sat rubbing his wrists, trying to soothe the rope burns. He was kept locked up in the county jail until his trial. Prudy filled him in whenever she brought him his supper but he only talked about going home. Ruby accompanied her one day and stood in the doorway as Prudy picked up his untouched meal. They decided to tell Becky he'd been found.

The court date was set for October 11, 1915, only a couple of weeks after Will turned himself in. When an innocent man is summoned by the court on such short notice, he doesn't have time to collect his thoughts, especially when he's caught between a rock and a hard place.

The prosecutor was from Penn County, but not from Hampton. He was a city prosecutor — a damn good one. Taking the advice of his brother, Will retained Cecil's attorney, Simon Sinclair, a lawyer who mostly settled land disputes and such. Doc wanted Will locked up for criminal assault. Sinclair's defense was entered as battery, caused by a moment of passion.

Will jerked when he heard the gavel hit.

"Would you lawyers please approach the bench?" the ruddy-faced man in a black robe blustered.

Will took in a deep breath as he scanned the courtroom. For a moment he thought he smelled Honey Boy's with its familiar traces of leather and livestock. Honey Boy had told him once that less than fifty years ago, the circuit judge held court in his place. That's when the other scents caught Will's attention — aftershave and perfume, folks from the city. He swallowed. This jury wasn't going to be twelve of his peers.

The prosecution didn't need any witness other than Doc Slayer. They advanced their case by cross examination of Will Krouse's witnesses — folks who unintentionally condemned Will as they testified to Will's outbursts of temper in the last few months. Even Mildred Gates, Will's best witness, cried when she attempted to explain how she had to wake Will and didn't reach the upstairs bedroom until the ruckus was pretty much over. The trial advanced to the final two witnesses.

"Do you swear to tell the whole truth and nothing but the truth, so help you God?" the bailiff asked.

"I do," Doc said, his hand resting on the Bible.

"Doctor Slayer, please tell the court, in your own words, why you believe the accused assaulted you," the prosecutor said.

"I believe that he was looking for someone to place blame on," Doc said.

"Would you expand on that for the court?" the prosecutor asked.

"Well, it's like this, the man's wife is dying of tuberculosis and she's pregnant. And that leaves him with a brood of children, and cattle, and land to tend with no one to help him," Doc said.

"I object, your Honor," Attorney Sinclair said.

"On what ground's, Mister Sinclair?" the judge asked.

"The circumstances of Mister Krouse's property and the condition of his wife are irrelevant to this case."

"If you let me continue, your Honor, I'll show the relevance," the prosecutor said.

"I'm going to overrule you for now, Mister Sinclair," the judge said. He looked over at the prosecutor. "For the time being, please continue."

"So Doctor Slayer, would you say that Mister Krouse was on the verge of a mental breakdown?" the prosecutor asked.

"Your Honor, I object. He's leading the witness," Attorney Sinclair said.

"I'll re-phrase my question, your Honor."

The judge gave the prosecutor a nod.

"How would you describe the accused at the time of your house call?" the prosecutor asked.

"When I first arrived, he was irritable and confused. The first thing he said was 'What took you so long?'" Doc Slayer rubbed the splint on his nose as he spoke. "Will Krouse is crazy and he should be locked up. The man's dangerous."

The judge glanced over at Attorney Sinclair after the prosecution finished. "Are you going to cross-examine, Mister Sinclair?"

"No, but I'd like to call Will Krouse to the stand."

On day two of the trial, that would prove to be a major mistake during the cross-examination.

"Where were you before you ran upstairs, Mister Krouse?" the prosecutor asked.

Will looked out the large pane glass window. The leaves on the sugar maples were falling, red and yellow. How was any of this going to save his family?

"Answer the question, Mister Krouse," the judge said.

"I was downstairs sleeping," Will said.

"And why were you sleeping while your ailing wife was being examined?" the prosecutor asked.

"I don't know," Will said.

"Please speak up, Mister Krouse, so that the court can hear you," the judge said.

"I don't know," Will repeated.

"What did you do when you finally decided to go upstairs and check on her?" the prosecutor asked.

"I kicked the door in," Will said.

"You didn't try knocking first?" the prosecutor asked.

"No. I couldn't, I mean ..." Will answered.

"Please just answer either Yes or No," the prosecutor said.

"No," Will said.

"What was Doctor Slayer doing when you burst into the bedroom?"

How could he forsake his childhood sweetheart, the mother of his children? Stories only got bigger with time in these bump in the road burgs. Could a good hundred years ever erase a scandalous moment of the present? Will felt the lump in his throat descend into the knots that twisted and turned deep inside his stomach. Did the judge expect him to relive that entire rape attempt on his Becky in front of the town of Hampton? He wiped the perspiration from his hands on the sides of his wool trousers.

"I don't know," Will said.

"Answer the question, Mister Krouse, or I'll hold you in contempt," the judge said. "Would you talk to your client, Mister Sinclair?"

Will's mind was miles away from the courtroom at that moment. The portly judge motioned the lawyers to his bench. "I'll see you two in my chambers," he said, pounding the gavel. He declared a twenty minute recess.

Upon hearing the sound of the gavel, the court was back in session. Will listened as the judge's words rang out.

"Will Krouse, please stand and face the bench. Do you have anything to say before I pass judgment?"

"Please, your Honor, let me see my dying wife, spare me jail, I need to see her."

Some of the jurors were drying their eyes outright. Others were trying their hardest to choke back their emotions.

"Please, I beg of you," Will said.

"Will Krouse, this ruling is extremely difficult for me, considering your circumstances." The judge cleared his throat before continuing. "The State finds you guilty of battery by reason of insanity. You are hereby committed to Long Pointe, an asylum for the insane. You are to remain there until their Board of Trustees sees fit that you should be released."

Will's knees buckled. Sheriff Gates had to brace him up. The twins sobbed. All Wendell could do was shake his head as he placed Will in handcuffs. Will hung his head and sobbed as Wendell lead him from the courtroom.

It would have been ordinary for the deputy to take Will to Long Pointe. It was a long trip. But Wendell needed to handle this himself. He stayed up late in his office with Prudy, making sure everything that had to get done would be done. He slept a few hours, harnessed the horses before dawn, and drove to the jail, put handcuffs on his haggard charge, then loaded him in.

The sun was beginning to rise. Frost from the night still coated the clay road. Every so often, the wagon would hit a deep rut. There had been major washouts along this road from the rain. It was going to be spring before these could be filled.

The sheriff looked over at his shackled prisoner and thought that this was going to be a rough trip in more ways than one.

No sound came from the gaunt, gray-faced man sitting next to him.

The sheriff tapped his shoulder. "Will, I could've packed your ass in the back, but I thought I'd do you a favor and let you ride up front on the buckboard with me."

Will's eyes remained fixed on the passing farmland.

Most of the corn had not been harvested because of the rain. There wasn't a slim chance that the farmers could get a wagon into the fields in their present condition, even if they used hardheaded mules or hard working Belgians.

Making sure the man next to him was awake, Wendell tugged on the chain attached to his wrist cuffs. "Do you hear me?"

"Ow."

"At least you're still alive."

Wendell took off his Stetson, replacing it in a slightly cocked position to block the sun from his eyes. If it weren't for the hat and star pinned to his jacket, he would look like just another farmer.

The man next to him managed to turn up the collar on his coat and continued his silent gaze.

"What's wrong? The mornin' air gettin' to you?"

No reply.

Wendell followed suit turning up his own collar. "If we're lucky, we should reach Long Pointe before sunset."

His passenger shifted his body at the mention of Long Pointe and let out a deep breath. It wasn't the morning air that caused him to shiver.

"Will, I want you talkin' to me before we get to that loony bin, or you won't get shit to eat tonight. How's that sound?"

Will didn't know what to say. He was overwhelmed by the beauty of the farmland, the smell of the wet soil, even the ruinous signs of the damaged crops.

One of the grays whinnied. "Okay girl, you talk to me then."

Wendell rubbed his kidneys each time the wagon's wheels hit a rut. "Let me know when you need to take a piss, and I'll pull up."

The man nodded.

They rode on in silence. It was difficult to tell the

time of day because the sky was not only clouded over but dark and menacing. Unconsciously, Wendell let the horses pick up their pace as they went down a hill, he wanted to make good time and maybe even avoid the rain.

At the bottom of the hill the wagon hit a deep rut. The horses reared up, pulling hard on the reins.

"Whoa there," yelled Wendell, as the wagon tipped.

Will grabbed for the iron ring his wrist cuffs were chained to. A flash of lightning shot across the sky and the wagon was on its side before the thunderous boom that followed. Will fell off the seat and was hit hard by the frame of the wagon as it rolled over.

He must have blacked out for a moment. When he opened his eyes, things were blurry. He waited a moment until he could see. The horses were terrified. With the next flash of lightning, they bucked, then reared back. Blood rushed from Will's wrists where the irons had cut in. He let the chain slide down through the iron ring that was still attached to the buckboard. Was there enough chain for him to drop to the ground?

The sheriff lay unconscious. His head hit a fieldstone that the wagon turned up from the muddy rut. Will took in a deep breath as he stretched his arms toward the sheriff's belt that held the key to his cuffs. He couldn't reach the key. He felt dizzy and sucked in some cold air.

His wrists were beginning to throb. He closed his eyes and pulled the chain as hard as he could. Pain shot up his arms.

Another clap of thunder caused the horses to neigh and kick the wagon. His hands reached the keys as the horses reared once again. Fate saw to it that the tongue of the wagon broke away from the animal's hitch. That stroke of luck alone saved the horses from their otherwise sure death.

"Easy, girls, easy. I'll have you unhitched in no time."

He rolled the sheriff over and slipped the key ring from his belt. "Stop shaking," he told himself, trying to get the key in the lock.

The cuffs fell open. He stood up and grabbed the horse's reins.

"That's it, easy does it." He unbuckled the leather straps that had broken free of the wagon and began stroking one of the horse's necks. "That's a girl."

He turned back to the sheriff. "Sheriff? Sheriff," he said, shaking his shoulder. Was he dead?

Another pain shot up his arms. He felt his blood running down his fingers. He ripped off a piece of his shirt and wrapped his wrists. He was free, for what it was worth.

He was too unsteady to move. His scalp wasn't cut,

but his head throbbed. He crawled half out of the wagon, into the rain. He couldn't say what had happened. Some papers had fallen out of the sheriff's coat pocket.

Will reached over, pulled them out and read the court order:

WILLARD A. KROUSE TO BE COMMITTED TO LONG POINTE INSANE ASYLUM

In the rain, in the middle of a field, the big horses stomping and snorting, he tried to make sense out of his circumstances. He could run. But where? Wendell needed attention. But why should he help the person who was taking him to Long Pointe? He wasn't crazy. Becky needed him.

He braced himself against the side of one of the horses and retched. He shivered in the rain and cold, then remembered something his father told him: "You can run to the edge of the earth but you never stop having to live with yourself, son."

Will rerigged the harnesses so that he could ride one horse and lead the other. There was only one place to go. Somehow, he managed to lift the sheriff onto the back of one horse and tied him there. Wendell was bleeding from his nose, mouth, and ears. He would die without help Will knew — but he was breathing. They set out along the road in the rain.

It was after dark when Will saw several old Victorian

buildings in the distance. The horses spooked as they made their way along the gravel road leading up to the largest building on the grounds. There were no lights in any of the other buildings. Will noticed the sky had gotten almost black. The orange harvest moon punched through the clouds as the wind picked up. A cluster of storm clouds smothered it again. Will stared at the buildings and felt cold. He had heard stories about Long Pointe. He could leave Wendell there and run away again, but that hadn't worked. He knew he was going to have to go through Long Pointe to get back to his home and his family. It was all a misunderstanding.

"Wendell, can you hear me? Whoa, girl, easy." Will leaned over and put his hand on the man's back. He was still breathing. Will dismounted and checked the harness again to make certain that Wendell wouldn't slip off his horse. He couldn't take another fall, no matter how slight.

Will wiped some of the blood from Wendell's left eye, then felt his temple. His pulse was weak.

Will rubbed his own left wrist where the chain had cut in. For the first time since the fall, he felt the throbbing. He held the reins in his good hand and walked through the gates of Long Pointe. A sharp pain ran from his left leg all the way up his spine. He shook his legs, one after the other, and grimaced. At least nothing was broken there, probably just a pulled muscle or a pinched nerve.

Will tied the horses to a post, limped to the double doors of the main building, and knocked. The three-story structure was the only building that still had some lights on in it. It was also the only one without iron bars covering the windows.

The door swung open. A man in a white duck cloth uniform glared at him. "Who the hell are you?" he asked.

"Will Krouse, is my name," he said. "The fellow on the horse is Sheriff Wendell Gates. He's been hurt pretty bad."

"Why are you here?"

"I'm his charge," Will said.

The rain began to pick up.

"Wait here until I get some help."

Will pulled his coat over his head as the heavy droplets began to pour down. It seemed as if he had been out in it forever.

Finally, another man in a uniform appeared. "Will who?"

"Krouse," Will answered.

"Help us get the sheriff inside," one of the men said.

"I can't, my wrist is broken."

"My God, man, don't just stand there then, get inside."

Another man walked up and handed Will a blanket

and a bundle. He pointed to a door in the middle of the hallway. "Go in there and get out of those wet clothes. You can put these on. I'll get someone to help you."

Will spotted a man wearing a derby looking back at him as Will stepped inside the room. Was that Doc? Then he turned toward the screams.

PART II

CHAPTER 11

Good men and women sometimes fail because evil takes over.

Insane asylums were built in America in the mid-eighteen hundreds. They were to be safe havens in which the mentally ill would be cared for and no longer be a danger to themselves or others. There was hope that they might even be healed. Society, in general, was afraid of anyone who was "abnormal." So, if the mentally ill were kept out of sight, they would be out of mind.

Most of these institutions were at least, in part, based on good intentions and with that in mind, Long Pointe was constructed in 1880.

What is it that makes inhumanity toward the sick and helpless possible? Is it power or greed? It was both at Long Pointe.

Will Krouse woke up the next morning strapped down in the infirmary. The other beds were empty, except for one across the aisle from him.

"Mornin' glory," a man spoke up. "I'm Crawford Steinwell, one of the star boarders here at Looney Pointe. What's your handle?"

"Will Krouse."

"Oh, yeah, you're the wacky who chose this resort over freedom."

Will strained his neck, looking for the face to match the voice. He felt the straps tighten around his chest as he moved. He let his head fall back.

Steinwell rolled over on his stomach when he heard footsteps.

Will gazed at the ceiling. The original white paint had yellowed over time. The touch-ups made it obvious. He turned his head and started counting the rows of beds.

He looked back up at the ceiling just as Doc Slayer spoke.

"How's my star patient today?" Doc asked, unbuckling the straps.

The crank on the bed squeaked as Doc turned it. He

pulled the chair next to Will's bed and set his black bag on it.

"Will, I'm going to give you something to ease your pain," Doc said.

"What is it?" Will asked.

"Open up," Doc said as he opened the corked vial and poured the liquid into Will's mouth. "It's the same thing I gave you and that little woman of yours at your house ... only a more generous portion."

Will's eyelids fluttered shut. Doc picked up his bag and walked over to Steinwell's bed and started to shake his shoulder when he heard him snoring. Doc read Steinwell's chart, then glanced at the blank paper on Will's clipboard, then left.

A tall, thin woman with a scowl on her face approached Will's bed. "Willard Krouse?" she said.

"He's sound asleep, Nurse Stout," Steinwell said.

She gave Will a hard shake. "He has to take his medicine," she said.

"What medicine?" Steinwell winked at her.

"I don't see it's any business of yours, but since you're so nosey, Crawford, they're pain pills," she said.

"Set them on his table and I'll see that he gets them when he wakes up."

"Steinwell, if you take these yourself, you're going to be in trouble. They're powerful."

"Do you see these stitches over this eye? They're for sneakin' a few sips of whiskey. I learned my lesson, beautiful."

Steinwell watched the tall woman turn and walk down the aisle. Her ass seems to be swinging a bit more. Or is it just my imagination? Steinwell took the pills out of the small paper cup and walked over to the sink and washed them down.

"Have a nice sleep, Will?" Steinwell asked.

"What time is it?" Will asked.

"You mean what day is it? You've been out almost two days. I was beginning to worry," Steinwell said.

Will gulped down the glass of water from his table.

"Why are you here, Steinwell?"

"Crawford," he smiled. "I'm nuts."

"No, I mean in the infirmary?"

"Gettin' over a bout of pneumonia."

Will noticed Crawford still had the remains of a black eye. His left eyebrow was shaved and stitched. Crawford continued to smile as Will gave him the once over. Long Pointe's newest patient was catching on to life inside. Steinwell looked to Will like a man who'd caught pneumonia after somebody cold-cocked him.

A few days later, a male attendant came for Will. He was a

man of few words, but he let Will know that Doctor Cooper wanted to see him. The doctor's name seemed familiar, but Will couldn't place it. While the attendant left the room for a moment, Crawford buzzed at Will and winked. He mouthed the words "Cooper ... Head Honcho."

The attendant walked Will down the hall to a shower room and told him to strip down as he turned the faucet handle.

Ice-cold water hit Will's body. His wrist throbbed.

"Try to keep that cast dry, you won't get another one," the attendant said.

The soap and water reminded him of washing up after a day in the field. The attendant turned off the water and threw him a towel.

Once Will had dressed, the attendant motioned him toward a wheelchair.

The attendant pushed the wheelchair down a wide hallway toward the Superintendent's office. Will fixed on the details of what he guessed was Long Pointe's main building. The walls were trimmed in dark oak. The polished wood floors creaked beneath them. The wall outside of Doctor Cooper's office displayed a large oil painting of a French battle scene. It needed leveled.

Will shaded his eyes as the morning sun flashed through one of the windows. The attendant knocked on the door. A voice responded through the half-opened transom.

The attendant pushed the door open and wheeled Will into the office. A stout man stood gazing out a large window behind an oversized desk. His back was to them.

He sent the attendant away and turned to face Will.

"Is that chest strap secure? I don't want you sliding out."

Will felt it with his good hand. "Yes, sir."

Doctor William Cooper sat down behind his desk. With his thinning gray hair, deep wrinkles and bags under his eyes, he looked to be in his mid-sixties.

"How's that arm of yours?" Doctor Cooper asked.

"My wrist is broken."

"Your arrival here was quite an account."

Will nodded.

"So, you do understand you need treatment?"

Will remained stoic. The point was not that he needed treatment. He needed someone to see, to believe, that he wasn't insane. He knew he didn't belong at Long Pointe.

"How's Sheriff Gates?" Will asked.

"He wasn't in very good shape, but he was well enough to go home the doctor from South Bend said. But let's talk about Doc Slayer," Cooper said. "Do you remember hitting the Doctor?"

"Not really," Will said, which was accurate.

"You're married and have children?"

"Yes."

"Tell me a little about your family."

"My wife is very ill ... and pregnant. I have three sons and a baby daughter." Will cleared his throat. "I need to know how my wife is."

"We'll see if we can get that information for you. But it's best not to think too much about your former life for now."

How could this man say his family was his "former life?"

"You were a dairy farmer, correct?" Cooper asked, talking as though Will were a dead man.

"Yes," Will answered.

"I've heard you ran a very good farm with little help," Cooper said. He got up and wheeled Will over to the windows behind his desk. Beyond, to the east of Clayport, there was an unbroken stretch of pastureland that ran clear to the horizon. "These fields go all the way to the Watomi River, some of the most fertile land in the state," Cooper said. "But it's not paying off. It's not helping people recover themselves because I don't have the organization to teach them skills. And if we can't make the land productive, I can't carry out our mission here. How's it look to you?" Cooper asked.

"It appears to be good dirt, but I'd have to smell it,"

Will said.

"What if I offered you an opportunity to farm once that wrist of yours is healed? We should be receiving our new equipment in time for spring."

"That looks like a pretty big piece of land," Will said.

"You'd have assistance, field hands," Cooper said. "They'd be people like you. Perhaps a bit more eccentric."

"How long you intend on keeping me here?" Will asked. Wasn't that the main question?

"I know you're not happy about the events that landed you here," Cooper said. "But we all must learn to play by the rules. Some types, say like yourself, worry too much. Mental breakdown remains somewhat of a mystery. What you need is rest and fresh air, not to be locked up like some of the other poor souls here. But you do need to be cared for. And in your case, it would be a good idea if you were to do some work, something to keep your mind occupied while you heal."

Will tapped his fingers on the arm rest.

"Suppose," Cooper said, "that I put you in charge of our herd."

"I've got my own farm to work," Will said.

"Let go of the past for now," Cooper said, "or you'll never be able to see the future."

Holding on to the past was what Will had been trying

to do his whole life. Will ran his hand through his hair.

"I raised dairy cows," Will said. "What have you got?"

"We have a mixed herd," Cooper said. "Some for milk, some for beef. Seventy head in all, mostly Angus. I don't know details; I'm not a cattleman."

At least he didn't lie. By the looks of his hands, he'd never handled farm animals of any type.

"Doctor Slayer spoke to me about you, and I'm not expecting difficulties. From what I hear, you're a bright young man."

Will stared at his cast while Cooper continued.

"Now our decision whether you're safe to release to the public — safe to yourself, to your family and friends — that will depend on you. If you display that bad temper that got you here, I'd say you're looking at quite a long stay. On the other hand ..."

"Does Doc Slayer have any say?"

"He's told me that he wants to help you get well," Cooper said.

Will licked his lips as he felt his mouth go dry.

Dr. Cooper covered his mouth as he yawned, then called for the attendant. "Take Mr. Krouse back to the infirmary and once he's out of that wheelchair, transfer him to Q Ward."

The attendant talked to himself as he wheeled Will

down the hall. "Don't know who this one is," the attendant rambled. "Damn lucky to stay in Q, I'd say. New ones don't hold up too good in V or S."

Will grasped his cast with his free hand to stop it from banging the arm rest. What did those letters stand for? He would know sooner or later. He was certain of that.

When they arrived back at the infirmary, the attendant jerked the wheelchair around. "These are the rules, Mister," the attendant said. "All the doors are kept bolted. Patients don't roam. Understand?"

"Yes."

"That's it for now, I'll have some new ones tomorrow."

Will climbed back into the bed and looked across the room for Steinwell. Steinwell's bed had been made. He could already see that the course of treatment for one was very different from that for another.

Dr. Cooper weighed the trade-offs. It was a delicate business, making an offer of considerable responsibility to a man who had assaulted someone who was not only a staff doctor, but a board member as well. The whole case was odd. If it were an ordinary assault, Will would have paid a fine, maybe served a few weeks in jail, and then gone back to his family; he had no prior police record. But

Doc Slayer had insisted Will was crazy from the beginning — Cooper believed there had to be more to the story. At times, it did seem that Will Krouse was a man who had spells or, as they said now, "mental episodes."

Those questions would be answered in time. As it stood, especially with Slayer on the board, Will's future at Long Pointe was questionable. Maybe all of that could be changed if Krouse was given a chance. Things had a way of working out and Cooper was sure he had the answer.

Dr. Cooper held on to his dreams for Long Pointe and its patients. He wanted them to have the best care, decent meals, and a chance to heal.

He recalled how the state legislators promised him the funds necessary to assure the patients' "physical, mental, and spiritual well-being," as they referred to it. He scratched his head and swatted at a fly buzzing around his ear. Five years at Long Pointe and he was still waiting for appropriations. He needed to find every way possible to combine his desire to heal with his need to make healing profitable.

He considered how pleased the mental health committee was when he suggested his plan to give the abler and more clear-minded patients something to do, instead of keeping them locked up. That was how Long Pointe's work program started. Not everyone was an easy sell.

Persuading a patient like Krouse was difficult enough. Persuading Cooper's staff of his ideas would be harder than selling the legislature itself.

Looking over his calendar, Dr. Cooper called Miss Whisman into his office, the director of day-to-day operations. Lena Whisman was a small featured woman, almost pretty save for her heavy eyebrows and the fact that she was often frowning. She dressed the same every day — white blouse with a navy skirt that draped to the toe of her black boots. The high collar on her blouse camouflaged her long neck. A coral cameo was pinned in the center. Her dark hair was always kept pulled back in a bun. Doctor Cooper felt a little wistful to see that her hair had started to turn gray, making her look like an old-maid. When she'd been hired, she was one of those "new women" — smart, assertive, and capable. She worked hard at running things, an impossible job, he was sure, filled with details he wanted to know nothing about.

He'd seen on his agenda that he had an interview that afternoon with Hanna Ames.

"Didn't you meet with her last week?" Cooper asked.

"I did," said Miss Whisman. Was he testing her?

"I assume she made a good impression," he said. "Or you wouldn't have asked her back."

Miss Whisman couldn't resist the temptation to take

a chair. It was a little improper, she knew, a little too familiar. So what?

"Her father is a very important contributor," Miss Whisman said. "I felt we owed it to him."

Charles Ames owned a successful woodturning factory in Clayport — you could see it from Long Pointe. Among a number of other things, he supplied the asylum with caskets.

"Owed it to him?" Cooper said.

"We need a veterinarian, Dr. Cooper," she said. "But it's a man's job."

"You always told me ..."

"She's a girl," Miss Whisman said, "without any experience."

"Well, she's graduated veterinary school, hasn't she?" Cooper asked. "I understood her credentials were excellent."

"Oh, yes, she has a degree. She graduated from a small college down state, Clayborne College of Veterinary Medicine."

"I've been told it's an excellent school," Cooper said. "Innovative."

Whisman wasn't done. "That may be, though she was an average student. Her records show she was somewhere in the middle of her class academically." She held the file out towards him.

"I want a veterinarian," Cooper said. "Not an English teacher."

"You'll see," Miss Whisman said, holding her ground. "She's articulate. But she's ... green, Dr. Cooper." She raised her eyebrows, letting him know she could say much more. "She's naïve, full of enthusiasm, full of idealism..."

"How old is she?" Dr. Cooper asked.

Miss Whisman shuffled some of the papers.

"I don't need her exact birth date, Miss Whisman."

"Twenty-one, maybe twenty-three at most," she answered.

"Describe her to me," he said.

"Blonde hair, blue eyes, very pretty actually. But also very young."

"Are you saying she's immature?"

"No, not at all, Doctor. In fact, she's a little naïve."

Doctor Cooper stood up and walked toward the window. Hanna Ames sounded better all the time.

"That'll be all, Miss Whisman. Leave her folder on my desk and bring her in when she arrives."

Miss Whisman took her time walking back to her office. She'd failed before to get her way, but she knew how to survive. "Well, I may not be in my twenties anymore, but at least I was at the top of my class."

Lena Whisman had a sense of misgiving that afternoon

when she introduced Hanna Ames to the Doctor. The young veterinarian arrived, driven by one of her father's employees. She wore a middy blouse and a long pleated skirt. The young man in the wagon couldn't keep his eyes off of her.

For Miss Whisman, Hanna's arrival was like a scene from a novel she'd read many times before. She'd hoped, at last, Dr. Cooper had gotten over his tendency to get involved with the young protégés. He was — she'd calculated once, twenty-five years older than she herself was — more than three times the age of Hanna Ames. She could see from the way he looked at Hanna that he would hire her.

"I'm pleased to meet you, Doctor Ames," Dr. Cooper said.

"Please, call me Hanna," she said. Although Hanna was thrilled to hear the title of "doctor" before her name, she knew no one truly thought of her as a real doctor.

Whisman excused herself. "The power of connections," she said under her breath. A girl hired because she was young and pretty, a girl hired because of her family, wasn't the kind of girl who would stay.

By the time that Miss Whisman was back at her desk, Hanna Ames, seated at the edge of her chair, was describing her struggle to persuade her father to let her become a veterinarian instead of a secretary or clerk. She recounted how he finally gave her his blessing, although he would not pay her way. She had persisted, working for room and board and volunteering her assistance to an aging veterinarian who was the doctor of last resort for dying horses and cattle, a man with magic hands who knew the languages of animals. Hanna laughed at herself falling asleep in class, but she stuck with it, graduating, when most of her professors said a girl couldn't do it.

Now here she was — one set of hurdles past, other challenges ahead of her. Her father, for all his pride in her, said no one would want a female veterinarian. She had considered returning to her college town of Clayborne to work with the old horse doctor but then she heard about Long Pointe, from of all people her father. For another quarter hour, Cooper heard her plans and her theories about the bond between human and animal. She was convinced that good care for the animals could not only make them more productive, but could heal the minds and spirits of their caretakers as well.

If Dr. Cooper was not positive he was enchanted by the time she finished, he at least knew he had found the right person.

"There's just one thing to know, Miss Ames," he said. "I have a hunch you know your animals, and Lord knows you've got energy enough for three. It sounds like you're a good daughter, so maybe I don't have to remind you of a few things about the human animal. We're jealous. We're lonely, and angry, and sometimes very unhappy. At a place like Long Pointe, there are factions. You make sure you have your loyalties in order here, and should we decide that we want to bring you on, remember you can always talk to me."

"My father always told me a person should know which side his bread is buttered on, or at the very least, where the butter comes from."

"Your father is a businessman with exceptional wisdom. That being said, I'll bid you a pleasant afternoon." Doctor Cooper escorted her out to the hallway. He pointed to a door at the opposite end of the corridor. "That's the director's office. You report back to Miss Whisman."

Just as she began to curtsey, he turned and walked back into his office, shutting the door behind him. He went to the window. He could see some smoke drifting from a tall chimney just across the river — her father's factory. Why couldn't they do some woodturning in their own shop? Why hadn't he ever thought of that? The wood-working business was very profitable he had heard. And wasn't it a godsend that a girl like that could just turn up at your doorstep?

Prudy leaned across the table to get a better look at Wendell's eye. "That's one nasty cut, Sheriff."

"Twenty-two stitches," he said.

"Does it hurt?" Prudy asked.

"Hell no, it tickles."

"My, my, ain't we in a foul mood," Ruby said. She whispered to Prudy, "Don't try talkin' to a bear, Sis."

Prudy stared at Wendell. "I was just askin'."

"I know, girls. It's just I'm not over the shock of it all yet."

Wendell had been in bed for four days. Mildred had gotten a neighbor to help Grandma Kepler and rode in to tend to him. Doc Slayer had patched him up but when a doctor came down from South Bend, he redid the stitches, claiming he would make Wendell handsome.

Although he healed quickly, Wendell was troubled. He couldn't get Will off his mind. Will had saved his life, which was more than Wendell had done for him. Late into the night, he would think it through, the right and wrong of it.

When Wendell could drive a wagon again, Mildred went back to Becky's children.

Ruby laid her hand on Wendell's. "Just consider yourself lucky it was Will you were arrestin' or you just might just be dead."

"I already told you I didn't arrest him. I was deliverin' him to the hospital."

Ruby threw up her hands. "Hospital? That's what

you call it? No, no, Sheriff, a hospital is where they took you after the accident. They didn't send Will to no real hospital."

"I know, I know," he said.

"You know the same as us. You just let other things get in your way," Ruby said. "Or should I say some other person?"

She touched the side of his face. "When do you think those can come out?"

"Doc said in a couple more weeks." He moved her hand aside. "You're givin' me a headache, woman. Let's not talk about Will anymore. It's done. At least for now."

"Have it your way, but it's bound to pop up again," Ruby said.

Afterwards, he would wish he had stayed at Honey Boy's.

Wendell was home asleep, when after midnight there was frantic knocking at the door. It was Ruby. She wasn't very clear, but Wendell understood that something had happened, that she needed him to come along.

Honey Boy's was quiet as a wake when Wendell arrived. Doc was there. Prudy sat at a table weeping. Honey Boy looked exhausted.

Doc seemed amused by it all. "Sheriff's here," he said.

"What happened?" Wendell asked Doc.

"Prudy seems to know most," Doc said.

Prudy raised her head. "All I know is I was in one of the rooms upstairs when I heard a gun go off, then a man screamin' something awful," Prudy said. "I cracked the door and saw Buck holdin' his leg, yellin'. Then I look at the other end of the hallway and there's Pa Wallace holdin' a double-barreled shotgun. He throws it down and runs over to Buck."

Ruby picked up the narrative: "Then she saw Hattie run past her Pa toward the front."

"Them Wallaces snuck in through the back," Honey Boy said. "They come here lookin' like bandits, thinkin' they could scare me into payin' 'em more for their liquor."

Wendell turned to Doc. Something made him feel that Doc was not going to give him the straight story, even though he had been there.

"Does this add up to you?" Wendell asked.

"It appears," said Doc, "that Pa thought that Buck was going to go knock on Honey Boy's door. Instead, Buck got confused, opens the wrong door, and sees Hattie in bed with some fella. He springs up, grabs his coat, slips something over his face and runs for the hallway. Then Buck yells, 'That bastard has Hattie.' Pa probably only intended to shoot at the ceiling ..."

"Where are Buck and his pa?" Wendell asked.

Prudy snuffled. "They're tryin' to track down Hattie."

Wendell scratched his head. He'd thought that this was only a fracas he was investigating. In all the turmoil, nobody mentioned the central fact, that Hattie was missing.

The first thing Hattie saw when she regained consciousness was a man wearing a trapper hat and bandana to mask his face, sitting on the seat in front of her. He snapped the reins. She remembered being shoved into the rig, then everything went blank.

Her body tossed as the buggy flew down the bumpy road. She tried to raise up to see where they were, but her body was wedged in between the rear seat and the floorboard. The night air had begun to settle in before they finally stopped. Hattie tried to scream as the man pulled her by her hair.

"Get out," he said, his bandana muffling his voice.

Hattie shivered in the cold night winds. She tried to spit the gag out of her mouth so she could talk, but all that came were throaty grumbles. She fell down as the man gave her a hard push.

"Get up," he said.

She tried to steady herself as he took hold of the back

of her neck and forced her through the dense woods. She heard the sound of rushing water and felt the temperature drop. The ruckus at Honey Boy's started coming back to her: the gunshot, Kurtz running, everyone screaming, someone pulling her down the back stairway, that's when everything went blank.

"I'm going to untie your hands, but if you make one wrong move, I'll cut your throat."

A sharp blade pressed up against her neck. "See?"

She mumbled and nodded. With her hands free, she rubbed the rope burns on her wrists.

"Get out of those clothes and put this on. Move it," the man said.

Hattie slipped the gown over her head, fumbling with the buttons. He opened the door to a small, windowless building and pushed her down on the earthen floor, tossing a blanket at her. The door bolted shut.

"I hear any noise at all, and you'll be one sorry bitch," he said.

She strained to listen as the sound of his footsteps disappeared back into the woods. She started wheezing, then took in several deep breaths, tightly wrapping herself in the blanket. She fell asleep out of sheer exhaustion only to be awakened by wailing and outbursts of giggling.

Hayward Kurtz was in the habit of coming into Hampton every so often, on business, and — he liked to claim — to regain his marbles. He arrived at Honey Boy's, bringing some of the frantic energy of Long Pointe with him.

Doc, not feeling ready to call it a night, not interested in going to Pansy's, sat and watched Kurtz polish off drink after drink.

"You know, Kurtz, a bright fellow like yourself could go a long way in life. I was talking to some of my colleagues at our board meeting about you."

"You were?"

Doc leaned across the table and motioned Kurtz in closer. "About a possible promotion and a fat raise to go along with it."

"Thanks, Doc," Kurtz slurred.

"I hear you use that blabbermouth Steinwell to get information," Doc said.

"Heck, he ain't nothin' but a souse. I mostly use him as a snitch."

"Well, once you take charge of the other attendants, I hope you'll find yourself a new one. A tattle with less wag." Doc raised his eyebrows and handed Kurtz a cigar. "Besides, you ought to know that it's never good to keep a drunkard around, they're too iffy. Get my drift?"

"Sure, Doc, Steinwell's as good as gone."

"Now tell me, what do you hear about Krouse?" he

asked.

"They'll be transferrin' him over to Q Ward any time now. He's on the mend."

"Don't be letting him heal too much," Doc said.

"Have I ever let you down, Doc?"

"Wendell's got Krouse on his conscience lately," Doc said. "It gets complicated, doesn't it, when a mental doesn't look mental?"

"You think he's really nuts?" Kurtz asked.

"He's at Long Pointe, ain't he? What's Wendell know, he wasn't there," Doc said, rubbing the bridge of his nose.

The barmaid approached their table. Doc waved her off and got up. "I'm going home to get a little sleep," he said.

"You sure that you don't want a nightcap?" Kurtz asked. "It's on me."

Doc sat down again. "That's what Hattie used to say, 'Time for a little nightcap.'"

"Hope she's okay," Kurtz said. "Must have run off, or took up with someone." He snickered, then began hiccupping.

"No other explanation," Doc said.

"Course she weren't ..." Kurtz hiccupped again.

"Hold your breath," Doc snapped.

"... nothin' but a fancy woman," Kurtz said. "Hey

Doc," he whispered. "You know how you told me I was, you know, like an ol' tom cat?" He slapped his knee. "Now there's another pregnant one out at Long Pointe. Good lookin', too ... for a loony."

"Gonna be a daddy, eh Kurtz?"

Kurtz slammed his hand down on the table. "Ain't that the cat's meow?"

"You might think so," Doc said. "But between you and me, pregnant women are a pain in the ass."

Wendell got himself to his office not long after dawn the next day. He began going through his files a second time. Since his accident, he'd woke lots of mornings shaking out the cobwebs.

He'd looked forward to a period of weeks or months that he could spend getting familiar with the files. They stood in cabinets, some mildewed, some yellowed, along two walls of the sheriff's office.

Wendell sent his deputy out to Beaver Hollow to try to find Buck and Pa while he did some research.

He'd made a list of people who had been at Honey Boy's the night of Hattie's disappearance and checked the files against the list of witnesses. This was, he knew, not likely to tell him who had abducted Hattie, but it might tell him something.

Then, he hit pay dirt. In the back of a drawer in a

cabinet stuffed with the older records, he found a series of misplaced files. He pulled them out and set them on his desk.

He spent more hours on these and into the afternoon, he realized he'd gone all day without eating or even stretching his legs. Finally, a break.

A second RAILSBACH, ANN file lay on the desk before him. She had been convicted of murdering her husband and sentenced to the asylum at Long Pointe.

Sinking back further into his chair, he grabbed the file and rested his boots up on the desk. He ran his fingers along the typed pages, stopping at a paragraph giving details on how her husband, Kendall, had beaten her repeatedly. Most of the time that was when he came home drunk, which was noted in red letters: OFTEN INEBRIATED AND DISORDERLY.

He continued running his finger down the list of dates until he came to the night of the murder, and re-examined the report and the news clippings attached.

It was after midnight when Ann heard a loud noise outside the house. She assumed it was her husband returning, drunk — as usual. She was half asleep, waiting for him to eventually stumble in. Hearing the second crash, she put on her robe and slippers and went to the kitchen window, where she saw shadows of two riders leaving. Ann stepped outside thinking that it was her husband riding off again. She heard noises coming from the cattle trough and walked over to it. That's when she saw an arm protruding from the water. All at once, Kendall's head popped up. She let out a scream and that was the last thing she remembered. The next morning, she ran to the nearest neighbor's farm and asked them to contact the sheriff's office.

At the trial, it was brought out by the prosecutor that she should have gone to the neighbor's that night. She claimed she was too scared. When asked why she didn't pull Kendall out, she said he was too heavy. The State's attorney convinced the jury that her story was all lies. He argued that Kendall Railsbach returned home drunk that night and stopped with his horse at the watering trough. While his horse was getting a drink, he probably leaned down to splash some water on his face, slipped and fell in, hitting his head on the side of the iron tank. The prosecutor explained the first noise Ann heard was his yelling for help. Once outside, she saw the situation as her chance to not only escape another beating, but to get rid of him permanently.

The prosecutor claimed she held his head under the water until no more bubbles surfaced. Then she went back into the house and waited until morning.

The defense asked the jury how Ann could have overpowered a man the size of her husband and why she never attempted to kill him in the past when he came home drunk. And finally, they questioned how it was that he had such a long, deep cut on the top of his head from a mere slip.

The jury concluded that Ann had more strength than her husband did due to his semi-conscious state. She never attempted murdering him in the past because the opportunity never arose. The jury had a problem with the size of the head gash, but the defense couldn't give them any explanations.

The State didn't want to hang a woman for first-degree murder on such circumstantial evidence, so Ann's scissor-bill attorney convinced her to plead guilty to man-slaughter by reason of insanity.

Then Wendell turned to the notes of the detective on the scene, cramped, small, and misspelled.

"I wonder why the defense attorney never brought up the felt hat layin' beside the horse tank?" The notes went on to say that the sweatband had the initial 'K' on it.

Could Hattie have been taken by the same men? Was Buck somehow in on it? Maybe. Maybe not. Who was the 'K' in the hat? Kendall? If Buck was in fact involved, he must have had some other purpose. He didn't necessarily like Buck, but Wendell had respect for Beaver Hollow men. If they wanted to take Hattie for some reason, there were much more efficient ways to do it than to come to

Honey Boy's. Somebody had planned this crime carefully, not expecting that Pa and Buck would be there. Somebody else had it in for Hattie. Wendell could not imagine who or why.

Wendell heard a horse whinny across the street. He looked out his window and saw Hayward Kurtz go into Doc's office. A few minutes later, he came back out and rode off. He glanced at the clock, then returned to his desk and the two files that consumed him: Ann Railsbach and Hattie Wallace. He rolled his tongue around his teeth. There were resemblances between the cases, but was there a real connection?

Wendell picked up Hattie's file and took out a piece of paper with some of his notes on it: 1. both young, good-looking girls; 2. mistreated by men; 3. Long Pointe connections, Ann had been sent there, Hattie's sister was an attendant there.

He felt a presence and realized that Doc was there, standing in the doorway. The clock started chiming.

"You look preoccupied, Sheriff. Want to skip dinner?" Doc asked.

Wendell slid the files into the top drawer of his desk and locked it. He tucked the key in his vest pocket.

"My stomach thinks my throat's cut," Wendell said. He pulled the shade and propped a faded sign in the window: BACK SOON.

199

Stepping into the street, Doc reached into his waist-coat and pulled out two cigars. "I miss our dinners, Wendell."

"Now that I'm sheriff, I don't have time like I did."

Doc struck a match with his thumbnail.

Wendell watched Doc turn his cigar, searing the tip before he stuck it in his mouth and began puffing. He noticed Doc's fingernails. They were clipped short and squarely filed. It reminded him of the twin's conversation about Hattie's painted nails — how long and beautiful they were. Prudy mentioned that Hattie even painted her toenails to match.

They moseyed down the street to Honey Boy's.

"The night Hattie disappeared, your rig went missin'," Wendell said. "But the next day someone from Long Pointe phoned my deputy and said it was spotted out there."

Doc's jaw muscles pulsed. "Your memory's going, Wendell. I thought we already went over this."

"I just want to make sure I got it straight. You said your rig was left overnight at the stable and that the stable boy messed up and hitched it behind Honey Boy's instead of taking it back to your house, right?"

"Like I told you before, he's not too bright," Doc said.

"But he can't seem to remember why he didn't take it to your house. Truth is, he don't even recall ever takin' it over to Honey Boy's."

"What'd I tell you?" Doc pointed to his temple and moved his finger in circles.

"Did you walk home, or over to Pansy's place that night?"

"Home. I was too pickled to go anywhere but to bed."

"Do you have any thoughts who might have run off with your rig, Doc?"

"Funny you should ask, because I saw Hayward Kurtz go upstairs with Hattie that night. And you know he's out at Long Pointe," Doc said. "Now Hayward wouldn't steal my rig. But he could have been too soused to notice whether he was on foot or horseback."

"That's true, but his own horse was gone. How would you account for that?"

"That one's over my head, Wendell. You're the detective."

Wendell said nothing. Doc had stopped just short of accusing Kurtz. Funny Doc didn't mention anything about Kurtz being at his office earlier.

They entered Honey Boy's and sat down without another word.

"Sheriff?"

"Yeah, Honey Boy?"

"Buck Wallace was in here a couple nights ago gettin'

himself all liquored up and cryin' about how he missed his sister. I'd keep an eye on that boy."

"Anything else?" Wendell asked.

"Just what everyone else knows about Buck and Hattie. I sure do miss that girl, Sheriff," Honey Boy said.

"I think I'll have me a whiskey, Honey Boy," Wendell said. He looked over at his companion. "Too early for you, Doc?"

"Nope." Doc gave Honey Boy a nod.

They ate in silence. A young barmaid cleared the empty plates from their table. Doc's eyes followed her as she walked back into the kitchen. Wendell watched Doc all the while.

"She should give some thought to working upstairs, huh, Sheriff?"

Wendell smiled. "How's everything going out at Long Pointe, Doc?"

"Busy. I'm out there pretty regular."

"Do you ever talk to Will?"

"Will's in bad shape, Wendell. He doesn't want to shower, he gobbles his food with his fingers. Hell, I've even heard the crazy bastard making salacious comments to some of the female patients. Offhand, I'd say his future doesn't look too bright."

Will's wrist was almost as good as new. He lay in bed, day

after day, growing ever more restless. Steinwell, on their one meeting, had seemed to be the one man who might be able to get him some inside information. But Steinwell had never come back.

Almost a week passed — utterly uneventful days — when Will heard a commotion in the hallway.

"Hold that door open for me," an older man wheeling a gurney toward the infirmary called out.

The attendant stood with his hand on the door handle, peering through the window. The man brought the gurney to a stop, but not before it hit against the closed door.

Will looked up at the attendant from the wheelchair. The attendant waved the man back and opened the door, pushing Will through. Will stared at the covered body on the gurney.

"Who's that?" the attendant asked.

"Some fella named Steinwell – Crawford Steinwell," the old man said. "Found him out by the ice house."

Will's eyes widened.

"What happened to him?" the attendant asked.

The old man pulled a card from the metal holder attached to the end of the cart. He ran his finger across it. "Hmmm, age twenty."

"I didn't ask his age," the attendant said.

The old man pulled back the white sheet. "He cut his

own throat ear to ear."

The last time Will saw him, Steinwell was joking and laughing. Why would he cut his own throat?

"Look how deep that cut is," the old man said. "I've done my share of butcherin' and it takes a mighty strong hand to make a slice like that. Don't you agree?"

"Don't be doing too much thinking, old man. That could get you in hot water," the attendant said. "Has someone contacted his kin?"

The old man looked at the card again. "He ain't got no kin. I'll bury him."

"Just get him out of here," the attendant said. "I've gotta get this one over to Q."

Wheeled down a labyrinth of hallways, Will wondered if he'd emerge alive. Steinwell hadn't killed himself; that was certain.

They entered a new corridor where there were many doors off the hallway. The attendant opened one and rolled Will in. "Someone will check on you later," the attendant said as he backed the wheelchair out of the room and slammed the steel door behind him.

Will sat down on a chair beside the bed and looked around, trying to make some sense out of things. The bed, chair, and table were all bolted to the floor. The chamber pot beneath the bed was the only thing not secured. The walls were bare. The iron lattice on the outside window had openings so tiny that Will could only see through it from up close.

After three or four hours, Will became aware that other doors in the hallway opened and shut often. Every few minutes or so, he could hear people pass in conversation. Will listened to his stomach growling while he waited. Waited for what? Near suppertime, he heard a knock and looked toward the door. He waited, then walked over to it and gave it a push. It opened. He stuck his head out in the hallway. There was the smell of food, coming from his left. Seeing no one, he walked in the direction of it.

Then, by instinct, he detoured. Walking to an outside door, he peered at the sky. It was overcast and red.

"Red at night, sailor's delight. Red in the morning, sailor's warning." There wouldn't be rain.

He was about to turn back when he noticed sparks from a fire crackling, then disappearing into the cold night air over in a wooded cove just beyond one of the buildings.

He stepped outside and walked behind a line of trees to get a better look.

Kurtz was taking a shortcut across the lawn from one wing of the building to another when he spotted Will and ducked in a doorway near the dining hall. He lit a cigarette and watched Will until he was out of sight, before continuing on his way.

Will hesitated as he approached the grave markers. Two fires were burning on the ground in a space about the size of a small rowboat. Will saw a shadow and stepped behind one of the large oaks.

"You might as well come on out. I seen you walkin' up," a gruff voice said, before spitting a long stream of tobacco juice into the air. A fat orange tabby darted behind one of the grave markers just as the juice splashed on it. The old man stomped his foot. "Damn, missed 'im."

The gravedigger looked down to see the old tom, walking back and forth, rubbing against his leg. The old man stood up straight, and used his fingernail to dislodge a piece of chaw from his stained teeth. He wiped his mouth, then shook Will's extended hand.

"You're the man from the infirmary," Will said. "I'm Will Krouse."

"I know who you are, but what the hell are you doin' in my graveyard?"

"I saw the fires and wondered what was going on," Will replied.

The gravedigger laughed. "You ever tried diggin' a hole when the ground's frozen?"

Will studied the man's weathered face.

"If I don't get this dirt warmed up, I ain't gonna have no place to put these caskets, now am I?"

Will eyed a few of the marked graves.

"Lookin' for someone in particular, mister?" the gravedigger asked.

"No, but I'm surprised at the size of this cemetery," Will said.

"Shouldn't be, we keep up with the best of 'em. Folks is just dyin' to get in."

The gravedigger spit some tobacco on one of the markers. The firelight hit upon his face, displaying a stream of brown juice running out the corner of his mouth and down his chin. He wiped it off with the frayed sleeve of his jacket.

"You know, son, most of the folks here at Long Pointe would be better off in my cemetery than locked up in one of them," he said, pointing a bony finger toward several brick buildings.

"How long you been here, mister?" Will asked.

"Since 1890, twenty-five years come the eleventh of November to be exact. And I ain't had any of my customers complain either. But nobody cares, why should you?"

"I better get over to the dining hall," Will said as he turned to leave.

The gravedigger spit on the marker again and called after Will, "Come back when you have more time, young fella ... you know, before it's too late."

"I'll be back for sure, old-timer, you can count on it."

Will walked toward the dining hall, wondering how the gravedigger knew his name.

"What's our girls up to this evening?" Kurtz asked the female attendant.

"It's been pretty quiet, Hayward," she replied.

"That'll change in a minute," he said, still brooding over the dressing down Miss Whisman had given him earlier that day.

"You're spending too much time away," she said. "Look at what happened to poor Steinwell."

Thinking about Steinwell made Kurtz anxious. "Take me over to those young ones' rooms," he told the attendant.

"Any certain one?" she asked.

"I don't give a shit, you pick." Kurtz followed her down the dark corridor that echoed with the crying and laughing.

The attendant stopped at one of the rooms and fumbled through her key ring.

"Come on, I don't have all night," he said.

She pushed open the door. A young woman sat on a chair in the corner, staring at the ceiling. Kurtz recognized the woman — Ann Railsbach. He could still picture the body bobbing in the horse tank, then remembered losing his hat. He wiped the sweat from his forehead.

Ann's arms dangled at her side.

"Okay woman, I don't have a lot of time. Let's get you out of that gown."

She said nothing.

"You alive?" he asked.

She remained quiet, her eyes still fixed on the ceiling. Standing in front of her chair, he reached down and raised her chin, then placed his hands under her arms. He lifted her up and pushed her against the wall. He pulled the gown over her head. His eyes roved her naked body.

"You must miss your old man, huh?"

He felt her breasts then ran his hands over her body. He unzipped his pants and pressed himself against her legs. All of a sudden, he felt a sharp pain in his shoulder. He let out a yell. Her teeth were clamped into his skin. She wouldn't let go. Blood poured down his arm.

"You bitch ..."

Kurtz clenched his fist and hit her in the nose. Blood flew from her nostrils, splattering on the wall. "Bitch," he yelled, striking her repeatedly. She fell to the floor, her head bouncing off the chair. He straddled her and bit down on her nipple. He slapped her across the mouth, splitting her lower lip, then wrapped his hand around her long hair, pinning her to the floor. He spread her legs and thrust himself into her. His body quivered. It was over. He dragged her up off the floor and threw her on the bed. He picked up her bloody gown and tossed it at her.

He knocked on the door and it opened instantly. "She's all yours," Kurtz said, pushing the attendant out of his way.

The female attendant entered the cell and saw the blood everywhere. She looked at the woman lying on the cot. Tears streamed down the young woman's cheeks past the drying blood. She never uttered a sound.

There was no dealing with these loonies, these women out of control. Who cares, Kurtz thought, it's not my problem.

Hanna had received the call from Dr. Cooper the morning after her interview. He made her a modest offer — she believed he'd like to have offered more. In a year, or two, he suggested, when things had evened out, he said he wanted to give her a handsome bonus.

For Hanna, the offer of an important job, close to home, at a place her father spoke so highly of, was irresistible. She had packed two trunks and arranged to move to Long Pointe the following week.

When she arrived, she was so busy that she hardly had time to meet other staff. Miss Whisman was not much at conversation. Dr. Cooper was on an extended leave, visiting asylums in the East. She was putting her office in order, checking off things on her notepad when a visitor arrived.

"Miss Hanna?"

She turned to see a colored boy standing just outside her office door, his straw hat in his hands. "May I help you?" she asked.

"Ma'am, I's Leroy Jefferson. I works de stables."

She noticed he had only a lightweight shirt on beneath his overalls. His dark skin glistened with tiny beads of perspiration.

"Miss Whisman told me ta see ya when I be through. You de lady in charge of de cows, ain't sha?" He reached into his back pocket for his handkerchief and wiped the sweat off his forehead. Every small move made the muscles on his arms flex.

"Well, Leroy, just what exactly do you do?" Hanna asked.

"I cleans and brushes de mules and horses and tosses hay in de loft."

"It's chilly outside. Where's your coat?"

"It be in the barn. I got hot. I's sorry, Miss."

He was maybe fifteen at the most by the looks of his skin and hairline. She walked over to him and held out her hand.

"It's okay; give me your hand, Leroy. I'm pleased to meet you," Hanna said, clasping his hand in between hers. She asked him to meet her tomorrow to show her the work he'd been doing. Leroy was going to be a great help; she'd been waiting for someone to come along who could give her the tittle-tattle.

The next day, Leroy showed her the new barn. On the way back, he introduced her to Rufus, an old man with huge calloused hands. Rufus did a little of everything at Long Pointe but his official duty was the graveyard, which was surprisingly large for an institution dedicated to healing.

"If you don't mind, I'm going to excuse myself. I have some things that need attending," Hanna said.

"Wha'cha wants me t'do?" Leroy asked.

"I'll meet you back at my office after supper and give you a list of regular chores. For now, I don't have any-thing for you." Hanna waved at them and headed off. She turned around to see Rufus handing Leroy a shovel and pointing down at the ground.

Hanna found herself approaching a barn, but it wasn't the one Leroy had shown her. She took a look inside. The beams were sagging a bit, but it still looked in good repair. There was new hay stacked high in one corner and leather hitches and harnesses hanging on the stalls. She walked to the rear where there was an open door. Peeking out, she saw a man bent over, working with barbwire.

"Hello," she called out.

He stood up and removed his canvas gloves. "I'm Will ..."

"Will Krouse," she cried out.

"I'll be, if it ain't Doctor Hanna Ames," he said. "What are you doing out here?"

"That's what I was just about to ask you," she smiled.

"I'm trying to get this fence fixed before winter sets in," he said. Will could see the puzzled look on her face. "You don't know, do you?" he asked.

"Know what?" she said.

"I'm a patient," Will said.

Hanna's mouth flew open as she reached for the wooden railing by the door. Will reached out in time to brace her up as her legs gave out.

"Easy, Hanna, I'm sorry. Come on, hold onto my arm. Let's go inside and sit down," he pointed to the baled hay. "Are you okay?"

"Just let me catch my breath," Hanna said. Hanna sat and listened as Will spoke.

A few days later, she had another guest. She was thumbing through the pages of a college textbook, reading up on tuberculosis, when a woman in a nurse's uniform came in.

"I'm sorry," said Hanna. "I didn't see you there."

"I confess, I've been watching you read," Pansy said. "Good book?"

"I'm reading up on tuberculosis. There's a lot of it going around."

"Cows get it too, don't they?" Pansy asked.

"That's right, cattle are just as susceptible as people."

"I imagine there's a lot to learn," Pansy said.

"There is a lot about farm economics," Hanna said. "That'll be the hardest part for me."

"If you need any help, just ask," Pansy said.

Hanna looked a little surprised.

"Oh," Pansy said, "my father was a banker."

They chatted. Pansy had been convinced to spend a month or two at Long Pointe, to help Doc get set up. It wasn't what she was accustomed to as far as comfort, but she'd been bribed with a diamond engagement ring.

For Pansy, Long Pointe sometimes felt like exile. She wondered why Hanna had taken the job.

As if Pansy had read her mind, Hanna said, "I guess I'm here because no men wanted the job." She didn't want to seem too eager by saying how thrilled she was to have been hired.

They swapped a few stories about people they met. They even gossiped a bit about Miss Whisman. Why didn't

Pansy mention Will? Finally, Hanna asked, "You know Will Krouse?"

She told Hanna she knew him before Will became a dangerous man. Pansy knew she had hit a nerve, but what?

CHAPTER 12

Wendell poured his third cup of coffee, eyeing the stack of paperwork in disarray on his desk. Some coffee spilled on the desk when he moved the hot cup away from his lips. "Damn it." He blotted the papers with his handkerchief.

He picked up the telephone receiver to call his deputy, paused, and then set it back down. It didn't matter how busy he was. This was something he'd have to do himself.

He unhitched his rig from the post outside and headed for the Kepler place. His thoughts focused for a brief instant on the court order that was tucked away in his coat pocket, then he practiced what he was going to say.

"Grandma it's not my doing, I'm just the messenger. You can't handle all your grandchildren by yourself, not with Becky bedridden and with child at the same time. Try to look at the bright side; you get to keep Sammy. I even agreed to let Mildred stay with you to help with Becky." He couldn't imagine the response and was certain that nothing he had to say would make things better.

Wendell turned it over in his mind so many times that when he looked up, he was startled to see he was approaching the Kepler place. He took off his Stetson as he made his way up to the front door. Mildred already had it open but didn't move aside. She had her coat on, with its collar turned up. He took a step back. "You goin' somewhere, Mildred?"

"No. Grandma saw you coming, so I told her I'd see what brought you. She's warming some biscuits and coffee but you don't look as if you'll be wanting any. I hope I'm wrong," she said. During the three days she'd tended him, they had managed to avoid talking about Will, Becky, and the children. But she knew that was what he'd come about.

Wendell pulled the court order from his pocket.

"Is Doc Slayer behind this?" Her voice was like steel hitting ice.

"Doc's well connected," Wendell said. That was, in truth, all he knew.

"Give it to me, Wendell."

"I should really give it to Grandma, it's her business."

Mildred's hand remained extended until he gave it to her.

"She gets to keep Samuel."

Mildred unfolded the papers. "How could anyone do this to Will and Becky?"

"Mildred ... It's the law. Once someone's been declared insane, things just happen. There's procedures that ..."

"But his family too? Wasn't it enough for him that he finally got Will?" Mildred looked up at the gray November sky. "You must have hated coming out here, but it's better that I tell Grandma."

"You sure, Millie?"

"Wendell, you be on your way before the boys come on out."

"I thought that maybe I'd say hello to them."

Mildred stood firm in front of the door.

"When are you taking them?" she asked.

"The Nighswanders want to come for Jacob tomorrow. Cecil promised he and Minnie would try to pick up Addie the same day. I'll be back Friday for Aaron. Can't put it off any longer." Wendell saw one of the curtains in the parlor move. "You sure I shouldn't talk to Grandma?"

"Wait 'til Friday," she said.

Although it had not been the best marriage, Wendell trusted his wife's judgment. Mildred gave him a pat on the shoulder.

Wendell climbed into his rig and headed back toward town. He knew things were far from over. His stomach gurgled around the knot that he felt inside. He tried to clear his mind by sucking in the morning air, only to have Hattie Wallace and Ann Railsbach take turns popping in and out of his head.

When he returned Friday, Mildred was upstairs with the boy.

He went outside and sat in the rig until she and Aaron came through the door. There were kisses and hugs mixed in with the tears. Then Wendell set the boy's bag in the back of the rig and they drove away.

Wendell finally spoke first. "Aaron, you've gotta believe me when I say I'm not one bit happy about this. It's a shitty job."

Aaron continued to stare at the horses. The last conversation Aaron had with his younger brothers was two days ago. Since that time, he hadn't spoken a word. For Wendell it was a long, silent day. Hours later, turning up a badly rutted road that Wendell scarcely knew, they arrived.

"Jump down, Aaron." Wendell looked at the run-down farm and shook his head. Couldn't they have found a better place for the boy? They had placed Aaron here, Wendell guessed, because he was becoming a strapping young man, perceived at the county offices as a potential worker, not as child who still needed nurturing.

Wendell reached into the back of the wagon, lifted out the small duffel bag, then handed it to Aaron. "Here's your belongin's, son." He tucked a gold pocket watch in the boy's overalls. "I retrieved this. It's your pa's."

The front door of the weathered farmhouse opened as they approached.

"Afternoon, sir, I'm Sheriff Gates from Penn County, and this here's Aaron Krouse."

A short man with beady eyes held out his hand. "Come on inside and meet the Missus." The man turned his head and shouted, "He's here."

"I'm comin'."

A heavyset woman in a wheelchair rolled out from behind a red velvet drape that hung over one of the door-ways. "My, aren't you a handsome boy. Come here and let me have a good look at you."

Wendell nudged Aaron. "Go on, do as you're told."

"How old are you, Aaron?" she asked.

"He's almost eleven, ma'am," Wendell said.

She looked up at the sheriff. "Don't he talk?"

"He hasn't since ... well, you folks know the story. Here's some papers for you to sign, sir, then I'll be on my way." They stepped into the kitchen and laid the papers down on the worn table cover. The old man made his mark. Wendell couldn't help but notice that, though it was suppertime, nothing was cooking. He stuffed the papers in his coat pocket, then covered his face with his handkerchief as if to blow his nose. He hoped to be on a better road before sunset.

The three of them watched as the sheriff's wagon disappeared.

"Shut the door, Aaron, and roll me back into the kitchen," she pointed. "I'll bet you're hungry."

"How long you gonna need him for?" the old man asked.

"Just long enough to show him around and get acquainted a little."

Once in the kitchen, she pulled some corn cakes out of a wooden breadbox and set them on the table, shoving a jar of molasses next to them. "Now you sit down and I'll get you a cup of coffee. Don't let me forget, I'll have to show you where you'll sleep."

"And when you're through with all that, send him out to the barn. I'll show him where he's gonna work," the man grunted as he walked through the kitchen and out the back door.

Aaron ate what she had set before him, remembering his pa telling him: "Son, when someone offers you something to eat or drink, it's not polite to refuse. It's just their way of being friendly."

"How's those taste, Aaron?" she asked.

"Good, ma'am. Thanks."

She picked up her paring knife. "I'm going back to eyeing out these potatoes, so when you're finished, you go on out to the barn and see what Mr. Lansdown has in mind for you."

"Yes, ma'am." Aaron wiped his mouth on his coat sleeve and headed out to the old leaning barn. Lansdown was waiting for him.

"Boy, one of your jobs will be to groom the horse and mule."

Aaron noticed whip marks on the animal's backs.

"Somethin' the matter, boy?"

"No, sir," Aaron replied.

"They tell me you know how to rig an animal for plowin'. That true?"

"Yes, sir."

"Good, then you'll be in charge of takin' care of the livestock, among other things."

"Yes, sir," Aaron said as he stroked the horse's nose. It raised its head, nudging Aaron's hand.

"He seems to like you, boy. That's good, I reckon."

Aaron's eyes fixed on a half-fallen shed just beyond the barn.

"Look around all you want, boy. From what I hear, this ain't what you're used to, but believe me, you'll get used to it," Lansdown said. "I did."

"Where will I be going to school, sir?" Aaron asked.

Lansdown snorted as he turned to walk away. He paused and looked back at Aaron. "Get this barn cleaned out, boy. I don't want to be tellin' you what needs doin' all the time. You got two eyes."

In her heart of hearts, Mildred did blame Wendell a little. It wasn't hard to blame the messenger who brought bad news. Within a week, though, she was glad that Wendell had moved as quickly as he had to get the kids away.

Grandma and Mildred understood now that Becky was dying. It wasn't only her labored breathing that told them so. It was the way she thought. All of the humor and grace of the Becky they loved was disappearing like a spent wick sputtering out. She could think of only Will and the children. Over and over, she would say, "I still want you to raise my baby, Millie. Would you do that for me?" However many times Mildred gave her promise, Becky still needed to hear it.

"Please don't talk like that, dear," Grandma said.

"Millie?" Becky asked.

"You know I'd do anything for you, Becky," Mildred said.

"And when Will gets better, would you see to it that he sees his new baby girl?"

Grandma Kepler couldn't bring herself to leave the room, but didn't want Becky seeing her cry anymore. She bit down on her bottom lip and prayed for strength.

"Mother, did you hear what I asked Millie to do?"

"Yes, my dear."

"I would leave her with you, but you have your hands full with Samuel."

"A baby girl?" Grandma said.

"Yes, Mother, I feel like it's going to be another girl. What happened to my family?"

Grandma Kepler stroked Becky's head. "Shhh, you don't need to be worryin' yourself. Just try to get some rest."

"I love you, Momma."

"I love you too, dear. You're my baby." Grandma sat down in the rocking chair. She'd sat there through two nights in a row now.

"Millie, don't leave," Becky said.

"I'm not going anywhere, dear." Mildred looked over at Grandma, then back at Becky. "Listen, she's already sound asleep."

They were quiet for a moment.

Becky released Mildred's hand and reached under her pillow. She unfolded the one page letter that Mildred gave her that night the half-breed came on Will's behalf. Mildred watched as Becky's eyes moved back and forth, taking in every word. Becky folded it back up.

"Oh, Will, you must know how much I love you, don't you? I miss him so, Millie," Becky said. She pressed the note into Mildred's hand. "You give this to my little Addie when she's old enough."

Mildred rode the next day to a farm nearby. There were sisters there. Thinking she might need help, Mildred offered each of them a dollar to come spend the night. Both girls stayed in Samuel's room, while Mildred took the rocking chair beside Becky. Grandma was persuaded to return to her own bed, but in the middle of the night, she was awakened by a baby's cry. She climbed out of bed just as Mildred walked into the room, carrying a tiny bundle in her arms. "It's a girl, Grandma."

"Oh, Becky, you were right," Grandma said.

Mildred handed the baby to Grandma.

"Becky named her Elizabeth."

"Elizabeth, my sweet grandbaby." Grandma Kepler carried the child back to Becky's room and bent down to kiss her daughter's forehead. "Is she ..."

"Yes, Grandma, she's gone."

Grandma's hands trembled as she handed the baby back to Mildred.

The neighbor girls started gathering up into a bundle the bedclothes the baby was born in. One reached over to cover Becky but Grandma stopped her. She knelt at her daughter's bedside and bowed her head.

When Will's real trouble came, it came without warning. He was trying to sort out if Thanksgiving had come or went when he heard the squeak of the door opening. He arose when he heard the voice.

"Get up, you crazy son-of-a-bitch," Kurtz yelled, kicking the corner of Will's bed. He had something in his hand and tried to strike Will with it.

Will rolled off onto the floor and grabbed Kurtz's leg. He pulled Kurtz down, smashing his fist in his face. It was the first time since he had arrived at Long Pointe that Will felt like a man again. The feeling didn't last long.

Kurtz screamed for help as blood flowed from his mouth. Within moments, two attendants rushed into the room. It took all three of them to get Will down. They thrashed him. Will tried to fend them off, but once they had his upper body restrained in a canvas camisole and straps around his ankles, he was helpless. They beat him until it seemed that his cries were coming from outside his body.

In time, the noise and voices began to fade away as darkness overcame him.

"You two take his sorry ass over to the Violent Ward," Kurtz said.

"What happened?" one of them asked.

"Krouse thinks he's an employee instead of a nut, but don't bother yourself with details," Kurtz said. "I come here to talk to him, Doc Slayer's orders."

The attendant knew better than to ask anything else.

When Will awoke, it was still dark. His body ached. The attendants left him lying on the floor of his new quarters in the V Ward, still restrained in the bloodied camisole. Before he attempted to raise himself, he moved his legs to see if any bones were broken. He turned his head back and forth, causing his neck to crack. He made the same movement again, this time shrugging his shoulders. Will felt a sharp pain in his rib cage as he twisted his torso. He was worried that his ribs might have been broken when the attendants were kicking him. The heavy canvas of the straightjacket gave him a little protection. All at once, Will felt the same darkness creeping back.

The next time Will awoke, he could see daylight coming through a small crack near the ceiling. He tried again to take account of his injuries, but it was futile. He was helpless. After a while, Will finally remained conscious. He knew that the days and nights were turning into weeks only because his pains began to subside. He was hungry and thirsty given the stingy amounts of mush and water they brought him. In time, he lost his appetite. His mouth was dry and crusted with blood.

He thought about how life was easily taken for granted. The smell of the room was nauseating. His soiled clothing, added to the foul odor of rotten food and vomit overcame him at times. He couldn't help thinking he was going to die and be buried in one of the gravedigger's unmarked graves. At times, dying was his hope. He repeated the Lord's Prayer over and over.

Hanna hadn't seen Will for over three weeks. She told Miss Whisman that she needed Will's help with the cattle. The director, in turn, remembering that Dr. Cooper had high hopes for the dairy farmer from Hampton, sent for him.

"Upsey daisy, Krouse," the attendant smiled.

Will braced himself on the bedpost as he swung one foot at a time on the floor. He stared at the attendant in silence, and then felt a stinging pain as the attendant's fist struck the back of his neck. His legs buckled as he fell face down onto the damp floor. The attendant grasped the collar of his shirt and pulled him up. He was conscious enough to hear the attendant spout out, "I ought to just kill you. It'd be my favor to you."

Will rubbed his neck. The threat of dying didn't seem to faze him.

When they arrived at the shower room, the attendant turned to his helper. "Hurry up and unlock his camisole. This one really reeks."

They stripped Will's clothes off of him and held his body under the ice-cold shower. The water felt like BBs hitting his body. He silenced his moans as he attempted to move his hands and arms.

"If he don't start helping us, I'm gonna use a scrub brush on him," one of the attendants said to the other.

The stiff bristles on the brush chafed against his raw skin. He started to regain the feeling in his arms, then in his hands. Will felt his face. He realized that he must have been locked up in the Violent Ward for some time because he had a soft beard.

Both the attendants laughed. "That's right, Krouse, you've been with us for a while."

The other attendant shut off the shower, led Will to a wooden chair, and pushed him down on it. "Do you think you can dress yourself, or do we have to do that, too?"

Will's voice was hoarse. "I'll do it."

The attendant threw a towel and fresh clothes at

him. Will saw the cuts and dark purple bruises all over his body as he dried himself off. He pressed on his ribs and decided they were not cracked. At least he hoped not. Once he was dressed, the attendants led him to the men's dining hall.

The three of them sat down at one of the long tables. A woman brought Will some lumpy oatmeal, along with some milk, bread, and a tin cup filled with coffee.

"You'll eat if you know what's good for you," one of the attendants said.

Will nibbled at his bread, but couldn't swallow without drinking his coffee. The attendants had to get Will in a little better shape before they took him to see Lena Whisman. Miss Whisman was known for making the attendants who got on her bad side eat in the patients' dining hall.

One of the attendants added more milk to Will's bowl, hoping to soften the sticky oats, and then poured some of it on the stale bread in Will's plate.

"Go on, try to eat your food. It should be easier for you now," the attendant said.

Will grimaced as he chewed, but he was able to finish half the oats, most of the soggy bread, and sip some coffee.

"Let's go," the attendant said. "We don't want to keep the director waiting."

The other took Will by his arm and pulled him up from the table. They led him over to the administration building.

The door to the director's office was open. Lena Whisman was sitting at her desk.

"Step inside," she said as she pointed at three chairs she had arranged. "It's been a while since I last saw you, Mr. Krouse. It looks like you've lost weight."

Will didn't answer.

"I'm sorry, Mr. Krouse, we'll have this conversation later, that's enough, for now."

One of the attendants stood and stepped forward.

Miss Whisman's eyes narrowed. "I want you men to take Mr. Krouse back to the Q Ward." She had guessed correctly that Kurtz had been confining Will to the Violent Ward. There was no other explanation for his condition. "Do you men understand?" she asked.

"Yes, Director Whisman," one of them responded.

She rose from her desk and escorted them to the door. "Q Ward," she repeated.

The second attendant went to fetch Kurtz from the V Ward. Kurtz made his way down the hallway to Q where he found the attendant who had brought Will back. Kurtz pushed him aside, stepped into the room and shut the door behind him. "So now you're back in Q without any restraints, huh? Tell you one thing, Krouse, you cause me any trouble at all — like sneaking out again — and you'll change things real fast. Then back to the V Ward you go. Trust me, Doc has a lot more say than that Whisman bitch."

Kurtz shoved Will against the wall. Too weak to resist, he slid to the floor. Kurtz stepped back and watched Will struggle to get up and lie down on the bed.

He hadn't had a bed in all the time that he had been confined to the Violent Ward, though he knew it might disappear as quickly as it had appeared. Will had become the most dangerous sort of man there is — one with nothing left to lose.

The keen powers of observation Kurtz felt he possessed were clouded that morning. He should have noticed that the first attendant had disappeared, or that the second attendant cringed as he passed by, walking away from Will's room. He'd barely turned the corner when he heard his name called. Reversing directions, he headed back towards the administrative offices.

The receptionist stood in the hallway, wringing her hands and looking distressed. "Miss Whisman wants to see you immediately," she said.

Miss Whisman waited at the door to her office as he walked in. She slammed it behind him and told him to sit down. Keeping her eyes on him, she took a seat at her desk.

"Kurtz, if I ever see or hear of you, or one of your cronies beating Will Krouse like you did, I'll have you before the board and see to it that you'll be neck-deep in troubles. Do you understand me?"

Her eyelids fluttered as she jumbled her words.

"Yes ma'am, but who said I'm to blame for his condition?"

"You oaf, do you think I'm blind? His clothes are bagging and there are bruises all over his face. I'm sure if the rest of his body were examined, it would look the same. Would you like for me to arrange an examination?"

Kurtz shifted his weight.

"What the hell were you trying to do anyway, kill him?"

"He ..." Kurtz began.

"Shut up and listen to me, you ignoramus. The V Ward is for violent patients, not for you to dish out violence. The final thing I have to say is that I'm holding you personally responsible for anything that happens to Will Krouse. Now get out."

Kurtz managed to hold his tongue. He hesitated as he held the doorknob, then took off in large strides down the hall. Kurtz was not a man who tolerated humiliation or frustration, at least not his own.

"Krouse had better be as good at farming as they say. Good or no, this candy-ass treatment don't set well with me. Don't lock him up, Kurtz. Let him have the run of the place, Kurtz."

Kurtz's not so private opinion was that a few of the damn crackbrains who made the decisions should be locked up themselves. And what was an old jenny doing running this place anyway? Once outside, he looked over toward Slayer's office. "Shit, I'm just following the doctor's orders," he mumbled to himself. Why was he always the one delivering all the beatings anyway? Doc didn't have the balls; that was why.

Kurtz stuck his head in Will's room in the Q Ward. "Do you want me to stay in here with you, Doc?" he asked.

"No, he's restrained," Doc said.

"I made sure we strapped him up good," Kurtz said.

"I can see you did, Kurtz. Now wait for me at the end of the corridor. I'll call you when I'm ready to leave," Doc said.

"Yes, sir."

Doc's eyes combed the dim room. Will managed to raise himself and sat at the edge of the bed, staring down at the floor.

"I don't know when we'll get to talk again, so I'll lay it out for you now, Will. At first, I was a little worried of what people might think with you being such a prominent dairyman in Penn County. 'Course there was no denying that you broke my nose, but you telling everyone I assaulted your wife? Come on, Will, I'm the respectable doctor."

Doc paced back and forth as he spoke.

"But let's forget all that. You run off to God knows where and then come back. I still don't know what happened to you, but whatever it was sure helped my testimony."

"Why are you doing this to me, Doc?" Will asked.

"You've got it backwards, Will. You got yourself to blame. You should've had better sense than to break the nose of a doctor, and for what? Feeling up a beautiful girl?"

"Don't you have any decency?" Will asked.

"As a matter of fact, I do. That's why I came to pay you a visit," Doc said. "I thought you should know that your precious Becky died in labor."

Will's body trembled.

"Happened a few weeks ago, something like that. I guess you don't get much news here."

"Where are my children?" Will asked. He couldn't bring himself to ask about their unborn child.

"Let's see, if I can remember. Your brother took your little girl, and that busybody mother-in-law of yours got to keep that little bed wetter, Samuel. You interested in knowing where Aaron and Jacob are?"

"Please ..." Will sobbed.

"Okay then, Jacob's with a swell family being well cared for, but it's clear the hell over by ... what's the name of that county? Doesn't matter. Now Aaron? He's a different story. They tell me he's a lot like you — hell-bent. He's living with an old sot and his crippled wife. A case could easily be made to have the old man committed. And her? Well, the old folk's home would probably be a step up for the old hag." Doc paused. "Are you paying attention, Will?"

"Yes," Will said.

"Then look at me when I'm speaking to you. I'm doing you a favor by telling you this, because it's against the rules. So if you ever say a word about this conversation to anyone, or so much as attempt to contact anyone outside of here, I promise you I'll go to all lengths to make sure Aaron winds up in the state's orphanage or worse. Am I getting through to you, Will? I believe your boy's already on record of running away several times. He's had to be disciplined."

Doc squinted his eyes. Will waited.

"That's right, let the wheels turn," Doc said. "Tell you what, I'm going to pay Doctor Cooper a visit and suggest that you be transferred back to the infirmary because of the physical harm you've done to yourself while in isolation." Doc turned toward the door. "Kurtz?"

Kurtz's footsteps echoed through the corridor as he hurried back to the room. "Yes, Doc?"

"I have to check in with Cooper. Would you see to it that Will's taken care of?" Doc winked at Kurtz. "Now don't get too carried away, the man needs to be able to farm this spring."

Doc turned back to Will. "Doctor Cooper tells me all you need is some fresh air and sunshine. I'm inclined to agree with him. But until spring, there really isn't much for you to do. That is when you farmers get moving, ain't it? Just think, you'll have all winter to recuperate."

Doc turned to walk out. "Be extra careful with that wrist of his, it seems to have healed very nicely. I wonder if he broke his nose banging his head on this concrete wall."

Kurtz looked at Will, then back at Doc. "But his nose ain't broke, Doc."

"It ain't?"

Kurtz thought for a moment, then shook his head and grinned. "Got ya."

Doc started humming as he stepped out into the corridor and closed the door behind him. He stopped and smiled when he heard a shrill cry coming from Will's room.

Doc's footsteps faded as some of the patients started banging on their doors and screaming out.

When Will came around, he could barely breathe.

Hanna gasped when Will walked into her office.

"Do I look that bad?" Will asked.

She couldn't help but to stare. One of Will's eyes had a distinct red dot next to the pupil. His nose still had a gash that was in the process of healing. His clothes were bagging on him.

"I'm sorry, I've been so worried about you." She moved around her desk and took his hand into her hands. "Please sit down, Will. Can I get you something to drink?" she asked.

He smelled the fresh coffee. "How about coffee?" he said.

Her hand trembled as she handed him the cup.

Will laughed. "That cup's going to be empty before it's back in my hands."

Hanna pulled a chair across from him. "Will, you must tell me what's been going on."

Will raised is eyebrows.

"I'm serious," Hanna said.

"Okay, Hanna," Will said. "Pretend that someone snatched you from your bed in the middle of the night and when you awoke, you found yourself in a camisole in a small room here at Long Pointe."

"I don't understand, Will."

"What would you do?" Will asked.

"I'd be scared and want out," she said.

"And how would you go about getting out?" he asked.

"At first I'd try to reason with whoever was in charge that I didn't belong here."

"If they didn't listen to you?" Will said.

"I would complain, maybe quarrel, until they did," she said.

"Scream and kick?" Will asked.

"Maybe ... probably," she said.

"See, Hanna, that's the problem with insane asylums. If you remain quiet, you're nuts. If you yell and carry on, you're nuts. If you cause trouble, they beat you. If you continue to cause trouble, they strap you down. If you're old and forgetful, you go to the C Ward. If you're a problem, V Ward. If you try to take your own life, S Ward. You're a veterinarian, Hanna. What's the best way to get a mule's attention, with a sugar cube, or a rod?"

"I'm not sure I understand," Hanna said.

Once Hanna had learned some of what went on in the asylum, she had to see it for herself.

Will remained silent as he and Hanna walked over to

the S Ward. Hearing a man raising his voice to someone, they stepped inside and stood in the shadows.

"I don't care if it's dinner time, I said open her room."

"But, Mr. Kurtz, she's asleep," the attendant replied.

The lights in the hallway were dim.

"What's going on, Will?" Hanna whispered.

"Shhh, Hanna. Be real quiet and follow me."

"I'm scared."

"Then go back to the barn," Will said.

"No, I'm staying with you."

"I want to get closer." Will grasped Hanna's hand and pulled her behind one of the columns. He could see Kurtz with a female attendant he didn't know.

"I told you to open it," Kurtz said.

"Please, Mr. Kurtz, she's asleep," the attendant repeated.

"So, I'll wake her."

"After your last visit we had to transfer her to the Suicide Ward."

"She ain't gonna kill herself, she just wants it easy. She knows she don't have to work as long as they keep her locked up in here. She's just lazy," Kurtz said.

"But here she's always strapped down, or in muffs, or a camisole."

"Quit arguin'," Kurtz said. He grabbed the attendant

by the back of her head and pulled her hair. She let out a scream.

"Shut up, bitch," he yelled as he yanked her hair a second time.

"Okay, okay, please stop. I'll unlock the door, Mr. Kurtz," she said.

Kurtz snatched the key ring from her hand. "You'll get 'em back when I'm finished."

"Please don't hurt her this time."

Kurtz eyed the attendant. "Get going," he said as he unlocked the door.

Will's own experiences told him that the other women in the ward would remain silent. They were either too scared, or simply thankful that nothing was going to happen to them. Men like Kurtz, Will had started to understand, were excited by fear.

Will turned to Hanna and wrapped his arm around her. He could feel her body trembling.

Ann Railsbach screamed, "Help, they're after me." Sweat streamed down her face. She gulped for air while twisting in the camisole.

"The goblins gettin' after you, bitch?" Kurtz asked.

"Please," Ann sobbed.

Kurtz closed the door behind him. The walls and doors were padded. She bolted up in the bed, wide-eyed.

"Rats were crawling on me."

"Stand up and turn around," Kurtz said as he fumbled through the key ring. He unlocked her arms and took off the straightjacket, tossing it on a chair.

"I'll help you forget that nightmare." Kurtz squeezed her breast.

Tears filled her eyes as she rubbed her arms that had been pulled too tight. She lifted her gown off, quivering as Kurtz's eyes roamed her naked body.

"Lay down," Kurtz said.

Her body tightened as his hands pressed hard on her shoulder blades. "See, was that so bad? That's a good girl. It better be like this from now on."

"Yes, yes, I promise," Ann said.

A few minutes passed after the door closed, then Will took Hanna's hand and walked to the outside door.

"Will, let's do something," Hanna choked out.

"Shhh ... We have to leave now."

Hanna pressed her hand over her mouth.

"I'm sorry that you had to see that," Will said.

Hanna sobbed as her body shook.

"If we would've tried to do anything back there, I'd have been back in V Ward and there's no telling what you'd be in for," Will said. "It's not always patients harming patients; it's the attendants, too."

"Can't we do something?" Hanna said.

Will put his arm around her as they walked to the barn. "Hanna, I want the name of that girl."

"How am I going to go about that?" Hanna asked.

"When the time's right, tell Miss Whisman that you saw a young lady who looks just like a girl you knew from school. Maybe we can get her out of the S Ward and have her help us."

"What if Whisman asks me about her qualifications?"

"Let me handle that," Will said.

Will set the paper weight back on the desk. "I've been doing some thinking, Hanna. The only way to help some of the patients is to make sure Long Pointe's farm makes a handsome profit. Those in charge won't bite the hand that feeds them."

"Don't you think that the staff will know what you're up to?"

"Not off the bat, but in time they will, but it'll be too late."

"Why?"

"Because I'll expand the operation so large, they won't be able to do without the help it'll take to keep it all going."

"Why wouldn't they hire their own workers?" she asked. "Greed. The patients are free labor. And the bigger the operation, the bigger the profits."

"But how's money going into the wrong folks' pockets going to benefit the patients?" Hanna asked.

"It's not, but the produce they'll be raising will. I'm going to see to it that the patients start getting fresh meat and vegetables."

"How?"

"Don't worry about that right now, Hanna, they'll want to go along with whatever we say when all the cash starts rolling into their coffers. Maybe I can even convince them that I'm not crazy, but if our plan is going to work, we're going to have to make sure we pick the right people. After all, the patients will be handling all the produce from the farm and caring for the livestock. Don't you see all the patients will at least be eating better?" Will asked.

"Do you really believe the staff is going to share?" Hanna asked.

"Not at first. We'll have to devise some system on the QT, but eventually ..." Will stopped.

"What is it, Will?"

"We'll need folks in the kitchen, slaughterhouse, and the fields to begin with. Some patients are already working in the woodshop and the sewing room," Will said.

"This just has to work," Hanna said.

"It will. There's everything to gain. You'll see," Will said.

Soon after the new year, Hanna and Will went to present their plan to Miss Whisman.

The theory of this new enterprise seemed all wrong to the director. The treatment of the mentally ill did not naturally fit with economic success. One or the other was sure to fail. Miss Whisman didn't much trust the young Hanna Ames. Moreover, the thought of giving a patient so much power seemed to her to be a dangerous move, and yet they were half way down that path already. Proper procedures had been violated. Dr. Cooper, for example, had given Hanna permission to get Will's meals.

She knew, though, how fond Dr. Cooper was of his own dream of a utopia for lunatics. The best she could do was to drag her feet a little so that when the whole bad idea collapsed in on itself she could say that she'd told them.

Called for an account of things, Will felt as though Miss Whisman expected him to play the part of a deranged patient needing guidance. He wasn't good at playing the crazy, so he ignored the issue and presented the facts as if he were at a Grange meeting. He reviewed the condition of the soil and the equipment, and talked about his inspection of the farm buildings. Most of them were in excellent state he reported, "Much better than some of the other buildings here," he said.

Whisman understood the sarcasm. The problem was that he was right.

Will talked about the farm equipment for a time, suggesting the purchase of a few items he had never dreamed he'd set his hands on. Hanna then talked about the condition of the herd, the rotation of pastures, and a number of other technical things that Miss Whisman didn't understand.

Miss Whisman filed her nails and took an occasional note. When they'd finished, she sat staring at them.

"So what do you want from me?" she asked.

Will had his answer ready. "It seems that Long Pointe's just about set up to run what could be a very profitable farming operation. All that's missing is good help. To make a profit, I'll need folks who'll be able to do the work, or at least ones who are willing to learn. I'd like to be able to talk to those patients myself."

Miss Whisman dropped her fingernail file as she sat up straight. "Now you listen to me, Krouse. Don't you think for a minute that you're in charge. I am. We don't encourage the inmates, pardon the expression, to run this asylum ... this facility."

"Ma'am, I didn't mean to give you the notion that I wanted to be in charge. Truth is, I'd like to leave right now, but I was under the opinion that I was to oversee the farm operation." The truth was that as much as his children filled his dreams, the tortured souls at Long Pointe haunted him.

"Are you going to cooperate with me, Mr. Krouse, or do you prefer to be treated as a mental?"

"Miss Whisman, if I don't have the say-so as far as who is going to do what, then I'm not going to be able to make this work. You might as well lock me up for good and throw away the key, or let the attendants at me." Will settled back in his chair. "I've already lost everything. Do you really think anything else scares me?" Everything about Long Pointe scared him.

She planted her hands on the edge of her desk. "Okay, Krouse, I'll talk to Dr. Cooper. This will take some organizing and you'll still have to check in with the attendants. But I'm warning you, our farm better be one of the best."

Hanna didn't like confrontation. She'd never seen Will like that.

"Hanna, the only reason I figure I'm even here is because someone up there has a grand plan."

"I believe you," Hanna said.

"I lost my wife, my kids, maybe even the farm my great grandfather came to this country for. My father is lying under a fieldstone in a pasture I used to walk across every morning, and now I'm here. I won't let them make me their slave."

"They need you, Will," Hanna said.

"And I believe that, Hanna. If they didn't, you sure as heck wouldn't be getting my meals from the staff's kitchen, nor would I be free to roam this place. I knew before we went to see Whisman that I wasn't going to let her browbeat me. You don't put a lunatic in charge of a veterinarian. A lot of it still doesn't make sense right now, but it will."

Will was sure that Dr. Cooper would give his permission. Dr. Cooper was a believer, like the Krouses who fled the old country, one who wouldn't pass up a chance to make his dream a reality.

Though Hanna and he were eating together during the work day, Will usually ate supper at the patient's dining hall. It made him less conspicuous and he could keep tabs on what they were eating.

Their meals consisted of some combination of the ingredients of hog slop — wilted coleslaw, sauerkraut, corn meal, lima bean soup, squash, potatoes. If they were served more than two of these items at one time, they considered it a treat. Water and black coffee was the drink. Many patients grabbed at their food like animals, spewing it all over the tables and the floor. Most of the time, leftovers were mixed in with their meals. The kitchens were filthy and, at times, the food was left out unattended. Will thought about all the food the able patients raised only going to spoil by uncaring officials.

The staff ate well. They got fresh fruit and produce from local farmers and there was even a bakery. One day, Will polished off his coffee and was about to leave when a young, blonde-haired man approached him. He introduced himself as David Owens.

Will extended his hand.

"I was wonderin' if you might give me some consideration as to working on the farm?"

"You ever farm, David?" Will asked.

"I've shod horses and milked cows for an uncle of mine. I'm a good worker."

"The director hasn't given me the okay yet to pick the help, but I believe she's going to. When she does, I'll add your name to the list. How's that?"

David smiled as he chomped down on an apple he pulled from his pocket. "You won't be sorry. I'll work hard, you'll see."

David Owens seemed like a good soul and a willing worker, whatever had got him here. He was cocky and Will thought the others would follow his lead.

Will walked back to Q Ward, pausing for an instant at the intersecting hallway that led to V Ward. He recalled being in solitary.

The matter of giving Will a free hand had been settled an hour after the interview with Miss Whisman. She'd gotten Dr. Cooper on the telephone, complaining of Will's arrogance and Hanna's rudeness. She agreed with Dr. Cooper that — in terms of precedent, morale, etc., etc. — it was, of course, unusual to let Will choose the patients he would work with. That would give him extraordinary powers not appropriate to a patient. But she knew there was no point in arguing when Cooper shouted into the receiver, "It can't work any other way. Do you want to choose the help yourself?" She did not, of course. "Perhaps," he suggested, "you'd like to run the farm yourself, Miss Whisman. Or maybe we could take your salary and use it to hire a highly qualified outside expert."

"I'm sorry, Doctor Cooper, you know best."

CHAPTER 13

Becky hadn't been in the ground two months when Cecil was back visiting his attorney. Simon Sinclair sat at his desk with the telephone receiver to his ear.

Cecil sat down and eavesdropped while he looked around. Against the wall were several shelves, sagging under the weight of volumes of worn law books. Stacks of files were everywhere. Sinclair was no dummy, Cecil decided.

The attorney hung up the phone, sat it back on his desk, then looked over at Cecil. "I'm afraid I have some bad news for you."

"And what would that be?" Cecil asked.

"We're wasting time and money advertising your brother's farm for auction."

"Why?" Cecil asked.

"That was Judge Percy. He received a telephone call from one of the Pennsylvania Railroad's Chicago attorneys. It appears that Will's farm isn't yours to sell."

"What?"

"Settle down, Cecil, I'm just passing along the information the Judge has from this railroad lawyer."

"Are you going to keep me in suspense?"

"About a year ago, the railroad was prepared to file papers with the court granting themselves access to cut an easement through Will's farm. It appears that your brother sought legal advice through an attorney friend of that Professor Knobbs. After looking over all the specifics, Knobbs's lawyer advised your brother that the railroad had a good chance of getting what they wanted and in his case, arbitration would be much better than litigation. To make a long story short, your brother not only decided to sell the railroad the right to intersect his farm, but he also sold them most of the farm."

"Damn it, Simon, why would the railroad people want all that land?"

"They didn't at first, but Will, Knobbs and his lawyer friend convinced the Pennsy's lawyers that the land could eventually be used to build some grain elevators, a passenger station, and switching yards for Penn County."

"That seems like a whole lot of acreage for what you just described."

"It would be, but that's not all. It seems the railroad people have been wanting to get in the coach building business for a long time. It's cheaper if they do it here than in a city. Are you starting to see the picture, Cecil?"

"This is bullshit."

"Maybe it is, Cecil, but there's not a whole lot we can do at this point."

"What the hell are you talking about, Simon? My brother was declared insane by the very same court where this railroad deal would have been filed. All you have to do is prove that Will was incompetent at the time he signed those agreements with Pennsy's lawyers."

"I wish it were that simple."

"And why isn't it?"

"Because it was only one day before Will gave you his Power of Attorney to handle his affairs that he signed the railroad contract. In layman's terms, if he didn't know what he was doing signing agreements with the Pennsy, then he didn't know what he was doing signing over his Power of Attorney to you, Cecil."

"Okay, Simon, even if all this crap is legal with Will's children being minors and Rebecca's death, I'm still the closest relative to pass assets to, right?"

"Partly right, Cecil."

"Now what?"

"Have you ever heard of an irrevocable trust?"

"No."

"That's what I'm going to need to look into, Cecil. Your brother set one up for his youngest child to inherit the trust assets when that child comes of age."

"That's crazy, Simon. Why wouldn't he make his oldest child the beneficiary?"

"Maybe he didn't feel that was the way to go."

"Well, I'm the oldest in our family."

"There's your answer," Simon said.

"Damn it, Simon, that's not funny. Besides, his youngest boy is Samuel, you know, the one I couldn't find a home for. So all I have to do is take him in, and then you can get me appointed as his guardian."

"Samuel isn't Will's youngest child and neither is Adeline. Did you forget your sister-in-law gave birth to a baby girl before she died?"

"Okay, so what's the difference? I'll take and adopt my new baby niece, what's her name. Right?" Cecil asked.

"Wrong. It appears that Rebecca's dying wish was for her baby, Elizabeth, to be raised by a Mrs. Mildred Gates."

"They can't do that to me. I'm Will's brother."

"They can and did," Simon said. "Remember me telling you that Knobbs steered your brother in the railroad matter by using his attorney?"

"Yes."

"Well, that's the same attorney who filed papers stating your sister-in-law's dying wish. Mildred is the legal guardian. That sort of document is a heartbreaker. It would be very powerful in any court of law."

"I'll tell you something you didn't think of, Simon."

"And that is?"

"Knobbs is looking out for his own interest for the simple reason that his farm is right next to my brother's, and he thinks he'll have control of all the land and assets if he's appointed that baby's guardian."

"Although you'd never know it from your own experience, it's not illegal to be a good businessman. But that's not what he wants anyway."

"How do you know?" Cecil asked.

"Because he's already filed papers stating that in the event of his death, all his assets are to go to Elizabeth Krouse's trust until she's of legal age."

"So are you saying I have no recourse, Simon?"

"I'm not saying it's hopeless. Maybe this professor will pass away; he's as shrewd as they come. Or maybe your brother will be declared sane again, then find some other way to mess things up."

"You've got no advice for me?"

"I'd say that you should keep your nose clean, work hard, and be the best damn stepfather in the state. You're going to have to make some serious amends to your brother and to all those kids."

Aaron turned the knob on the lantern. The flame on the wick sputtered and went out. He had been up before daylight. By the time he had milked the last cow, the sky was beginning to get light. He poured the last bucket into the large dairy can.

He remembered back, picturing his ma hollering at him and his brothers from the foot of the stairs. "You boys scoot, breakfast is almost ready. Don't forget to wash behind your ears. Today's a school day."

He could still see his pa winking at him across the breakfast table, "You watch out for Jacob" and his brother saying, "I can watch out for myself, Pa."

Aaron jumped when he heard Oat Lansdown's voice.

"What are you doin', boy? Sleepin'?"

The old man's words hung in the cold January air.

"No, sir. I was just about to tote this can over to the milk house. Am I going to school today?"

"Not today, there's too much to do. Besides, ain't you had enough book learnin'?"

Aaron picked up the can and nodded.

"Did you get yourself any breakfast?" Lansdown asked.

"Yes, sir," Aaron answered.

The old man never asked what he ate, only if he did. No need to, it was always the same: corn bread and molasses. The only thing different was that he was drinking coffee instead of milk. The milk was to be sold. Aaron smiled.

"What's so funny, boy?" Lansdown asked.

"I was just thinking how those old barn cats come running every time they hear the milk hitting the pail."

"Don't you be givin' those damn cats milk. I only let them stay around to keep the mice away. Let them hunt for their food."

"I don't," Aaron said. Weren't they funny looking, licking their whiskers whenever he squirted them with the cow's teat?

"I'm goin' back up to the house to help Mrs. Lansdown. You go on and get busy."

Aaron watched him head toward the house. He lifted the milk pail and gulped down the remainder, wiping his mouth on his coat sleeve.

Aaron had thought about running away, but remembered the sheriff telling him that if he did, he could end up in a worse place, maybe even the State Reform School for Boys. He wondered how much worse things could be.

He was already up before daybreak and never finished with his chores until dark. Some nights he was even too tired to say his prayers. He looked toward the sky and asked his mother to forgive him.

They let him go to her funeral. Jacob wasn't there. Aaron wondered if he ever would see him again. When the prayers and weeping were finished, old man Lansdown, who'd sat outside during the entire service, drove him back to the farm. Before nightfall, Aaron was mucking out the stalls. When the old man came down with a lantern, he cuffed him in the face for having been too slow.

Aaron flexed his arms, feeling his biceps. He tightened his neck and put his hand on his shoulder, working his muscles. "Jacob would be surprised how strong I'm gettin'."

Maybe it was because Jacob was younger that life with his family seemed further away from him in time than it did for Aaron. He struggled to hold on to the memory of it.

Jacob's good fortune seemed to be designed to carry him a long way away from his starting point. He was now living in a principal's home. There was no question of skipping school for him. Every morning the boy opened his eyes to the smiling face of Mrs. Nighswander. She would lean over and smooth back his hair. "Shake a leg," she would say, "the principal likes to be at school early."

Jacob wondered if Aaron was living with a family as fine as the Nighswanders. Max Nighswander and his wife were in their fifties. Jacob remembered Mr. Nighswander telling him, "Today's my birthday. I'm a half century old." Mrs. Nighswander was pleased when she discovered that Jacob and her husband were born in the same month. They had no children of their own.

For a principal, Mister Nighswander knew quite a bit about farming, although not as much as Aaron. He farmed just enough land on their 40 acres to eat from. Now Jacob attended school in the same building as the upper grades. Grades four through eight were taught in the same rooms on the main level. Grades nine through twelve were on the upper floor. He wondered if that was the reason they referred to it as a 'high school.' He remembered how much Aaron had liked school and wished that he were here.

Jacob opened the back door of the summer kitchen and hollered, "Tiny. Here, Tiny."

A little beagle came running across the yard.

"Jacob, don't you let that dog in the house," Mrs. Nighswander reminded him.

"I won't, Mother."

Jacob didn't mind calling her mother. It made her happy. She knew she would never be able to replace his real mother and had even told him so. Sometimes when he cried at night, she would tell him that if Aaron were ever looking for a new place to stay, she was sure Mr. Nighswander would take him in too.

His new family had a car. It was the first car Jacob had ever ridden in. Every morning Max Nighswander walked to the front of the Studebaker coach and inserted the S-shaped rod into the bumper hole. He gave a couple of cranks and the engine started running. "Hop in," he would say.

"How would you like to sit on my lap and steer her?" Max would sometimes ask.

Jacob could remember sitting on his pa's lap, holding the Belgians' reins. He would have cried, but he was too excited. He would jump into the principal's lap.

After a few months passed, Aaron was never really mentioned. Jacob eventually stopped crying, but never stopped thinking about his brother. Mrs. Nighswander said his prayers with him every night. Jacob would bless everyone in his new family, including Tiny. Once she left his room, he would continue, "Bless Samuel, Aaron, little Addie, and my ma and pa." To make sure God knew who he meant, he added, "Will Krouse."

When the first snow came just after Thanksgiving and then when the big winds set in before Christmas, Samuel would sit on the bottom porch step of Grandma Kepler's house, kicking up snow with his shoe, making little snowmen until his face was beet red. She couldn't keep him in all day, though the thought that he might catch a cold, and then tuberculosis, was Grandma Kepler's waking nightmare. She would watch him from the window until she couldn't bear it any longer and then find some excuse. Rapping on the glass she'd call, "Sammy, why don't you come inside and help your granny rip some rags? My old fingers are achin' today."

He would thaw and dry and she would look at him with amazement. His auburn hair was growing every which way. The older he got, the more he looked like Becky. Samuel liked to help. He'd fetch her hairbrush, an apple from the cellar, a knife to peel it, asking questions all the time. The bad times for her came when he asked for news of Aaron, Jacob, and Addie. He'd want to know where his mother and his father were. Answering each of those questions was painful in its own way.

He'd tell her how he wanted to see his brothers and it seemed wrong that he had no contact with anyone but her.

"Do you think I'll get to see my brothers again?" he would ask.

She wondered if she should take him to see Addie, but maybe it was best to leave well enough alone. What would happen if Cecil and Minnie were to decide they wanted Samuel now?

Within a few months, Addie stopped crying for her parents. Her Uncle Cecil and Aunt Minnie became her new "Papa" and "Mama," and their sons treated her as their own baby sister.

Minnie, who hadn't been offered much joy in life, found a way to make this blessing into something tragic. She'd toss and turn, then get up early to sit in her rocker and worry about the arrangements. Most of her regret focused on Cecil. She couldn't understand why they hadn't taken all the children. They had room.

In hindsight, she'd been right in her thinking. Cecil would have had a better chance at the family land if he'd adopted the kids. Though he'd wanted them at first, he was just as happy not to have to deal with Will's boys. They were young and full of energy. The kind that would have taken a lot of training.

"They're not even together ..." Minnie would lament.

"No one wanted two boys their age, especially brothers," Cecil said.

"Poor Samuel," she said.

"What are you *poorin'* about? He's with his grandmother. No one else would take him, he's a bed wetter."

"He never was before all this happened, losing both

his ma and pa, now his brothers and baby sister. Can't you at least talk to your brother?"

"He's not allowed any visitors, he's lost his mind. And if you keep frettin', you will too. You wanted a little girl and now you have one. What else can I do?"

"Maybe all the children should have stayed with Becky's mother."

"Stop it, Minnie, that woman is too old to take care of all those children."

"She didn't have a choice."

"I'm finished talking about this, the sun's comin' up and I've got plenty of work to do. Pull yourself together. I hear the boys startin' to move around. They'll be wanting some breakfast."

Minnie's great talent was for making a sow's ear out of a silk purse, Cecil thought. Sometimes he wondered if he personally wasn't the best example of her fine work.

The thermometer on the shed read ten degrees below zero. He set the lantern down in front of the door. It was a perfect night. He had been able to keep her alive, waiting for the weather to change. The local journal said the frigid spell would last for at least a week.

Hattie was huddled in the corner when she heard the bolt snapping open. The lantern's glow exposed the matchbox on the dirt floor. Reaching down, he picked it up, sliding it open.

"My lucky two-headed match, you little thief."

Her eyes were dark and sunken for lack of food. She wobbled as he lifted her by the gown's collar, dragging her out and lifting her in the horse tank that he had tied on a sled. He pulled it to the steep bank above the river's edge. The first bucket of water hit her in the face, taking her breath away.

All the fight was drained from her. Once the water line raised above her head, he placed a heavy fieldstone on her chest. Her whimpers ceased. He watched all her air bubbles disappear, then glanced at his pocket watch.

He returned early the next morning. Overnight, the water turned into a solid ice block. Her open eyes were looking up through the crystal clear ice. He tipped the tank over, kicking the block loose. Pushing it with his boot, it slid down the snowy bank, hitting the rapids and swirling out of sight.

"Pregnant, huh?"

He pulled the empty tank back up to the shed, gathered Hattie's kerosene soaked clothes and stuck them inside his coat. He looked around before he came out of the woods and walked over to the Convalescent Ward. He went inside and headed straight for the boiler room.

The flames from the boiler shot out as he opened the iron grate to toss her dress and the trapper's hat in. He watched them ignite, then turn to ashes. Walking back out into the cold of the night, he pulled his wool scarf up around his neck.

CHAPTER 14

Will thought of having the meeting in secret, but decided that less attention would be drawn if it took place in Hanna's office. He knew eventually he would need Stella Wallace on board. Hattie was an old friend of his, he was certain he could count on her kid sister. Will looked around the office: Rufus Rimleek, David Owens, Captain McConnell, Mettie Walker, then Hanna Ames and Leroy Jefferson. Could he trust all of them? He wasn't sure of Owens, or the Walker woman. Could he get their trust?

"Everyone here stands to gain by working as a team," Will said.

"What's in it for me?" David asked.

"Yeah, how about me?" Mettie added.

"I thought you wanted to work, David," Will said.

David cocked his head back. "Just asking," he said.

Will's eyes turned to the Walker woman, but she turned her head before he made contact.

"If this is going to work out, we're all going to have to depend on each other. And anything that is said stays in this room. I'm sure that in time we'll have others joining us, but you're the core group," Will said. "If everything goes as planned, us patients will have more freedom and all patients will have better food and care."

Hanna raised her hand.

"Hanna?" Will said.

"I just wanted to stress what Will said about keeping this amongst ourselves," Hanna said. She continued, "I'm sure that you all are aware that there are patients that might unintentionally spill the beans. They will benefit from our efforts also."

"Well put," Rufus said.

"David Owens will be my straw boss. Captain, you're going to work in the slaughterhouse. Mettie, you're in charge of the kitchen. And Leroy and Rufus will work directly with me as my Hanna will."

Everyone looked over at Hanna.

"Okay, settle down, everyone ... *our* Hanna," Will said.

Hanna met Will as he was dragging out of the barn. She rubbed the back of her neck. She knew how he felt. They sat outside and talked anyway.

"Will, come winter, what happens to the patients that you pick to farm?"

"Your guess is as good as mine, Hanna. I reckon that most of them'll be locked up."

She continued to rub her neck.

"Hanna, taking away a person's goods and little things taken for granted like combing your hair and brushing your teeth is wrong. But robbing them of their dignity is sinful."

"What makes one human being treat another like that?" she asked.

"You were taught how to care for animals while you were at college. I had my father and grandfather to teach me. You wouldn't break an animal's spirit for the Hell of it, Hanna. You wouldn't take pleasure in seeing one suffer. They leave patients locked up for two weeks or more, strapped down. I've seen patients punished because they asked for food or water, or just because they cried out for help. The attendants don't want to be bothered."

"What can we do?" she asked. "Do you think the officials know?"

"I believe some do and some don't. Then there are others who don't much care."

They sat and held hands as they watched the orange glow disappear from the sky. They'd had another long day and were weary. They both needed sleep, especially Will. It was his only escape from Long Pointe.

Hanna walked back to her room. If the two of them couldn't bring peace to the poor souls at Long Pointe, how could the world ever expect to find peace or happiness? Her mind spun with thoughts — thoughts about the patients, thoughts about Will, and his family. After she said her prayers, Will remained on her mind until she dropped off.

After talking to Rufus and a patient working in the woodshop, Will had a newly designed rectangular casket built in secret. The carpenter removed the bottom, added short struts on the inside, replaced the bottom and then added a second bottom on the inside. He covered the interior with padding.

Rufus had to have the idea explained three times.

"You've heard of a false bottom jewelry case where people hide their gems and things, right?" Will asked.

"So you want a dead body on top, and room for another below?" Rufus asked.

"Yes, but the space below is for the escapee," Will said.

"And then?"

"We use those caskets for smuggling someone out when we send a body outside of Long Pointe," Will said.

Rufus grinned. "It's kind of like Moses and the bulrushes, ain't it?" he said. Having a Biblical connection made the idea seem much more rational.

None of the officials seemed to notice, or even care about, the difference in the way this casket looked. The only person who even asked was one of the carpenters. He was a feebleminded man who hadn't spoken for years until he got his hands on tools again and then he came alive. He started asking questions. Will finally took him aside and told him that the casket was designed for pairs, for mothers who lost their babies, or for twins. The double casket suggested that those buried together would remain together in the world to come.

Now all he had to do was recruit a living patient who was willing to test the system.

"Look here, Hanna." Will's hand was extended to his waist. "Knee high by the fourth of July. This is going to be a very good crop of corn."

"Where'd that saying come from, Will?" Hanna asked.

"Who knows, but it's a good one. Owens tells me that when the patients pick some of the orchards apples, they eat the entire apple, core and all so there's no evidence laying about," Will smiled.

"I'll tell you one thing, Will, even the employee's food has improved since Mettie's cooking," Hanna said.

"The Old Captain has been sneaking out beef and pork for the patients," Will said.

"What if he gets caught?" Hanna asked.

"It's all over then. But my money's on him. After all, any man that survived four years of that war knows something," Will said.

"You know, Will, this spring our herd dropped ten calves, and the other animals have done equally as well," Hanna said.

"While we're on the subject, are you making certain that no one suspects you of ordering extra medicines for the patients?" Will asked.

"Are you kidding me, Will? No one pays two hoots to a horse doctor," she laughed.

"That's what you think." Will squeezed her hand.

Doc had been careless about his story, therefore Pansy, Miss Whisman, and Wendell all had different versions of his whereabouts. He'd been called to Chicago, actually, by his mother's distant relatives, the Shultzes.

It was because he was family that Doc was entertained. Henrich Shultz knew Doc's appreciation for the fine cigars and brandy he kept in his office. But Doc was only a poor relation to Henrich Shultz, who needed to terminate this business arrangement.

Henrich said he knew that Earl would understand. It was a small amount of money for a large risk. Doc had to agree, or he'd look like a bumpkin. Shultz asked that Doc shut things down quietly, pay off the Pennsy railroad dicks or throw a scare into them.

Doc took it all in stride. He'd gotten tired of the penny-ante moonshine deal himself and he had a new proposition that he thought might interest Henrich Shultz — maybe even impress him. The herds of cattle and swine at Long Pointe, Doc saw, if properly cared for, would never be subject to a full accounting. He was pretty sure there was a way to skim off livestock for the family enterprise.

Pleased with himself after his meeting with Henrich, Doc took the train straight back to Hampton. He made a quick stop at home, then left before dawn to drive straight to the hospital. He'd been gone long enough.

Will woke up feeling the wet mattress underneath him. The smell made his nostrils flare.

Kurtz had found him in the dining hall.

"Eat your mush," Kurtz told him.

Will stared at the squirming larvae on his plate and shoved it off the table. Even before it hit the floor, tables and benches were being overturned. Cups and bowls flew across the room.

Kurtz blew his whistle. "Stop it, stop it," he yelled.

Several more attendants rushed into the dining hall and began bludgeoning other patients. Men were hee-hawing and screaming, running around and jumping on tables. Almost as fast as it had started, it ended. You could have heard a pin drop as the patients filed back into their rooms.

Kurtz and another attendant dragged Will back to his room and strapped him in a camisole. They restrained his arms behind his back. Kurtz hit him until he blacked out.

He'd gashed his leg open when Kurtz flung him against the jagged bedpost. An attendant came that night with some water. Will, trying to sit on the edge of the bed, realized he could hardly move his leg. It was too swollen. He asked the attendant to send a doctor. He closed his eyes and started counting to one hundred. Even with the throbbing, he drifted off to sleep. He was awakened by someone shaking his bed.

"Did you want to see me, Will?" Doc Slayer asked, standing at the foot of the bed. He held a handkerchief over his nose.

Will nodded.

"What about?"

"My leg is cut pretty bad. The pain ..."

Doc saw the open wound and looked away. "I hear you were stirring up trouble again over at the dining hall."

"I ..." Will felt the dried blood on his lip bust open and begin to ooze.

"They tell me you fell down some stairs, Will. What were you doing, trying to leave us?"

Blood dripped onto the straightjacket. "Are you going to bandage my leg?"

"I don't have time right now, Will." Doc bent down and lifted the torn flap on Will's pant leg. "It looks like it's infected."

"Please, help me, this camisole ..."

"Keep it elevated," Doc said as he turned to leave the room. The door slammed shut behind him.

Will rolled on his side to get a better look at his leg. When he caught a glimpse of the oozing blackened wound, he fainted.

A few days earlier, Hanna had noticed the receptionist in tears. She covered her tearfulness well but Hanna, who rarely missed anything, noticed her either staring off into space or weeping every time she passed. She had started to speak to her and then held back, thinking she might be out of place.

When more days passed and the woman seemed not

to be feeling any better, Hanna asked her to come along on a trip to Clayport. Miss Whisman was out of the office for that day and so, without attracting any attention, they took a carriage and headed down the road.

"The fresh air will do you a world of good," Hanna said.

The woman broke into tears.

"Now, now," Hanna said, handing her a fresh hankie. "Sometimes it's best to get things off your mind."

"Doctor Slayer had Kurtz beat Will Krouse within an inch of his life," she said.

"Who told you that?" Hanna asked.

"One of the better attendants. I probably would have shut it all out, except I know some of the Keplers. And that Krouse boy married one of their lovely daughters."

Hanna pulled off the road and took in every word. There were gaps and omissions in the woman's story. The most terrifying and unbelievable part came last.

"I heard it myself, Doctor Slayer telling Will that he couldn't do anything about his leg, that he didn't have the time," the woman said. "That poor boy," she added.

Hanna forgot the pretense of driving into town and turned the carriage around. On the way back up the drive to Long Pointe, she spotted Leroy. The boy waved and Hanna called him over. A moment later, Leroy was at the reins of the carriage and Hanna was running toward the cemetery.

"Rufus, Rufus," she yelled.

The gravedigger was waist deep in a hole. "Over here, child," he waved.

"Will's in trouble," Hanna said, gasping to catch her breath.

"He must be, he's here, ain't he?" Rufus laid his shovel down and climbed out of the grave. "What kind of trouble?"

"The receptionist told me they beat him pretty bad, then locked him up."

"Is that woman at it again?" Rufus spit and rubbed his gray, stubbled face.

"You think she's making things up?" Hanna asked.

Rufus puzzled over the question for a moment. "Nope," he said. "I think she's probably tellin' the truth."

Leroy was approaching in the buggy.

Hanna rattled on, desperate to make a plan. Rufus tried to calm her down. He asked who on staff was still here. Dr. Cooper, Miss Whisman, Doc Slayer all were away. Kurtz was here. Stella?

Hanna hadn't met Stella, who often worked nights.

"Stella finds things out," Rufus said, turning to Leroy. "Leroy, where the hell is Miss Stella?"

"I seen her," Leroy said. "She jus' come back. She be over in Hampton wid some friends."

"We're gonna need to talk to her," Rufus said.

Hanna's eyes began to well up.

"Missy, you're gonna have to stop that cryin', or I ain't gonna be able to help. Will's tough, he'll make it."

They sent Leroy to find Stella. Stella hadn't made contact with Will since he arrived. When she wasn't doing office work, she was working in the Women's Ward. Will's troubles, which followed closely on the disappearance of her sister, made her want to stay away from him; she didn't like being reminded.

Stella had a friend, one of the male attendants. She talked with him and in less than an hour, she came running out to the cemetery.

Stella's friend reported that Will had not only been beaten up, but that he had gotten a deep gash in his leg. Doc Slayer said it was fine, but everybody who went near his room claimed it stank. What they smelled was the start of gangrene.

"Is that what the doctor said?" Rufus asked.

"He's not around. He left here sometime after he looked in on Will," Hanna said.

"Where'd he go?" Rufus asked.

Stella spoke up. "No one knows ... maybe to his office in Hampton would be my guess."

"How 'bout Dr. Cooper?"

"He's out of town for the week," Hanna said. "And he doesn't practice medicine anyway, Rufus."

Rufus turned the situation over in his mind. The women waited for him to come up with a plan; they had no one else to go to.

Finally, Rufus asked Stella to find George McConnell.

They agreed to meet in an hour. Hanna went back to her room while Leroy brought in some of the milking cows.

Rufus looked up at the sky, rubbing his stomach. It was almost suppertime. He sat down on the pile of dirt beside the grave and rested his eyes.

Finally, he heard Stella and Hanna approaching. They were pushing a rattan wheelchair with McConnell in it. With his thick gray hair and bushy sideburns, he looked like he was still in the Civil War.

"Hanna, you get on back to your office," Rufus said.

"But I want to stay and help."

"I know you do, but you're new, it's too risky. You go on back."

Hanna did as she was told.

"How do, Captain," Rufus said. "Now, Stella, I want you to pay heed to Captain McConnell."

The Captain leaned forward in the wheelchair.

"You're not crippled up, are you Captain?" Rufus

asked.

Stella interrupted. "No, he's fine. The wheelchair's just an excuse. I'm taking him to supper."

The old soldier put his hand to his ear. "I'm a might deaf ... cannon thunder."

Rufus cupped his hand to the captain's ear. "That's not a problem," he said. "We want you to talk. Now go on and tell her what you told me about them battle wounds."

The old man had to have his memory prodded several times. When it came back to him, he told the story with great vigor. "Miss Stella, there was this terrible battle back in sixty-two. Them Rebs were kickin' the hell out of us at Shiloh ..."

"No, no," Rufus cut in. "I want you to tell her how that field doctor showed you how to treat them open wounds. Or better yet, one that's gone to black 'n green festerin' and smellin' foul."

"You mean the gangrene?"

"That's right, Captain, gangrene. Now listen up, Stella."

The Captain delighted in having an audience. "Well, this here's what you call the battlefield cure. First, you get you some fresh maggots and pack them directly into the wound, then bandage it to hold those critters in. Them little worms'll start eating all that dead flesh in no time.

That boy'll be good as new in a week or so."

Stella covered her mouth.

"You're going to have to be the one to pack that gash, Stella," Rufus said. "You're the only one who can get to him."

"Oh, Lord, I can't do it."

"Will Krouse's life depends on it. There's still a good chance he might lose that leg," Rufus said.

"Where would I find maggots?" Stella asked.

"That's the easy part," the old captain said. "In our food — just pick 'em out of the garbage."

"You can get a bandage from that attendant friend of yours," Rufus said.

"Is anyone going to help me?" she asked.

The captain pointed to the sky. "Him."

"You and the captain better git, Stella," Rufus said.

"One more thing," the captain said. "After a day or so, you need to clean out the dead maggots and re-pack it with live ones. Gotta use the hungry ones."

"How will I know if it's time?" she asked.

"They won't be squirmin'."

Rufus watched Stella wheel the old soldier in the direction of the dining hall. Could she stomach the job? He recalled the time he and the Captain were discussing how each of them ended up at Long Pointe.

"You know, Rufus, I get drunk and carry on, so they

call me loony and lock me up. General Grant drinks and raises hell, and I'll be damned if they don't go and make him president of these United States."

The rat seemed to have been there for days. Will was sure it was the same one since it always came alone. It would scuttle across the floor, then get up on its legs to sniff Will's wound. When he would move suddenly, or make a noise, the animal would run away but over time, it got bolder.

During hours of sleeplessness, he and the rat played their game. Gangrene was the third partner, infecting Will's blood, working toward making Will into food for the rodent.

Near evening of the day she talked to Rufus, Stella made her way down the dimly lit corridor, ignoring the crying, laughing, and groaning of the patients as she passed by their rooms. One thing she couldn't ignore were the smells. Human sweat and waste lingered in the air. She watched where she walked, remembering the time she didn't and something ran across her shoe. She shuddered.

She stopped at one of the doors, peering through a small barred window. "Will, psst, Will, it's me, Stella."

She heard a faint voice from inside. She slid the key in its hole, careful not to make any noise. The door hinges squeaked as she pushed it open. She stopped for a moment, then opened it just enough to turn sideways and squeeze in.

"I need to change that bandage, Will."

He lay motionless on the stained mattress. She took a deep breath and swallowed as she felt a lump rising in her throat.

Stella knelt beside the bed and stroked Will's hair. "I have to turn you over," she whispered.

Will's thoughts had slowed to something almost viscous, collecting like pitch or tar in pools in his head. Why was Stella here? When had he last seen her?

She carried a matchbox full of maggots that she set on the floor. In the end, she'd had Leroy collect them, something he'd done reluctantly — nevertheless, he did it for her. She'd borrowed the key from the attendant, but it came at a price, and she knew she was in serious danger being here. She went to work right away and started to lift Will's weakened frame when she heard footsteps coming from down the hall.

"Will, please," she said, "I have to hide."

She rolled him over and pulled his body on top of hers. Her heart beat so hard, she was sure whoever was coming would hear it. The key rattled in the lock.

"Krouse? You still alive, you bastard?"

It was Hayward Kurtz.

"That you, Doc? Please, help me," Will said. Then Stella felt him rise up, almost as if he were having a convulsion. He dove toward the floor at the foot of his bed.

"Hey, Kurtz, you pansy asshole," one of the patients down the hall called out.

Stella heard him take the key back out. Simultaneously, Will convulsed again.

"Who said that?" Kurtz asked.

"He did," someone yelled back.

A different voice called out, "I did."

Kurtz stepped back out to the middle of the corridor. "Shut up, you loonies."

All at once, yells and screams of, "I did" echoed up and down the corridor. Then, it was quiet. Will moved again and seemed to Stella to rise up, almost as if he were levitating. He slammed his hand down on the floor. A piercing squeal filled the room.

Kurtz moved back towards the door and fumbled for the key. He peeked in the room through the opening in the door. Will held his dead rat in his hand, its blood running down his wrist to the flat stone he was holding.

"Aren't you going to come in?" Will asked. His voice was hoarse. He swung the rat back and forth, then tossed it at the closed door.

Kurtz jumped back. "Not this time, Will. I'll just leave you to eat your supper."

Stella waited until Kurtz was gone, then slid out from underneath Will. She swallowed hard, then licked her dry lips.

Covering her nose with her arm, she pulled the bandage from his leg. She poured raw alcohol on the wound and dried it with a clean piece of gauze. Will seemed to feel nothing.

She pulled on a glove and forced two fingers into the gash, flipping out the dead ones. She almost choked.

Will patted her shoulder.

Stella opened the matchbox and shook the live maggots into the gash. She tied a clean wrapping around his leg, making sure it was tight. "There, it's done." She let out a deep breath.

Will's eyes were hollow. She dabbed a wet cloth around his cut lip, then wiped his face.

"You're going to be all right," Stella said. "Don't touch it. I'll be back."

She felt Will's forehead. He was burning with fever and mumbling. She leaned close to Will's lips to listen.

"Louie Three, Louie Three, Louie ..."

She gathered her things and paused at the door. "Don't you die on us, Will Krouse." She locked the door, then braced her hands against the dank wall, and puked.

Through the tedious hours of his working day, there was only one thing on Doc's mind and he was glad when Kurtz appeared to bring it to his attention.

"While you were away, Doc, well, I need to talk to you about Krouse."

"Let's go check in on him, Hayward."

"He's in the infirmary. His leg ..."

"I know, it's a shame. But it'll probably have to come off."

Kurtz looked confused. "What do you mean?"

"If I don't amputate, the gangrene will kill him."

"But he don't have gangrene anymore, Doctor."

"What?"

"He's all better. They say the wound's healing and he's resting."

"How do you know all this?"

"I overheard Doctor Cooper. He said that sometimes the Lord works in mysterious ways and it just wasn't Will's time to go," Kurtz said.

"Come with me," Doc said as he rushed off toward the infirmary.

Will was strapped down. He looked healthier than Doc had seen him in months. "How are you feeling, Will?" Doc asked.

"A lot better."

"Who took care of that leg for you?"

"No one."

"That's hard to believe. When I last saw you, it looked pretty bad. Let me have a look." Doc unwrapped the bandage and saw the new pink flesh. "Put him in a camisole, Kurtz, and let him spend the night in the V Ward." Doc shook his head. "It's too far gone, I'll have to saw it off. We'll be getting you ready for surgery first thing in the morning."

"I have to give it to you, plow boy, this year's harvest was bigger than ever," Kurtz said. "But with winter right around the corner, there's not much for a one-legged crackerjack like yourself to do."

The smell of liquor was thick on Kurtz's breath.

"Come on, it's almost dark."

Will knew he had to take Kurtz by surprise. His head was spinning. He had to make his move before Kurtz locked him down.

Kurtz pushed the heavy door open with his boot. That's when Will turned, kicking him in the groin. Will felt his knuckles crack as they landed on Kurtz's jaw. Kurtz fell to the floor senseless.

"Get the hell out of here, Will. Go back to the infirmary," Owens said. "Mettie, get Kurtz's key ring and unlock those two rooms," Owens pointed.

Will moved behind a pillar.

"This ought to make a nice necktie for you, Kurtz, you piece of shit," Owens said. "Come on, get up."

Will heard Kurtz being slapped.

"Get up, I said." Owens put his hand over Kurtz's mouth. "One little sound out of you, and I'm not gonna make this fast. I'll skin you alive, piece by piece. Understand, Kurtzie?"

Kurtz's chin bobbed up and down, feeling the curved blade against his throat.

"Good," Owens said as he tossed the loose end of a rope over the ceiling beam. "Come on, boys, let's hang him."

Will became aware of the stillness of the ward. "Don't worry, Will, there won't be any screamin'. Everyone wants him strung up."

Will shuddered. There was a deep gurgling sound before Kurtz's head hit the girder. Kurtz's flailing arms and legs fell limp. The air filled with the stench of Kurtz's bowels releasing. The ward doors opened. Will waited before making his way to the door. He checked before stepping outside, then headed back to the infirmary. Behind him were the faint sounds of clapping and hysterical laughter. Will covered his ears.

CHAPTER 15

"Have you ever thought about getting married again?" Hanna asked.

"Now there's a thought. You know someone who'd like to marry a mental?" Will asked.

"You're not a mental. And besides I just might be that someone," Hanna said.

"You know we're good friends."

"Can't good friends be married?" she asked.

"I'm sure they can and are," he replied.

"Then marry me."

Will grinned.

"Did that strike you as funny?"

"No, not at all, Hanna. I like a woman who speaks her mind. Becky ..." He stopped himself.

"Don't worry about telling me what Becky was like. She was quite a woman from what I hear."

"It's not just that. I have daydreams ..." Will paused. "Daydreams of me and my boys hitching up a plow to the Belgians again and going into the field at dawn."

"I want to be in your dreams, too."

"You are, Hanna."

It wasn't that Will didn't love her. He didn't feel free to love, just yet.

"You'll be getting out," Hanna said.

He lowered his head so as not to show his smile. "I've had a few thoughts ..."

Stella was sitting at a desk in the small room outside the main door into the women's ward C. She stood up as she saw Will approach.

"Stella, I stopped by to thank you."

Stella placed her hand over Will's mouth. "You don't need to say anything, Will. Many times things are best left unsaid," Stella said.

Will knew by the sadness in her eyes that she was aware of what took place behind the locked doors. This wasn't the time to ask about her sister, Hattie, either. He handed her the apple that he'd been polishing on the way over. "Some day we'll have a long talk at one of those Beaver Hollow shindigs," Will said.

"I'd like that, Will."

Will headed back to the barn. Hanna ran up to him. "Her name is Ann Railsbach."

"Was Miss Whisman suspicious?" Will asked.

"I didn't need to talk to her," Hanna said. "Rufus told me."

Rufus told Hanna that Kurtz had bragged to him about his exploits. He showed the old man scratches on his face that some of the "little wildcats" had given him and told Rufus he could have girls too — if he weren't too old to cut the mustard.

"Where is she now?" Will asked.

"Back in the Q Ward."

"Why'd they transfer her there?"

"She's pregnant."

There was something else on Will's mind. Something Hanna mentioned in passing, something that might be important.

"Hanna told me she came by when you were burying a coffin with the Mettie Walker baby written on it."

Rufus spat. "What's so unusual about a casket in a hole? That's where it belongs, Will."

"She said there was only one baby in that casket.

There was another baby, Rufus."

"You're gonna cause me a lot of trouble, ain't you?"

"I just want to know what you know," Will said.

"Why does Hanna need to be involved?"

"She wants to help."

"Thou shalt not be curious," Rufus said.

"Tell me about Mettie Walker's other baby," Will said.

"Leave our Hanna out of it," Rufus said. "You do that, and I'll tell you what you want to know."

"Suppose something happens to you, Rufus. Nobody'll ever know how things work out here."

"I'm gonna give you just an outline, son, for your own peace of mind. There's a half dozen different courses of treatment here. There's treatment for folks like you and me, people who maybe ain't as crazy as lots of them outside, or even lots of them who works here. We get to seem free, though we ain't. Then there's treatment for the other kind, the violent, crazy ones, the ones stickin' pins in themselves. We don't usually see those 'til I bury 'em. But they're here.

"I was nothin' but a drunk when I come here, though most thought I was crazy. I wasn't so much loony as drinkin' too much. After bein' locked up for a couple of months, I quit my screamin' and hollerin'. Then one day a good meanin' attendant — they used to have a lot of them back then — helped me out. I told him I felt pretty good whenever one of his attendant buddies weren't kickin' the hell out of me. So to do me a favor, he found me an out-of-door job. Long Pointe was in need of a bone yard at the time. One of the bigwigs called me into the office and they asked me what I'd done in my former life and gave me the responsibility and the title of gravedigger-in-chief. A few years later, I even got my own quarters. Had 'em ever since."

Will stood with his hands in his pockets.

"By the time I sobered up, it was already too late to go back. Most of my family and friends had turned against me. Too much water under the bridge."

"So you decided to stay here?" Will asked.

"Son, I didn't decide anything. Haven't you been listenin'? My fate was decided the day I set foot in this place. That's why I said we have somethin' in common. They found a purpose for me. They wouldn't let me go now for nothin' and now it seems they've found one for you too.

"For women it depends. Women don't run free at Long Pointe like you and me. The attendants like to keep them locked up and scared out of their minds. There's reasons for that, but I don't understand 'em. The more afraid women are, the more attention they get — I'm talkin' about that kind of attention Kurtz used to be so generous with. They get took over to S Ward. They beat 'em and violate them, and then there's the miracle: Sometimes these women get pregnant."

"They treat the pregnant ones different?" Will asked.

"They stop havin' their way with them after a while. But they don't get no midwife." He paused. Thinking of these matters made the old man shiver. "You seen any mothers 'round here?" he asked. "You seen any babes at the breast? The mothers, by the time they give birth, they're in bad shape; they're missin' teeth, sometimes their hair. But those babies ... a baby like that, with a fine, strong, intelligent father like one of these attendant fellas is a thing of value."

Will turned it over in his head and then he remembered something. "Is that what happened to the other twin?"

"Hanna knew one of Mettie Walker's babies lived?" Rufus asked.

"She was there when Dr. Slayer delivered it."

"She was assistin' him?"

"No. She happened to be across the hall from the delivery room and heard Slayer talking to someone on the telephone."

"Did she know who he was talkin' to, Will?"

"She didn't."

"That may be just as well."

"Hanna, I'll be back for dinner," Will said.

"Where you headed, Will?"

"The day room," Will said.

"Stella, what are you doing standing in the hall?" Will asked.

Stella's eyes widened. Will placed his hand on Stella's arm and pulled her body away from the small wire meshed door window. "My God, Stella, open the door," Will said.

Will's eyes quickly shifted to Mettie Walker. The giggling and cat-calling that filled the room stopped.

"Mettie, give me those scissors," Will said.

Mettie Walker was a large woman. The early gray strands in her red hair gave it an orange shade due to it being chopped off in uneven cuts.

"Somebody give Pansy her dress," Will demanded.

"It wouldn't do her no good. I cut it to pieces," Mettie said as she cut a handful of hair from Pansy's head.

"Stop it," Will said as his eyes watched the hair drop to the floor.

Mettie pulled the scissors away as Will reached out.

"Ask this bitch what her and that sawbones lover of hers did with my baby," Mettie said.

"I told you, your baby died," Pansy sobbed.

"You liar, I had twins. Ask Stella."

"Miss Wallace," Will shouted.

"I'm right behind you, Will," Stella said.

"What the hell is she talking about?" Will asked.

"I delivered her first twin in her room two days before the next one arrived over at the infirmary," Stella said.

"Stella, tell her to give you those scissors," Will said.

Stella took them out of Mettie's hand.

"Who's side you on, Will Krouse?" Mettie said.

"Come on, girls, break this up and go back to your rooms before an attendant drops by," Will said.

"Oh, don't worry about them. The pretty nurse can handle 'em. Doc and those guards are thicker than thieves," Mettie said.

One of the women snickered, "Kurtz was a dirty man."

Will took off his coat and hung it over Pansy's shoulders. "Stella, hurry take her over to Hanna and get her dressed. Mettie, you come with me, I want to talk to you," Will said.

"About my twin?" Mettie asked.

"Yes." Will patted her back.

"Come in."

Will heard Doctor Cooper's voice coming through the door transom.

"What can I do for you today, Mister Krouse?" Doctor Cooper grinned and motioned for Will to be seated.

"Thanksgiving will be in three days, Doctor Cooper,"

Will said.

"So?"

"Since we had such an abundant harvest, I thought that maybe my crew could enjoy a nice Thanksgiving dinner with all the trimmings," Will said.

Doctor Cooper scratched his head. "Why not? Most of the employees will be going home for Thanksgiving, except an unfortunate skeleton crew."

"Thanks, Doctor Cooper," Will said as he headed out the door.

"Hold on there, Will. Let's not be blabbing this all over the place," Doctor Cooper said.

The attendant kicked at ol' Tom, but hit the toe of his boot hard on the tree that the tabby jumped behind. "Son-of-a-bitch, everyone goes home for turkey, but I stay here."

The attendant heard noise coming from the dining hall. Looking in the windows, he saw every table occupied. He began shaking the doorknob. "Will Krouse, open this door," he shouted.

Will and Hanna sat silent, holding hands as the patients ate their first turkey dinner at Long Pointe. It would have looked pretty much like a church picnic if it wasn't for some of the patient's gowns.

Will walked over to the entrance as the door broke off its hinges. "You better be careful, you're the only attendant on duty in this area," Will said.

"Your coming with me, Krouse," the attendant said.

Will released Hanna's hand.

"No, Will," Hanna said.

"Don't worry, Hanna, it'll be all right," Will said.

"That's what you think," the attendant said as he snapped the steel cuffs on Will's wrists.

David Owens stopped when he saw the piece of cardboard covering the dayroom's door window. He put his ear to the door, then walked over to the water fountain across the hallway. Turning the handle, he watched the water dribble from the spigot. He rushed back to the dining hall.

"Mettie, Will's in trouble. The water ..." Owens said.

"I know David, there's no water pressure here in the kitchen, either."

Will stopped trying to get up after the water knocked him down the second time. He shielded his eyes as he slid across the wet dayroom floor. The attendant laughed as he aimed the heavy fire hose.

"See, Krouse, there's always a cost or payback," the attendant said. "Get your ass up. We need to dry you off," the attendant said. That was two weeks ago.

"Upsey daisy, Krouse, it's time to get ready for Christmas."

"Get the hell up," Doc Slayer said.

The attendant rubbed his eyes. "What time is it?"

"Morning. Now get the hell up," Doc repeated.

"Where are we going? It's still dark out," the attendant said.

"You'll see." Doc opened the door to the dayroom and pointed. "Who's responsible for that?"

Sitting in the corner was a fully decorated Christmas tree.

"There's one in every ward and also the patient's dining hall," Doc said.

"Don't ask me. Maybe Doctor Cooper knows," the attendant said.

"He don't know shit, but I have an idea. Come with me," Doc said.

They walked outside.

"See that?" Doc pointed over to seven pine tree stumps. "I told Krouse to have one cut down for Pansy and me ... one, not seven. You get Krouse, he's got some explaining to do."

"Then what?" the attendant asked.

"Oh, don't you worry. I'll think of something."

When Cooper went on leave again, and with the intentional indifference of Miss Whisman, Doc had one of the attendants lock Krouse down.

Doc claimed he never should be allowed any freedom at all, knowing how violent he could be. He ordered the attendant to put Will in a camisole so he could talk with him. After the attendant had done so, Doc made sure he postponed his visit for a day. When Doc arrived, Will was in discomfort, his mouth was dry and his body was aching all over.

Will twisted in the camisole as he sat at the edge of the bed.

"Tight, huh? It has to be, because you're a violent fellow, Will." Doc took a seat in a chair in the corner of the room furthest from Will. "Now where shall I begin? Oh, yes, how about work? Doctor Cooper is very pleased with the job you've done with the farm, but he won't be needing you again till spring.

"This is going to be a change for you, isn't it? I mean, being locked up again. My professional opinion is that there's a risk you'll try to run."

"I've talked with Cooper," Will began.

Doc cut him off. "What were you thinking helping Wendell anyway? That just makes me think you really do need help. Reporting to a loony bin all on your own? Tell me, does that sound sane?"

"Wendell needed my help," Will said.

"And what about your family, Will? They didn't? Well, those kids sure as hell need somebody's help. Imagine, having to grow up with no parents. Such a pity, such a waste."

Will tried lunging forward.

"Don't do something foolish, Will. Remember last time."

Will lifted his legs back on the bed.

"That reminds me, how's that leg of yours?" Doc asked. "It's amazing how your body keeps healing itself. Makes me wonder ..."

Through the heart of winter, Will spent almost all his time locked up. Hanna ran out of excuses to get him out.

Ann Railsbach spent the same months lying in the Women's Ward. Her baby was due in the summer if she was still alive by then. One day Stella opened the door to her room, pausing before she entered. Stella had been her favorite attendant, she'd promised to look out for her. Then Kurtz raped her and Stella disappeared.

"Where have you been?" Ann asked.

"There was nothing I could do," Stella said.

"I'm pregnant," Ann said. "I think it belongs to the attendant that Kurtz used to bring along with him. What's going to happen to me?"

Stella stared at her.

"Everyone knows that women in here die during childbirth. But what happens with their babies? I'm only twenty-two years old, but I hope your Dr. Slayer puts me to sleep for good."

Ann began to retell the story of her case, but Stella already knew it — the drunken husband with a belt, the way he drowned in the cattle tank, and the trial. Prudy once had taken the file from the sheriff's office and the two had read it upstairs at Honey Boy's. They figured that Wendell somehow connected it with Hattie's disappearance.

"I want to help you, Ann."

"Then get me some clean clothes and bed sheets."

"Okay," Stella replied.

Stella wondered whether or not Sheriff Gates was still interested in Ann's story. The matter of the missing babies might be worth investigating.

Then, of course, Ann would sometimes say that she had murdered her husband, though another man's hat was found on the scene — an almost sure sign that someone else had been there the night of her husband's death.

Maybe, Stella thought, it was just as well to let the whole thing lie. Ann was upset right now. Mothers dying in childbirth — that happened everywhere. A woman like Ann with her kind of history, with too much time to think, might imagine anything. Clean sheets and combed hair, that was about as much as one could offer.

CHAPTER 16

In February, Wendell left his deputy to run the office and took the train to Indianapolis, where he had attended several meetings as Penn County's Republican Party chairman. That was how he got the welcome news.

When he came back, he stopped at his house just long enough to shave and change clothes and then met Ruby at the courthouse. She was taking notes of a County Commissioner's meeting on plans for the orphan's home so Wendell went to Honey Boy's first.

"Hey, Sheriff, come over and have a drink," Doc motioned.

Doc pulled out a couple of cigars. He lit his and

leaned to light Wendell's, laying the matchbox down on the table. Wendell picked it up.

"Gas Light Club," he read. "Good spot, Doc?" Wendell slid the box lid open. Doc snatched the box from his hand.

"Grab us a couple more whiskeys, Honey Boy."

Wendell covered his glass. "Not me, I gotta run. Ruby's waitin' for me. Catch ya' later."

He wanted to get her away from everything, to get her undivided attention, for once. Though there was snow on the ground and a threat of more in the air, he took her to the edge of town, opened up the old schoolhouse, and sat her down on a bench inside.

"You must have something really important on your mind to carry me all the way out here, Wendell," Ruby said. "It's my favorite place, though I usually save comin' for the summer."

"Honey Boy fried us some chicken," Wendell said.

"Wendell, you didn't bring me out here to eat chicken, did you?"

"I was meetin' people in the capital," he said. He used to call the city he'd returned from "Indianapolis," like everybody else, but that changed once he was in politics.

"Say what you have to say, darlin'."

"All right, Ruby. I know where your son is."

Her cheeks flushed. He began rubbing her hands,

then patted her face.

"Take a deep breath, Ruby."

"Don't say anything else yet, Wendell. Did Honey Boy give us anything to drink with that chicken?"

"No, he didn't need to. Here," he said, handing her his flask.

She took a gulp and started coughing. Wendell patted her on the back.

"He's a cadet at a military academy down in Virginia. He's the son — I mean a State Senator named Blackburn and his wife are the folks who adopted him. His first name's Henry, after the senator."

"Is he healthy? Never mind, that's silly — of course he's in good health if he's at a military academy."

"Ruby, there's more. Your son knows that his mother was very young when she had him and had no choice but to sell him to a gypsy by the name of Zelda."

"How did he find out?" Ruby asked.

"The Senator is up for re-election and it appears someone from his opponent's camp decided to start a mudslingin' campaign."

"Oh my God, my poor boy," Ruby said, raising her hand to cover her mouth. "Who would do such a thing?"

"Unfortunately, a number of dirty politicians."

"Why would Zelda be tellin' anyone anything?" Ruby asked.

"Money," Wendell said.

"So now they're tryin' to ruin Senator Blackburn?"

"Yes, but it's not goin' to work. When Blackburn and his wife took your boy in, they were already in their thirties and didn't have any other children. They made sure that his adoption was legal and done through the court. But Ruby, here's the important thing. I want you to know they are two of the finest people that I ever met. Blackburn's eventually going to run for the United States Senate. He's very well respected."

"Wait until they find out the mother of their son is a whore."

"Was, Ruby, was."

She started crying.

"I hate seein' you do this to yourself," Wendell said.

She finally asked him to tell the Blackburns she wasn't a bad person.

"That's why we're here, Ruby. I wanted your permission to tell them that I know you, and to say what a fine woman you are."

"I'll bet Henry is a handsome young man."

Wendell took Ruby in his arms. "He has to be, you're his ma," he said. For now, Wendell thought it best that he not go into his and the Senator's conversation about the court trials of Will Krouse and Ann Railsbach.

After the first big thaw, Hanna was able to make the case that she needed Will's services. His arms looked thin. He worked hard and spent time with Hanna teaching her how to drive a tractor, then a team.

"How do you plow the rows so straight?" Hanna asked.

Will threw a crumbled candy bar wrapper in the furrow. Her chattering reminded him of Aaron at times. "You start at one end of the field and pick a point at the other end. Then you keep the tractor lined up with that point. I measure every new row using the tractor's wheels."

Sometimes Will would stop the tractor, freeing himself of its racket and fumes, and walk off down the field, imagining the rumps of the Belgians in front of him. The red-tailed hawk ascending to the sky in the distance reminded him of home.

"Someone said that they put you in the Convalescent Ward, Will," Hanna said.

"They transferred me back to Q Ward," Will said.

It was Doc Slayer who had him transferred to the Convalescent Ward, knowing he would isolate Will from all outside contact, plus, as one of the attendants told him, Doc was still fuming over Will's resolve. Will was locked down day and night, and only an attendant was authorized take him back and forth to the dining hall.

Will didn't know what other god-awful punishment might be in store for him, but over the two months he thought about his family and Hanna.

"Hanna, there's enough eggs in this coop for everyone, so fill your basket to the brim. By the way, the Captain tells me that Doc Slayer is stealing more cows and hogs," Will said. "Everyone is working extra hard, but it doesn't seem to be getting us anywhere."

"What do you mean? The patients are eating better now," Hanna said.

"I can't disagree with that, but we're still having to sneak around," Will said.

"What do they do with the shells after they peel them?" Hanna asked.

"Rufus collects them from the dayroom and buries them," Will grinned. "Come on, Hanna, let's get these eggs over to Mettie Walker and then take a walk down by the river. Hanna, sooner or later, I'm going to have to talk to Doctor Cooper before this place does drive me nuts. It's been over two years and I can't seem to see the light at the end of the tunnel. By the way, rumor is Doc's having the elderly patients transferred to the C Ward."

For Dr. Cooper, there were much bigger issues. Long Pointe's Board of Directors could not come to agreement on whether or not to house its elderly patients in one common ward. After several heated arguments between Doctor Cooper and Dr. Slayer Jr., Slayer won the vote and the elderly patients were eventually transferred to the convalescent building where those patients that were crippled stayed. Slayer had brought in figures calculating how to keep the patients at minimal cost, what the economic effect would be if Long Pointe could choose to treat only those who paid, or those who had a reasonable chance of recovery. From a business point of view, older patients were a liability. Lost in the debate was compassion.

It was an inevitability, it seemed to Cooper. The over-crowded C Ward always smelled. The paint on the frame building was peeling and its windows were permanently sealed with dried runs of paint. The lack of fresh air only added to the stench inside. Newly hired attendants were usually the ones assigned to the Convalescent Ward since the more experienced ones refused.

No visitors ever came to the C Ward. Once a patient was transferred there, his or her surviving family was informed that their loved ones had become totally unaware of their existence, completely detached from reality. They were technically living, effectively dead. Patients housed in the nearby wards knew better because they could hear their screams and cries throughout the night.

In the spring of 1917, the country now at war, Dr. Cooper had at last found a team of people who could make his dream for Long Pointe come true. That summer brought tragedy.

It started without warning, as Rufus remembered. He was sitting propped up against a tree in the cemetery when he thought he saw someone walking around the outside of the Convalescent Ward. The shadows restricted his view and he was too tired to find out.

The old ward building had two sets of double doors, one at the front and one at the rear. There was also an outside door to the boiler room. The man checked the rear exit first; it was bolted shut. Next, he tried the front doors. They were unlocked. He went inside and approached the attendant who sat in a chair, reading. She stood up when she noticed him.

"I need to see the patient register," the man in the white uniform said. She retrieved it for him. He ran his finger down the list, stopping at: KROUSE, WILL. "Have you checked the roll yet this evening?"

She didn't answer.

"Well, young lady?" he snapped.

"Yes," she replied.

He led her outside. "You're fortunate that I just happened over here. You've got a couple of patients wandering around outside without their gowns," he said. "It appears you haven't been very thorough checking the roll. What's your name, young lady?"

"I'm sorry, sir, am I in trouble?" she asked.

"How long have you been working here?"

"Only a few weeks, sir."

"Your first day on the job you should have known that these patients are difficult to handle," he said.

"Yes, sir, I was told by one of the senior attendants that I should strap the walkers down."

"Don't you have rooms to check?" he asked.

"Yes, sir, I do and I'm sorry, I'll lock the doors," she said.

"Make certain you do. Stay inside and read on your own time," he said as he turned around to leave. "Wait, someone left a can of alkaline water outside the boiler room." He pointed to the boiler room door.

"What's that?" she asked.

"They use it to make soap."

She bent down and grabbed the handle. "It smells like gasoline."

"Just see that it gets put back where it belongs."

He waited until she put the can back inside the boiler room, giving her time to lock all the doors. He took several small pieces of balsa wood out of his pant pocket and jammed them into the keyhole of the rear door. Pulling a syringe from his jacket, he injected gasoline into the keyhole. The wood swelled.

He did the same to the front doors, then walked back around to the side of the building near the boiler room. He took out a tiny oilcan filled with gasoline and squirted some through the cracks in the weathered door jams. The boards soaked it up. It wouldn't be long before the boiler's flames picked up the fumes.

An hour or so later, just after nightfall, Leroy was nearly thrown from the tree when he heard the explosion. He wrapped his arms around a large limb and watched the panes of glass burst out of the Convalescent Ward followed by flames shooting out into the night. One of the patients stood at a window slapping at her burning hair. He covered his ears to silence the screams, yet his eyes remained fixed on the horrors before him. He watched as their hands grabbed at, then released the iron mesh that covered the windows.

Inside the building, the attendant struggled to force her key into the jammed lock. Within minutes, the entire two-story building was ablaze. Patients banged on the doors of their rooms, begging to be freed.

A hunchbacked man stood urinating on the floor. "Help me put this out," he cried.

Another laughed and pointed upward, "Look, look, it's the fourth horse. We're in the fiery furnace of Hell," he said before being swallowed by the flames.

Leroy held his trembling hand over his mouth, watching the building swell and then crumble to the ground.

It wasn't just the sight of the fire that haunted Leroy. He'd recognized the man who set it. He'd wondered what that man was doing in an attendant's uniform, carrying an oilcan. But Leroy remembered his daddy telling him: "Don't get mixed up in the white man's business." He slid out of the tree, crouched down, and ran toward the barn.

"Mister Will, it's on fire."

Will saw the smoke rolling into the sky before Leroy was able to point to the C Ward.

"I seen him do it," Leroy puffed.

"Slow down, Leroy, catch your breath and sit down," Will said.

"It be Doctor Slayer," Leroy said. "What if he seen me?"

"Calm down, Leroy and tell me exactly what you saw," Will said.

"Dat's everythin' der is, Mister Will."

"Leroy, we'll keep this quiet. Don't repeat a word of this to anyone. Okay?" Will placed his hand on Leroy's shoulder.

"Yessa', dat's zackly what my daddy wud say."

"What made you tell then?" Will asked.

"I reckon it's another thing my daddy tol' me. One day we wuz sparrin'. I wuz dancin', an' a bobbin', an' weavin' 'round da ring when daddy's punch comes from nowhere, an' land smack dab on my chin. He reach down and hep me to my feet sayin', 'Son, you can run but you can't hide.' I guess dat goes fo outside da ring too, doan it?"

Doctor Cooper had Will bring in half his farm crew to help to dig graves. Will got a tractor, dug a trench and, in the grimmest event in the history of the institution, laid the unclaimed and unidentified bodies in a long, common grave.

Will asked if Rufus knew the number of dead.

"Son, that rat-infested fire trap was supposed to house forty — that's all," Rufus said. "Never seventy-five. Some of them didn't even have beds."

Rufus had stored away only a dozen or so regulation caskets; "pinchers," he called them because the head was wider than the narrow foot. Miss Whisman had called Hanna's father in Clayport and asked him to send as many as he could. The ones they rushed would be rectangular, more expensive because they were bigger, but more quickly built. The design change couldn't have come at a better time.

Will got his crew and a dozen other patients together to

clean up the remains of the Convalescent Ward. He listened in as they each came up with their own take on how the fire started when Rufus tapped him on his shoulder.

"What Rufus?" Will said.

"Oh, I thought that maybe you had something on your mind since you were just standing there with your foot on the shovel," Rufus said.

"I was just thinking about ..."

"Will, I have some news for you. Why don't you take a break and follow me over to my office?" Hanna said.

Will looked at Rufus.

"Oh, go on. Me and the others can finish up for today."

Will was almost afraid to hear.

"Your two oldest boys are still in Indiana. I was able to get addresses."

"Doc Slayer told me ..."

"Doc Slayer makes things up," she said. "You know that better than anybody. Your brother and his wife are only keeping your oldest daughter, Addie, until you're released. Your baby daughter, Elizabeth, is living with Grandma Kepler and Mildred."

"Baby?"

"Your wife gave birth just before she died. The baby lived. It was a miracle, Will."

Will waited until he caught his breath before he

spoke. "Why is Mildred still with Grandma? I don't understand."

"They said she finally gave up on the sheriff, something to do with the Garner twins. And Mildred agreed to raise your baby. Your wife put something down in writing, something that has legal standing."

"Who did you talk to?" Will asked.

"A few people," Hanna said. "I got the most of the details from Professor Knobbs. It sounded to me as though he'd thought of everything."

Will started to say something, then took a deep breath. She reached for his hand and held it.

Walking outside, he looked up toward the sky. Hanna had decided to spare Will the bad news.

Will, Hanna, and Rufus had planned on getting Ann Railsbach out of Long Pointe before she had her baby.

"Ann's baby is almost due. Is everything worked out?" Hanna asked.

"Kind of. I decided that now would be as good a time as any to put our plan in use."

"Did you tell Rufus?" Hanna asked.

"Not yet, I wanted to run it by you first. It will be dangerous," he said.

"Do we have any choice?" she asked.

"Not if she wants to keep her baby."

CHAPTER 17

Ann Railsbach went into labor a month early. For the first few hours, the ward attendant ignored Ann's pleas for help. When she finally went to a supervisor, the supervisor sent two attendants to put Ann on a gurney and wheel her out of the ward. She sent another to go fetch Doc Slayer, who happened to be on call.

Doc was happy to be interrupted; deliveries interested him. Moreover, after a moment, he realized why the name Ann Railsbach seemed familiar. He remembered her case from when it was news. He remembered, too, that both Wendell and Kurtz had mentioned the woman to him, though for two very different reasons.

Doc asked the attendant to tell Pansy to meet him in the infirmary at her convenience. He strolled across the grounds to the building. It was not yet entirely furnished. There were cabinets installed but never enough basic equipment. In a side room, there were tanks of oxygen, ether, and other combustibles, supplies one couldn't afford as a private practitioner.

When Doc entered the delivery room, Ann was lying on a table in considerable discomfort. A young attendant was trying to get her to drink some water, mostly spilling it onto her face. Doc asked her to time the periods between the contractions. He looked through several drawers until he found a forceps, a clamp, and a scalpel. By the time he had gathered his instruments, Stella had arrived.

"I can do this," she said, "if you're busy."

Doc asked her if she had a medical degree and she replied that where she grew up, women delivered their own babies and she'd had lots of practice. Doc told her to fetch some clean sheets. When she came back, he told her to leave.

She hesitated and there was a moment when he thought she might defy him. Who had she talked to? he wondered. What did she know? She didn't trust him. "I enjoy this," he said. "My father delivered hundreds of babies. If your parents had gotten in touch with him and offered to pay him a chicken, he might have delivered you, even." He insisted she go back to her regular assignment.

Pansy had arrived by then and put on a fresh surgical apron. Stella tried to catch Pansy's eye. She didn't want to leave Ann alone. She also knew she was powerless. She left the room, ducked into a large closet down the hall, and tried to listen.

The contractions were every four minutes now. Doc stepped into the small office to look for the file on Ann, so he'd have it ready.

When the contractions were a minute apart, Doc returned. Ann was exhausted and in pain. She stopped pushing, so Doc tried to pull the baby out with forceps. Pansy noticed his hands. They were smallish and narrow, good hands for assisting a childbirth, she thought, if he had any patience. His father's hands were similar. "You'll teach him patience, I know," Doc Slayer Sr. told Pansy. He was wrong.

Doc told her to push. Ann roused herself and pushed one more time and when she did so, Doc was able to pull the baby into the world.

It was clear immediately that something was wrong. Even for a premature baby, it was too small, too bluish, and deeply wrinkled. Doc slapped it on the bottom a couple of times and Ann raised her head, smiling.

"Stillborn," Doc said.

He clamped the umbilical cord, cut it, and handed the tiny being to Pansy. "He's been dead for a week," he said. "We should consider taking better care of ourselves around here."

Pansy held onto the child, looking lost for a moment. Doc took Ann's pulse. Not satisfied, he did another search of the cabinets and found a bottle. He pulled a handkerchief from his pocket and poured the bottle's contents into it.

Ann's color was not good and she was bleeding quite a bit. Doc sent the attendant to get fresh sheets.

"I need some surgical sponges," he said to Pansy. "There's some in my office, in my bag. Just set that thing aside and go get them, please." Pansy suggested sending someone else but Doc insisted she go, telling her to hurry.

Pansy wrapped the baby in a towel and placed it in a basket. "I can stay," she said. "There's lots to do here."

"I'm fine," Doc said.

Pansy paused in the doorway and took in the room. The pale woman, the sheets, soaked in blood, the lifeless baby, and Doc clamping his handkerchief down hard on Ann's face. Her legs started to kick and Pansy, feeling something unprofessional, something like terror, ran for his office.

When she returned it was all over. The attendant

had returned and replaced the sheets. Stella was there, too, pulling another sheet over Ann's face. Doc was in the office, filling out some forms.

Pansy opened the office door. She wanted to know everything. "She went into shock," Doc said. "I thought with the smelling salts over her nose, I could jolt her out of apoplexy."

"What did she die of?"

"It looked like a stroke coming on."

"She was awful young to have a stroke," Pansy said.

"I know, but didn't you see her body go into convulsions?" he asked.

"It was bad enough that she lost her baby, but to lose her own life, too? Why do so many die?"

Doc shook his head and closed up the file. He stuck something in an envelope and sealed it.

"Poor nutrition, bad habits, maybe. I think that it's probably a good thing. The human race," he said, "has to constantly work to improve itself."

The attendants now had Ann's covered body on a gurney. They wheeled her off in the direction of the morgue.

"Maybe it was for the best, Doc," Pansy said. "She was raped."

"Who told you that?" he asked.

"I thought you did."

"I never said that. No one knows what these patients are up to every minute of the day."

"I remember seeing her a few months back. She was all bruised and had cuts on her face," Pansy said.

"That's right. One of the attendants told me she fell down some stairs in the Suicide Ward," Doc said.

"She was so young," Pansy said.

Doc threw the file at the desktop. "What do you want me to do about it, Pansy?"

"You did your best, Doc."

Did he really think she didn't know the difference between the odor of smelling salts and chloroform?

"I'm going to list the cause of death as apoplexy on the death certificate," Doc said.

"What about the baby boy?" she asked.

In the aftermath of the fire, Miss Whisman began to think that her job would send her to an early grave. For the first time in her life, she began to wish she had not wanted to become one of the "new women," that she had stayed where she grew up, married whomever would have her, and had children.

The horror of the explosion had been hard to think about. The administrative difficulties of identifying who had died, who needed to be contacted, which bodies had to be shipped away, would have given even an archaeologist cause for concern. There were volunteers from one of the Clayport churches and a silent, pasty, young man from the county coroner's office who set up shop in her office. Long after the common grave had been filled, they were still writing letters.

The stench, of charred timber and whatever else, lingered in the heavy summer air.

Then there came the letters and calls from the families, people whose sense of outrage was magnified by their own guilt for having neglected their poor, crazy kin.

Among the others came one from a lawyer in Penn County wanting to know about Ann Railsbach. She was on none of the volunteers' lists, so they had no particulars to give him and in less than twenty-four hours, Lena Whisman found herself looking at the possibility of a lawsuit. Ann Railsbach's parents had received a letter informing them that their daughter perished in the fire. It was signed by Earl Slayer Jr., M.D. They requested whatever remained of the body be returned, but no one knew where it was. The truth was that Miss Whisman, if she knew the name Ann Railsbach to begin with, didn't know that she had died — in the fire, or otherwise.

Two attendants said that the last they saw of her was when she'd gone into labor and was taken to the infirmary. Doc and Pansy were on their way back to Hampton and Stella wasn't on duty, so she had traveled to Clayport for the day. She didn't return until evening and all she could say was that she'd been told the day afterward that Ann died in childbirth. For a moment, the phrase, "died in childbirth" hung in the air in Miss Whisman's office. It was one of the things that most troubled Miss Whisman — the fact that patients became pregnant and so many of their number died.

By nine in the evening, having exhausted every other resource, Lena Whisman was seething and ended up looking for the man she should have gone to in the first place: Rufus Rimleek.

Rufus was dozing in his private quarters when there came a pounding at the door — Miss Whisman with her demands for facts and her accusations. Well, yes, he said, half awake, he had buried Ann Railsbach and wasn't that a good thing — to get her safely in the ground and on her way back to her Maker since she'd lived so tragically? To Miss Whisman she was merely a human item on a list of administrative responsibilities.

As soon as Miss Whisman left, Rufus pulled on his boots and ran to the barn.

He got there as Will was closing things up for the evening. Will had never seen Rufus so rattled. He told Will what happened.

"I didn't know they wanted Ann sent back home,"

Rufus said.

"Nobody told you?" Will asked.

"Guess I didn't give 'em enough time. She and her baby were layin' over in the morgue. Soon as I saw 'em, I buried 'em. Did it this afternoon, Will."

"Why so fast?"

"Once I let an old woman lay over there for two days and when I finally got to her, the rats had gnawed half her face off. Besides, there are still remains from that fire waitin' to be put in caskets and sent off. I didn't know when I'd have the time."

Will shook his head. "Who's asking for them?"

"Families and friends. Now that they're dead, they want 'em back. I figured someone forgot to put her name on a list, now they're lookin' for a scapegoat. I have to dig her up," Rufus said.

"I'll help you first thing in the morning," Will said.

"No, I want to bring the casket up now, while it's dark. Then I can start drivin' before sun up."

"Where are you taking her?" Will asked.

"Doutt's Funeral Home, in Hampton."

Will thought of Becky. He imagined that Doutt's took care of her arrangements.

"Will, her folks already scheduled a funeral for her," Rufus said.

Gaining consciousness, Ann was confused. Everything was pitch black. She rubbed her eyes, her elbows hitting the sides of some sort of enclosure. She felt around and realized she was in a wooden casket. She smelled fresh earth. Shadowy images raced through her mind. She remembered hearing the doctor say something about her baby being dead. Then he put a cloth over her nose and mouth. The last thing she remembered was choking and not being able to get any air.

She wiggled her toes and felt something soft, something small.

"Oh my God, my baby." She screamed, then started gasping for air. She stopped herself, realizing what little air there was left.

Will and Rufus walked back to the cemetery, stopping at a shed Rufus kept under lock and key to get two shovels. Rufus looked around at all the freshly dug mounds of earth, pointed to one, and started to dig.

"It won't take as long as it usually does," Rufus said.

"Why do you say that?"

"She's down only three or four feet."

"I thought they were supposed to be buried at least six feet under."

"Sometimes, but in winter it's hard diggin' when the

ground's frozen."

"But it's summer, Rufus," Will said.

The dirt had just been dug which made things go faster. Will's shovel handle broke on the second spadeful. He ran back to the barn and got another – not the right kind, but one that would do. When he returned, Rufus was already down a foot and a half. Will dug down deeper while Rufus rested. It was cramped, two men digging up a grave, they got in one another's way, but they discovered a system and dug a little deeper when Rufus stopped all of a sudden.

"Somethin' ain't right," he said.

"What?" Will asked.

The old man's eyes darted back and forth. "I wasn't this close to that tree." Both hopped out of the hole. Rufus scratched his head. He had a system for identifying fresh gravesites by writing the names of the deceased on a scrap of paper and using a tack to attach it to a peg. He would pound it into the ground at the head and leave it there until he got around to setting a permanent marker. Rufus searched the ground and found the peg that had been pounded into this grave. Not having his glasses, he handed it to Will to read: "Ezra Zerkels."

Will wiped the sweat from his brow, scowling at Rufus, then began tossing the dirt back in. Rufus pulled on his shirt sleeve and pointed to a fresh grave a couple lots over. He reached down, pulled up a peg, and held it for Will to see.

"Ann Railsbach," Will said.

"I made a mistake, that's all."

"Step back, Rufus." Will started shoveling.

"See? We're more than halfway already," Rufus said.

Ann turned an ear toward the faint voices. She felt her heart pounding. She put her face close to the lid and opened her mouth, trying to suck in more air. She screamed.

Will straightened up and looked around. "You hear that, Rufus? Somebody's screaming."

"There's always someone screamin' around this place," Rufus said. "It's a loony bin."

"No, it's coming from there." Will pointed down, then began shoveling. His shovel blade hit wood. Screams poured out from the open grave. They cleared the loose dirt from the top of the casket with their hands.

"Lift it on the count of three ... one, two, three, lift." They lifted the box up on the grass. "Hurry, open it," Will said.

Rufus pried the lid off with the tip of his shovel. Ann bolted up, screaming and flailing her arms. Will cupped his hand over her mouth and lifted her in his arms.

"Easy does it, Ann, it's over, we're here. Shhh, you're

all right now."

Her body went limp.

"How the hell did this happen?" Will asked.

"How should I know? That girl was dead when I buried her. I wonder if that baby is still alive, too." Rufus picked up the half-wrapped body that he'd placed at her feet.

"It's already gone stiff, Rufus. Leave it be."

Will laid Ann down in the grass. "You going to put that babe back into the casket and bury it?"

"Waste of a good casket. It'd clean up. I'd say this little fella would be all right as he is. Goin' to meet his Maker pretty much the way he left him."

Will rubbed Ann's hands and patted her cheeks.

Rufus imagined the scene in the world hereafter. "'Turned out to be a short trip,' they'll say, 'You ain't been gone long, have you, baby Railsbach? You have time to get named?'" He looked around for something he could put over the tiny body but saw nothing. He took off his straw hat which covered all but the tiny feet of the infant. He caught Will watching.

"They don't like it," Rufus said, "when they get dirt in their face." He threw several handfuls of dirt over the straw, then used the shovel to rake enough so that the hat was covered.

Will turned back to Ann. She was still unconscious

but she was breathing. "This ever happen before?" Will asked.

"No," Rufus said. "It's a first for me, but I don't know about others ... gravediggers, that is."

"I'll carry her over to the barn. You get Hanna and meet me there," Will said.

"What should I tell Hanna?"

"Tell her to bring her black bag."

Rufus hurried off in the direction of Hanna's quarters.

Will picked her up off the ground. "You're going home, Ann."

Minutes later, Hanna and Rufus met up with Will in the barn. Ann was lying on some fresh straw he'd dragged into one of the back stalls.

"Is she all right?" Hanna asked.

"I think so, but she's still out. Do you have something that'll bring her around?" Will asked.

"Yes, smelling salts," Hanna reached into her bag and pulled out a vial. She sat down beside Ann, slid her arm behind her shoulders, and waved the bottle beneath Ann's nose. Her body flinched, then she started coughing and opened her eyes. Hanna pulled another bottle from her bag. "Drink some of this, Ann."

"Rufus, bring us a pail of water and a clean rag from

the shelf next to the horse stalls," Will said. "Hurry."

"You're going to be just fine, dear," Hanna said as Ann wiped her eyes. Hanna held her handkerchief to Ann's nose. "Blow."

Rufus returned with the bucket. Hanna helped prop her up against one of the bales of hay. "Take another drink, dear," Hanna said as she stroked Ann's hair and dabbed her face with the wet cloth.

"My baby was laying at my feet. Is he really dead?" Ann sobbed.

"I'm sorry, Ann," Hanna said.

The drink that Hanna had been giving Ann started to take effect. Her eyes closed and opened several times before she finally drifted off to sleep. Hanna put the bottle to her own lips and took a sip, then passed it to Will.

"What is this?" Will asked.

"Brandy."

He took a long pull on the bottle and offered it to Rufus. "Thanks, but no thanks," Rufus said.

Rufus and Will found Leroy and went back to the cemetery, leaving Hanna to tend to Ann. They set Leroy to filling up the hole, while they carried the coffin back to the morgue. It was dirty and there were splinters at the edge where Rufus had pried the lid off so they put it in the back, under several new coffins. They pulled out a new false bottom one and rested it on pair of sawhorses.

Rufus said, half to himself, half to Will, "Now what do you do when you don't have a body?"

Near the site of the boiler in C Ward — a boiler, Rufus noted, that should have never been fired up on a warm summer day — there had been several bodies near such intense heat that there wasn't much left but bone. The young man from the coroner's office had brought out several canvas bags and separated out the bones into three distinct individuals. The bone crumbled in his hands as he worked and when he got them back to the morgue, Rufus put them into ceramic urns that Long Pointe had bought years ago from a traveling salesman of mortuary supplies. They put one of the urns inside the casket and nailed it shut.

Rufus took a step back and bowed his head. Will looked over at him.

"Them ashes is still our bodies," Rufus told him.

When Ann awoke, they filled her in on their plans. But there was still a lot to do before she would be safe. It was about midnight when Rufus backed the truck out of the morgue garage. He got out to shut the garage door when an attendant suddenly came up behind him. The way he smelled told Rufus that he was just coming back from a Clayport watering hole and was half in the bag.

"Hold on there, Rufus, whatcha got in the back of that truck?" the attendant asked.

"A casket," Rufus said.

"Open them rear doors for me."

"I'm already late," Rufus said. "I gotta get to Hampton by dawn."

"Anything in it?" the attendant asked.

"Remains," Rufus said.

"Let me see," the attendant said. All employees had been ordered by Miss Whisman to check anyone, or anything, that looked suspicious. Rufus stood at the back of the truck.

"Open it, old man."

"Ann Railsbach," Rufus said, making sure the attendant would hear him.

"That's Railsbach?" The attendant remembered paying her a visit with Kurtz.

"Yep. Takin' her over to Hampton to bury her proper," Rufus said.

A wooden toolbox sat up against the cab of the truck. Some of the tools had somehow fallen out and were strewn about the bed of the truck. Rufus looked for his pry bar.

"Ann Railsbach, dead in childbirth. Tragic story," Rufus said, shaking his head. "I expect you'd like a peek. Didn't you know her?"

The attendant felt queasy. Part of him wanted to see

the body. "She was a looker," he said. "... for a loony. Let's get it open now, old man. Shake a leg."

Rufus wondered if he was strong enough to take him. He picked up the pry bar. "I could see where she mighta been kinda pretty," Rufus said. "Too bad the rats got to her."

"Rats?" the attendant said.

"That funeral parlor sure got their work cut out for 'em." Rufus paused. "What they do, I hear, is they take hot wax and pour it, right into the eye socket where the rats been feedin' and when it cools, they carve it and paint it and powder it. Now with her, with her nose chewed off, they're gonna have to think of something..."

The attendant's stomach started to spasm. "Just get goin' old man," he said.

The attendant walked behind a tree as Rufus pulled away and threw up.

Rufus drove through the gates. Once he was out of sight, he pulled over and ran to the back of the truck. "Ann?" he called as he opened the rear doors.

He pried open the lid of the coffin. It was empty. Rufus stepped back. At that very moment, the lid of the toolbox rose and Ann sat up.

"How'd ya get in there?" Rufus asked.

"I heard that attendant, so I got out as quick as I

could," Ann said. "Anyway, coffins give me the creeps."

The old man put his arm around her shoulder. "Come on up front and ride with me."

She curled up on the seat beside him all the way across the flat landscape, field after field, between Long Pointe and Hampton. She'd given birth a few days ago. Her breasts and her belly ached. She'd been buried, dug up, smuggled out of Long Pointe, and she was exhausted. When she finally fell asleep, Rufus slowed the truck, pulled off his coat and covered her.

When Ann awoke, the truck was stopped in front of a house and Rufus wasn't to be seen. She looked through the back window. The coffin was gone. They had apparently already been to, and left, Doutt's Funeral Home. She stretched and started to get out when she saw Rufus and a woman coming down from the porch.

Mildred stopped half way. Rufus walked back to the truck. "Ann, you're about to meet some of the nicest folks you ever met," he said as he took her hand.

"Is this your niece?" Ann asked.

"Yep," Rufus answered.

Grandma came out, smiling, and hugged Ann. "Glad you're here, honey," Grandma said.

"You ladies go on, I have to be gettin' back to Long Pointe before I'm missed."

Mildred walked him to the truck. He didn't have to tell her Ann's whole story for her to get the idea. Mildred didn't know Rufus well, but he had become somewhat of a legend in her family, a survivor. She trusted him as we trust people who've been through a lot.

"You did right, Uncle," Mildred said. "We're happy to help any way we can, especially if it's somebody who's close to Will."

"I know Ann will fill you in on Will and everything else," Rufus said. He cranked the truck and was on his way.

Mildred stayed outside waving until he was out of sight.

When she got back into the house, Grandma already had Ann's bath water waiting.

"We'll put her in the room next to yours after she's had a chance to clean up," Grandma said.

"Callie's old room?" Mildred said.

"Yes, dear."

Ann was awakened by a baby's cry. She caught her breath and then sat up in bed and began weeping. Grandma rushed into the room, followed by Mildred.

Grandma sat down on the edge of the bed, stroking Ann's hair. "Everything's all right, child."

Ann looked over at Mildred who was cradling a baby

and humming, trying to calm it.

"She won't stop fussin'," Grandma said. "Oh Lord, I think she has Becky's consumption." She finally said it.

"Why? Is there blood?" Ann asked.

"No," Grandma said.

"It sounds like whooping cough. Has she been exposed?" Ann asked.

"No," Grandma said.

"Grandma, didn't Molly Prater's baby have the whooping cough?" Mildred asked.

Grandma sighed as she put her hand to her lips.

"Whose baby you holding?" Ann asked.

"It's my granddaughter, Elizabeth," Grandma said.

"Will's baby girl?" Ann asked.

"Yes," Grandma said.

Ann opened her arms and motioned with her hands. Mildred laid the baby in them. Ann unbuttoned her gown and held Elizabeth to her breast. The baby immediately began to suckle.

Will shut the tractor engine down when he noticed Hanna running toward him across the field, flailing her arms. She leaned on the tractor tire to catch her breath. "Will, Ann's safe at the Kepler place."

"That's great news, Hanna, I couldn't get her off my mind," Will said.

"I have more good news. No, great news," Hanna said.

Will jumped down from the tractor and took Hanna's hand in his. "Tell me."

"Your baby daughter's doing fine, just fine. In fact, Ann is nursing her," Hanna said. She saw the expression on his face. "What's wrong, Will? Did I say something wrong?"

"No, no. Haven't you ever been sad and happy at the same time? Ann and my baby girl, that's the best news I've heard in a long time. But now that I know Ann's safe, I guess I'm feeling a little sorry for myself," Will said.

Hanna lifted his hat and pushed his hair back inside.

"I'll be okay, Hanna. I have to keep telling myself that our plan is working and there's going to be a good harvest. The patients are getting the benefits. They're eating better and working."

"You're right, Will, now you have more time to think about seeing your children," Hanna said.

"Don't worry, I've been doing all sorts of thinking," Will said. "You want to picnic under our tree?" he pointed.

"I'd love to, Will."

Ann had plenty of time to sort things out during her stay at the Kepler place. For the first time in a long time, she felt safe. One morning she came downstairs as Grandma pulled a freshly baked blueberry pie from the oven.

Ann closed her eyes and sniffed. "Mmm, that's making my mouth water, Grandma."

"We'll have to wait until it cools, Annie."

Nobody had called her that since she was a child.

"Your house always smells so good," Ann said.

Grandma Kepler sat the pie pan on the table. The wooden top was scorched with brown burn rings from countless others.

Ann walked up from behind and wrapped her arms around Grandma's waist.

Grandma turned to face Ann. She could see the little girl in Ann's eyes as she stroked her cheek. "Having you and Mildred here is a blessing."

There was something more than charity at work. Ann put them in touch with Will. However awful the stories she told — and she didn't know everything — any sense that he was in the world and well gave them hope that his family might someday unite again.

What she reminded them of was Will's quick wit. There was no doubt that he knew about the farm work they had him doing. But he also understood the politics of Long Pointe. "If he hadn't," Ann said, "I wouldn't be here right now."

Mildred came into the kitchen and stood behind

Grandma's chair, putting her hands on her shoulders. She saw that Grandma had been crying.

"Well," Grandma said, "I believe in my heart that the Lord has a purpose for Will."

"So do I," Ann said.

"Amen," Mildred said, smiling at Ann. "Look how much he's already done."

"Will's a strong and determined man," Grandma said. "Praise the Lord."

Though it was never said, everyone understood that baby Elizabeth was tying Ann to the past and that it was time for Ann to move on. There were other things as well. That girlishness that Ann had somehow hung onto cheered Grandma up, but it was too soon to risk her heart loving another young woman. Ann was too much like Becky and Callie. It was good to know that Ann lived in the world, they could be close later but it was better now to love each other at a distance.

Professor Knobbs had gotten involved in planning Ann's future. He had sat, like the old professor he was, and talked to her about what she had done and liked to do in her short life. He then wrote a long letter to a friend in Indianapolis. That Thanksgiving, the reply came back that they had hoped for. Ann was joining the Red Cross.

CHAPTER 18

A year into World War I, the newspapers were still giving all their space to news of it. There were posters everywhere asking young men to sign up, asking for volunteers. The war office demanded on knowing what the farms were producing. Long Pointe was officially informed that they had to make a quota for cattle to be slaughtered, dressed, and shipped east for our boys overseas. Discrepancies on the books were forgotten — for now. Even on the farms farthest from the scenes of action, and for people too old to be directly touched by world events, many felt the effect of the war.

Grandma Kepler received a letter one day. Samuel

had misplaced her glasses, so she took the envelope and handed it to Mildred.

They sat down at the table to make sure they could give it their full attention. It was from Ann.

Mildred read, "'June, 1918. Dear Grandma and Millie, I hope this letter finds everyone well. I met a handsome soldier boy in France. Can you believe I'm really in France? His name is Henry Blackburn and he's from Indianapolis. He's serving here in the Rainbow Division. After only knowing him for one month, we got married. Or at least I think we did (ha ha) because the minister spoke French. The ceremony took place in a small town right in the minister's home. And don't worry, I told Henry all about me. It's such a small world. He told me he's Ruby Garner's son. Stella used to tell me stories about the twins to cheer me up. Please share this letter with Ruby. I won't go into everything now, but someday I will. A lot of the soldiers are in the hospital with pneumonia, grippe, or trench foot. The sickness here is killing more boys than the German bullets. This war is nothing like I thought it would be. It's like a big adventure. On the ship over we all sang *Over There* and *Goodbye Broadway.* It's very sad. Millie, tell Ruby that I'm taking good care of Henry. And in the hospital where I work, if he did get sick, I could get him in right away. But no more of that, it's bad luck talking about troubles. And Grandma, he's going to help me get my good name back. I love you all and won't ever forget what you did for me. Tell the Professor hello for me. I'll be looking for your letters. XOXOXO, Annie (Railsbach) Blackburn.'"

The "Railsbach" was crossed out several times.

Grandma's voice cracked but she tried to remain calm. "Well, that was a nice letter wasn't it?"

"Very newsy," said Mildred, wiping her eyes.

"You be sure to get that letter to Ruby."

"I won't forget," Mildred said. There were tears running down the cheeks of both of them and they were both grinning. Then all of a sudden, Grandma let out a whoop, and Mildred answered with a higher-pitched whoop. Realizing they might scare the baby, they rushed to the door and stood on the porch whooping, and laughing, and weeping, and holding tight to the support pillars of the roof to keep themselves from rolling around on the ground. They pointed at each other, laughing until they thought they would burst. It had been a long time since either had had an occasion for this kind of joy.

There was a kind of delay in about almost everything that Leroy did — thought before action. He had learned never to do anything rash, without studying it first, because that was when he usually got into trouble. One morning Leroy opened his eyes and saw his future, like the pot of gold at the end of a rainbow, waiting for him. He ran to find someone to tell.

"Mister Will," Leroy called out as he came sprinting into the barn.

"What is it, Leroy?"

"What's dis say?" He handed Will a tattered business card his daddy had given him shortly before his death.

"It says, SALLIE DE ANGELO, FIGHT MANAGER, BOXING PROMOTER, BROADWAY GYM, GARY, INDIANA."

"I's gonna be a prize fighter, Mister Will."

"When did you decide that?"

"My daddy use to talk 'bout goin' to Gary."

"I take it you're not interested in farming anymore?"

"No'sa."

"Tell me, when's this all going to happen?" Will asked.

"Soon's I can," Leroy said.

"Tell you what, Leroy, in the meantime I'll find an old gunny sack and fill it with some straw. We'll hang it up on one of the rafters over at the old barn for you to punch on."

"You gonna help me den?" Leroy asked.

"As long as you're sights are set on being the world champion."

Leroy smiled and tucked the card back in his

pocket.

"Come on, Leroy, let's you and me pitch some of those bales down from the loft for the cattle."

"Can I do it m'self?"

"That's the best offer I've had today," Will laughed.

All Leroy could think about in the months to come was how he was going to be the champ. Now all he had to figure out was how he was going to get to Gary.

Will and Hanna finished surveying the farm. "Hanna, this looks like the best crop ever," Will said. "The patients are now getting the better meals served. Hell, at times they even get beef and pork," he added.

"When are you going to talk to Doctor Cooper?" She smiled as she felt Will's fingers tapping on her shoulder.

"There's no time like the present. You want to go with?" Will asked.

"Thank you, but I think Doctor Cooper might not fancy that."

"I'll see you later then," Will said.

"Will, don't the patients eat the same food as the employees?" Cooper asked.

Will's eyes looked at the bottle of brandy sitting on Cooper's desk.

"Now Will, you know that the patients can't have

alcoholic beverages."

"Oh, I didn't even notice that. I was just thinking about being here almost three years and our original conversation about fresh air, sunshine, and hard work," Will said.

"You even got church services every so often. You can't say that I haven't bent the rules for you," Cooper said.

"But Doctor Cooper, I want to go home to my family."

"I'll tell you what, Will, you and I will continue this conversation after harvest time," Cooper said.

"But ..."

"After harvest, Will."

"What did Doctor Cooper say, Will?"

Will leaned back against the big oak and pulled Hanna's back against his chest. He turned her head with her pigtails. Her neck felt warm on his lips.

"Will?"

Her lips parted as he kissed her. She swung her legs over his. He shifted and braced her back. She gave him a peck on his cheek. "Tell me, Will."

"I've decided to make an honest woman out of you, Hanna." He squeezed her thigh. "I accept your proposal. I love you with all my being."

345

"Oh, Will Krouse, I love you so much."

"Without you, Hanna, I couldn't have made it."

"Oh Will, your family in time will love me as I love them."

"We'll tell our families after the harvest," he said.

"So Cooper agreed?" Hanna said.

A few days later, they went down to the barn as a light drizzle started to fall. All day there had been big wall clouds moving across the sky to the north, concealing the afternoon sun. The two climbed up to the loft.

Hanna wrapped her arms around Will's neck and pulled his body down next to hers on the straw. Her lips parted as she pressed them against his. She ran her tongue inside his lips, drawing him even closer.

Will felt the warmth of Hanna's breath as she yielded her body to his. Whatever thoughts she had surrendered themselves to his caresses. Her body sensed feelings and pleasures she had never known. All time stopped as tiny explosions came in waves. She felt Will's muscles finally relax.

She pressed her lips to his ear. "I love you, Will Krouse. I've always loved ..." She continued to search his lips with her tongue.

He pulled back and nudged her neck with his chin. "I love you too, Hanna."

"Will, look how dark the sky is getting."

He stopped for a moment and realized that it was too quiet. He looked outside and saw the first funnel cloud. There was no time to move to the root cellar. He pulled her away from the door and held her close.

"Look Will, there's three of them." Hanna huddled against him, trembling.

The funnels swirled as they bounced across the fields.

"Keep your head down, Hanna," Will said, putting his jacket around her.

The barn shook. Loose boards and shingles flew. A big swoosh of air passed by, then it was over as fast as it came. When they looked up, the massive funnel clouds were headed away from them down the Watomi River.

Hanna crawled to the door of the loft. Will followed. "Will, the crops ..."

Pieces of cornstalks and wheat drifted down from the sky, looking as if a thresher had gone awry.

"Are you all right, Hanna?" he asked as he embraced her.

"Yes," she said.

They stood and looked out at the scattered crops.

"It's over, dear," Will said.

"What's over?"

"My ever getting out of here. Just look," Will said.

"Don't say that, Will. Look."

Will raised his head and looked out the loft window. Owens and the others were carrying sacks, gathering up the fallen corn. Hanna was jumping up and down, pointing.

"There's more of them coming from the dining hall."

Will jammed his hands down into his pants, ripping his threadbare pocket. Hanna turned to look as she heard the rock hit the floor. Will picked it up and rubbed his fingers over the grooves of dried blood.

"Louie Three got out of the cave," Will said.

"What are you talking about, Will?"

"Louie Three got out," Will smiled.

They decided to survey the damage.

Will noticed something as they passed the old icehouse. He pulled Hanna back.

"What is it, Will?"

"That's strange," he said, staring at a livestock trough.

"What's so unusual about a horse tank?" Hanna asked.

"Nothing, except that there aren't any animals to water out here."

"Come on." She tugged on his hand.

"Wait a minute, Hanna, something doesn't seem right

here," Will said as he placed his foot on the edge of the tank. "This tank ain't that old."

"So?"

He bent down to take a closer look.

"Come on, Will, it'll be dark soon and I want to see the river."

Will spotted something lodged beneath the inner rim of the tank. Hanna knelt down beside him.

"What do those look like to you?" he asked.

Hanna put her arm around his. "Oh my God, Will, they look like fingernails ... a woman's painted finger-nails." She stood up and pulled on Will's shirt. "Let's go, I'm scared."

"Hold on, Hanna." He persisted and pried one of the nails free. "Don't breathe a word about this to anyone," he said. "I've gotta talk to Sheriff Gates."

Will was in the barn rubbing down a bridle with saddle soap when Wendell walked in.

"I thought the tractor replaced all that," Wendell said.

"Machines break down," Will said.

"Well, are you gonna tell me about what you found?" Wendell asked.

"Didn't Stella fill you in?" Will said.

"I told him what I knew," Stella said.

"Then there's not much for me to say, is there?" Will said. "Besides, are you going to believe a lunatic?"

"I'll get right to the point. Who's fingernail do you believe it is?"

"Hattie's," Will said.

"Why Hattie's?" Wendell asked.

"Tell him, Stella," Will said.

"Everyone knows she got that nail polish from some traveling salesman as he was passing through Hampton," Stella said.

"Hampton?" Wendell asked.

"More particular, Honey Boy's," Stella said.

Will interrupted. "You know as well as I do, Sheriff, that we ain't got no store in these parts with anything like that."

They were right. In Hampton, a girl from Beaver Hollow wouldn't find any nail polish period.

"Do either of you have a thought just who might have killed Hattie?" Wendell asked.

"Same three I always thought, Kurtz, Buck, or ..."

"Or Doc?" Wendell finished.

"Since you brought up Doc, maybe you ought to poke your nose into the C Ward fire," Will said.

"What do you know about that?" Wendell asked.

"There's a witness who saw Doc around that old building that night, right before the explosion," Will said.

"And Doc was wearing an attendant's uniform."

"Is this witness a patient?" Wendell asked.

"Not everyone out here's a patient, Wendell."

"Who then?"

"Who's going to believe someone against a doctor?" Will said.

"Then why even mention it?" Wendell said.

"I guess I was just thinking about how I got railroaded out here," Will said.

"Whether you believe me or not, I've been working on your case," Wendell said.

"It's been nearly three years, Wendell."

"Let me ask you something, Will, didn't you own a felt hat?" Wendell asked.

"You know I did," Will said. "So what."

"I'm hoping to reopen Ann Railsbach's case, too," Wendell said. "And there was something in the report about a man's brown hat. It wasn't mentioned at her trial."

"So?" Will said.

"It had the letter 'K' branded on the inside of the headband," Wendell said.

"That's how your helping me? My last name's Krouse and I owned a brown dress hat?" Will said.

"Now don't go jumpin' the gun, Will. I just wanted to hear you say your last name is Krouse," Wendell said.

"What are you getting at, Wendell?"

"I wanted you to tell me what I already figured, and that is if'n a man were to put his initial in his hat, it would be the initial of his last name, not his first," Wendell said.

"That seems right to me," Will said.

"Well, Honey Boy tells me Ann's husband's drinkin' pal was none other than Kurtz," Wendell said.

"You can't hang a man twice," Will said.

"No, but that's enough evidence to reopen Ann's case," Wendell said.

"Ann flew the coop," Will said.

"Which brings me to my last two questions, Will. Do you know where Ann is, and do you know who hung Kurtz?"

"No and no," Will said.

"Stella, are you positive that Hattie didn't say where she was going?" Wendell asked.

"Yes," Stella said.

"You found nothing strange in her letter?" Wendell said.

"No ... wait, her P.S.," Stella said.

"P.S.?" Wendell asked.

"She wrote, 'Don't worry, Sis, I have my lucky two-headed match'," Stella said.

What was that two-headed match doing in Doc's

possession?

Doc watched the three of them talking from his parked car. He reached into his pocket and pulled out a cigar. As he began to light it, he picked up the two-headed match. What's Stella doing there? He held out the double-headed match. Did Hattie show her this? Yes, that's it. Wendell saw this back at Honey Boy's when he was fumbling around with the box. Did he open it? Yes, the son-of-a-bitch had to see it.

Doc struck the two-headed match and lit his cigar. Doc turned the matchstick until the flames crawled up to the other end and burst into a flame. He lowered the window and threw the charred stick out. Lucky, huh? Not for you, Krouse.

He pulled back the gearshift and released the clutch. He sped down the drive toward Hampton. He looked in the rearview mirror. Wendell turned to look as he heard the car's gears grind.

PART III

CHAPTER 19

One morning Will had to send five more head down to the slaughterhouse, some of them should have been a year older. He had long since stopped believing these were feeding our boys overseas.

He went up in the evening and talked to Dr. Cooper, asking his permission to go to the slaughterhouse the next day. He made up some story about looking at the color of the freshly slaughtered beef to determine whether they were getting the right feed. Besides, he told Cooper, he'd seen the accounts of what their cattle were dressing out at; he believed the slaughterhouse was robbing them. Cooper, delighted to find a way to make or save money, said Will could go as long as he took an attendant. Will chose Andrew, the oldest and deafest of them. That night, when he told Hanna he was going, she insisted on coming along. Slaughterhouses are ugly places he started to tell her, and then he stopped himself.

David Owen cut the five out of the herd at dawn. Andrew overslept. By the time they reached the slaughterhouse, the nasty work was done and the carcasses were hung on big hooks upside down being bled. Andrew sat in the wagon and dozed. Hanna, conscious of wanting not to be sick, held her nose. She had seen swine butchered when she was a child, but the scale of this was much bigger. Will stepped up to examine the heaviest carcass, which was closest to him. Then he said to Hanna, "I've decided that I'm leaving."

"And you're taking me with you," Hanna said.

"No," he said.

"Will, that wasn't meant to be a question. I'm going with you, so you may as well tell me your plan."

"I'm going to dress out a steer, get inside the cavity and have myself delivered to the sheriff's place. You are aware that every so often Doc sends him one?"

She nodded.

He examined the body cavity of the animal, thinking he'd just fit.

"So tell me how no one's going to notice you inside,

or the extra weight for that matter," Hanna said.

"First of all, the delivery men are going to be told that inside the carcass is a butchered hog."

"And how is no one going to see you?" she asked.

"I'll be wrapped in the brown paper they pack the meat in. Of course, I'll need someone to tie up the bundle — I mean me — with some cord."

"What's going to happen when you get to the sheriff's place? Is he going to unwrap you and shake your hand?"

"Very funny, Hanna. He won't even know."

"No? Then who will?" she asked.

"The twins," Will said.

"Have you already spoken to them about this?"

"No, Hanna, I'm counting on you to do that for me."

"What will you do once you get to the sheriff's?" Hanna asked.

"The twins have to be there when the delivery truck comes. They'll tell the deliverymen to put the package in the old shed behind Wendell's house. I remember it being there from when I was a boy. Then I'll come out later in the evening."

"How do you know that shed is still there?" Hanna asked.

"Farmers never tear anything down, Hanna. I'd bet my life on it."

"You probably are," Hanna said. "So, I tell the twins,

the twins help you get away, and then ..."

"Then I'll get myself over to the railroad tracks, wait for the nine o'clock freight, hop a boxcar, and I'm on my way. That's why you're not going with me now, Hanna."

"Give me one good reason why not?"

"Because riding the rails is dangerous. I'll send for you once I get settled."

"Where?" she asked.

He scratched his head. "I haven't figured that out yet. It's not good to get too far ahead of yourself."

"I've listened to you, now I need you to listen to me, Will," Hanna said, glaring at him. "I'm going with you."

Early the next morning, two men in a delivery truck arrived at Long Pointe to pick up the dressed out steer. It took three men to lift the large package of meat onto the truck.

"Why's this thing so damn heavy?" the driver asked.

"It says here on the delivery papers that it's stuffed with packaged pork," his helper replied as they jumped into the truck cab.

"Hold on, men," Doc said. "I want to check that delivery."

"We'll help."

"Stay put, I'll handle this myself." Doc opened the two wide double doors and saw the hanging steer. He took out his long scalpel and began plunging the knife into the carcass. Don't he think I know what's going on around here? He slammed the doors shut.

"Everything's okay, men."

"What?" they said.

"Turn that damn ignition off and maybe we could all hear better."

"Sorry, Doc."

Hanna watched the truck pull away. She finished packing her bag and headed toward the graveyard.

Rufus spotted her walking up as he was moving some things around in the back of his truck. "It's only noon," he said.

"I'm too nervous to sit still," Hanna said.

"It'll be a while before I get you over to the sheriff's place. I have to deliver one of these new coffins to Doutt's Funeral Home first."

"There's not a dead body in it, is there?" Hanna asked.

Rufus spat. "Not yet." He went back to arranging his things. "Well, if you're not gonna sit, get on in and we'll be on our way."

Hanna hopped into the passenger seat. Rufus smiled. Will's got himself a good one.

Prudy had gotten a call the day before. She and Ruby had

had to scramble to make an excuse for taking time off
— and for showing up at Wendell's place. When the truck
pulled up the drive, Wendell was still home.

"Who is it, girls?" Wendell asked.

"Just the delivery truck," Ruby said.

"What's bein' delivered?" he asked.

"I think it's the side of beef that was comin' from
Long Pointe," Ruby said.

"I don't know what you're talkin' about," he said.

"See, I told you," Ruby said. "Gettin' forgetful. Me
and Prudy will tell 'em what to do with it."

"I was just gatherin' up my paperwork," Wendell said.
"I'm ready to leave. Come on, I'll walk out with you."

"Okay," they answered.

The twins were waving goodbye to him when the
driver of the truck yelled out his window. "Hey, Sheriff,
hold up. We might need a hand."

"Me and Sis will help you," Ruby said.

Wendell stopped the prowl car and got out. He walked
to the back of the delivery truck.

"Where do you want it?" the driver asked.

"In that shed," Wendell said, pointing to the small
structure behind the house.

The three men picked it up and carried it to the shed.
Ruby held the door open for them.

"Why's it so heavy?" Wendell asked as they hung it

on a block and tackle.

"There's a butchered hog inside," the man said.

"Let's see," Wendell said.

"But it's wrapped," Prudy said.

"Well, it looks like it's coming unwrapped with all those holes."

"No," Ruby yelled. "Wendell, please leave it wrapped. It'll keep the bugs off it."

"There's no bugs in here," Wendell said.

The driver pulled out his jackknife and cut the string. The brown wrapping paper fell open. "That's a hell of a lot of pork loins they sent you, Sheriff," the driver said.

It was late in the afternoon when Rufus got to the sheriff's place.

"Give me a hand, Hanna," Rufus said.

He opened the rear door of the truck. Hanna helped him remove the false bottom of the casket.

"You can come on out now, son," Rufus said.

The twins ran outside about the time Will was making his exit from the truck.

"My God, Will, I told Sis I nearly peed my pants when the delivery men opened that package," Ruby said.

"We had a slight change of plans, girls. Rufus found out that Doc was having all beef leaving Long Pointe inspected," Will said.

"Thank God for Rufus," Prudy said.

"Hurry you two, get into the shed before someone sees you. Prudy and I are goin' with Wendell to Honey Boy's tonight, but we'll get you to the tracks before then," Ruby said.

"We'll let it start gettin' dark first," Prudy said.

"I've gotta get back to Long Pointe after I drop these caskets off," Rufus said. "It won't be long before they know you're missin', Will. With the crops bein' ruined, there was bound to be changes."

"Wait, Rufus." Will tossed him a cake of tobacco. "Take care of yourself and that ol' tomcat of yours."

Rufus nodded as he tugged the brim of his hat and jumped into the truck.

Pansy dropped off a letter with Miss Whisman with the instruction that it be given to Dr. Cooper as soon as he arrived that morning. She made another stop at the employee's dining hall and found Stella there having breakfast. Stella invited her to sit down.

"I can't, honey. I have to get over to the infirmary. Doc's expecting me," Pansy said, handing Stella a plain white envelope. "I need you to make sure Sheriff Gates gets this. It's extremely important to the patients here."

Stella dropped her fork as she took the envelope and slid it into her handbag. Pansy turned and left without saying another word.

She found Doc who was in the infirmary. Some poor fellow — another of Doc's victims she suspected — had taken a nasty fall, broken both legs and gotten pretty banged up in the face. Doc had just finished attending to him. They'd had to anesthetize him while they set the broken bones. Pansy waited until the attendants cleared the room before closing the door behind her. She looked gaunt.

In her hand was a box of matches. She held the head of one against the side of the box.

"What the hell do you think you're doing, Pansy?"

"They're just matches." She smiled.

"I can see what they are, but what are you doing with them in here?" he asked.

She put her finger to her lips, "Shhh ... don't make any sudden moves, Doc."

She turned the knobs up on both the ether and the oxygen tanks.

"Are you crazy, Pansy?"

"We both are, Doc. That's why we're here at Long Pointe. I thought that you'd change. Your father told me you just needed some time and I believed him. He told me that I'd be good for you and, in this way, I am. The end of you will be good for everybody.

"Let me read you something from a letter I ran across

in your father's files." She wept as she read a long letter from a woman whose daughter lost a child. The writer of the letter connected Earl Jr. to the misfortune.

Doc sized up the situation. He couldn't get to the door without crossing the room. Pansy let the letter drop to the floor.

"I left a letter to Dr. Cooper explaining how you've been stealing beef, amongst other things from Long Pointe. Will told me. I bet you're sorry now that you ever had him put out here. I said that you were working alone because I didn't want to involve your good friend, Wendell."

"And to think of what you did to poor Hattie," Pansy said.

His mind raced. Could he get the matches away from her? Maybe he could run.

"And what have you got to say about Will? Whose fault was that, Doc? If it wasn't for him saving me, I wouldn't be here to light this match. It's almost funny, isn't it?"

"I don't want to die." Doc fell to his knees.

"Who does?" she asked, striking the match.

CHAPTER 20

There was a shallow spring that fed into a small pond across the road on Lansdown's property. Aaron cupped his hand as he reached into the running water to get a drink. He ran his hand through his hair as the cool spring water streamed down his face. He remembered the times he would be allowed to skip school so he could help his pa farm. That was then, but school was now a place he looked forward to attending whenever he was given the chance. Working alone all day gave him plenty of time to daydream.

Lansdown gave him a thrashing with a bridle strap one time for knocking over a milk bucket. Mrs. Lansdown rubbed some of her homemade ointment on the cuts on Aaron's back once her husband fell into a drunken sleep. That was the first of many beatings. She would always tell Aaron, "I wish I could help you, but I'm crippled and if he throws me out, I'll have no place to go."

At first, Aaron hated seeing the old man drunk, but, in time, he decided it was actually better having him that way. The beatings finally stopped when Lansdown came to the realization that Aaron was bigger and stronger than he was. Whenever he wasn't thinking about the day he would be reunited with his family, Aaron thought about running away.

His schoolmaster talked about the war that was going on over in Europe and how America would win it. If only he were a little older. He felt his smooth jawline and the peach fuzz on his upper lip. Why wouldn't they take him? After all, he was already five eight and a hundred and forty pounds.

He recalled one winter night that Mrs. Lansdown wheeled herself into his bedroom, screaming that Oat had fallen outside by the barn. Aaron pretended to be asleep, but she was in a tizzy and ghost white.

"Who's going to take care of me? I'll be all alone," she kept repeating.

She didn't know it at the time, but she was right. Aaron had already come to the decision that he was leaving the Lansdown's for good, as soon as the time was right. He eventually got up and carried the old man back inside. For his good deed, Mrs. Lansdown promised to bake him an apple pie.

Aaron watched the water bubbling over the rocks. He was taught that it was wrong to hate, but he couldn't help thinking that if there ever was a son-of-a-bitch that deserved to be dead, it was Oat Lansdown. Aaron dried his feet with his kerchief and started to put on his boots when he heard Lansdown's voice coming from the thicket.

"Boy, what do you think you're doing?"

Aaron grasped a large fieldstone and held it up over his head, waiting.

Leroy hopped a freight train, leaving Long Pointe. He knew the ways to remain hidden, riding between cars, or on the roof of the boxcars when the railroad detectives checked the train. There were no signs of other hobos. A few sooners had headed south already, hoping to stay clear of the colder weather. Those tramps who lived in shanty town near the tracks stayed on until they were either run off, or burn out.

Leroy hopped the train headed west. A few hours into his journey, he spotted a boy who looked to be a few years younger than him running alongside the boxcar. Something made him want to help this boy.

"Run, faster," Leroy said, reaching out for the boy's hand. They locked hands and Leroy pulled him in.

The boy took a moment to catch his breath before he spoke.

"My name's Aaron ... Aaron Krouse."

"I's Leroy Jefferson."

"What's a colored boy doing in Penn County?" Aaron asked.

"I's comin' from Long Pointe. I's used to be de stable boy there," Leroy said.

Aaron pulled out his father's pocket watch. When he flipped open the case, the moonlight reflected off its crystal. He put it to his ear, then wound it.

Aaron knew all about Long Pointe. One night when Oat was drunk and cussing out his wife about Aaron, he shouted at her that the boy was crazy just like his father out at Long Pointe. A few days later, at school, a classmate told Aaron that Long Pointe was a place for crazies. Aaron had never been able to put it together — why would Oat say his father was in a loony bin? Maybe this was his chance to make sense of it.

"It's 9 o'clock, Leroy. Where you headed?" Aaron asked.

"I'z on my way to Gary, Indiana. How 'bout you?"

"Don't know yet, but I had to get away from the folks who took me in. Thought crossed my mind of killing the old buzzard."

"Gosh, why?"

"He worked me hard and beat me. Besides, one day I'm going to see my family again," Aaron said. They listened to the echo of the wheels on the rails as the train passed through a tunnel. "You ever hear the name Will Krouse?" Aaron asked. He just managed to get the name out of his throat.

"Mister Will Krouse done left Long Pointe."

Aaron's heart was pounding. "You know my pa?"

"I sure do," Leroy said. "He be a good man."

"Do you know where he's going?"

"All I knows is he always talk 'bout seein' his family."

Leroy pointed at Aaron's watch. "You'z bes' put dat in yo' boot so dem bos doan' steal it."

They sat with their backs up against the wooden slats. Aaron fidgeted with his watch, then stuck it back in his pocket.

"What time it be now?" Leroy asked.

"It's almost ten," Aaron said.

Leroy smiled.

"What's so funny?" Aaron asked.

"I sees dat you an' Mister Will's kin. He be a thinker, too."

"Is he all right?" Aaron asked.

Leroy told Aaron everything he knew about Will as he knew him at Long Pointe.

Aaron rubbed his eyes, fighting to stay awake. Within minutes, the boy was curled up and snoring.

Aaron was awakened by the banging of the boxcars as the train began to slow. He squinted in the early sun, then yawned. Leroy was gone. He felt in his bibs for his watch and pulled out a couple of rolled up dollars. The watch was gone.

He got to his feet and stretched, then walked toward the door of the boxcar. Something was in his boot. He reached inside and pulled out the watch. Leroy.

Aaron's stomach growled. He looked out and saw the wooden water tank. HAMPTON. He licked his dry lips and looked at the watch: six o'clock.

He remembered Leroy telling him to get off the train whenever it slowed down, came to a stop, or approached buildings. He closed his eyes and leaped.

Leroy had jumped out of the boxcar just before Hampton and hopped on another train headed west. A couple of hours later, he was picking himself up and looking around. He dusted off his coat and britches, then began walking along the railroad tracks. Red and yellow flames surrounded by clouds of dark smoke billowed from towering smokestacks of the factories below. The air smelled of ash. It reminded him of the smell of the train he had just hopped off.

The caboose's red lights were now barely visible. Leroy licked his finger and held it up in the wind. He turned and began walking toward the stacks ... and glory.

Ruby parked the car in a cornfield near Honey Boy's at dusk. It would be awhile before the 9 o'clock train arrived, but everyone was nervous and they couldn't stay at the house any longer. Will and Hanna got out of the car. The twins hugged and kissed them. Ruby handed Hanna a sealed envelope.

"Don't open it now, dear. It's from Sis and me. Wait until you're on your way," Ruby said.

"Thank you," Hanna said.

"Will, I'll get word to your boys. I'll tell them where to find you," Ruby said.

"I'm counting on you girls," Will said.

"Okay Prudy, powder them pretty eyes. We have to make it back home before Wendell gets there," Ruby said.

Will and Hanna laid in the field, waiting for the 9 o'clock freight train.

Will heard a whistle in the distance. "Here she comes, Hanna. Are you ready?" Will reached over and squeezed her arm.

She patted his hand.

They got up and rushed toward the tracks. Will jumped into one of the boxcars as the train slowed. Hanna ran alongside the train, reaching for Will's hand. The car's couplers started banging as the train began to brake.

"Why is it stopping, Will?"

"I don't know, Hanna. Just give me your hand," Will said. "It's too late now."

Perhaps it was the ongoing investigations, or just habit that made Wendell start to long for the old days when he worked the railroads. He'd listen for the train every night. Sometimes he would just drive down by the tracks to watch it thunder by.

Wendell had come back to his house to find the twins there waiting for him. Just before 9:00, they got into the girl's car to drive to Honey Boy's. The twins were chattering as Ruby turned onto Main Street.

"Shush, the train's stopped," Wendell said.

"So?" Ruby said.

"Something's wrong, or it wouldn't have stopped. I'm gettin' out to have a look-see. You girls stay here," Wendell said as he exited the car.

"Not on your life," Ruby said as she did a U-turn and pulled off the main street into the station. The twins got out and followed him, eavesdropping as he talked to the conductor.

"What made you stop?" Wendell asked.

"The engineer thought he saw something on the tracks up ahead, probably a cow or deer," the conductor said. "Wait, he's waving me on now."

"Okay, I was just checkin'," Wendell said.

"That reminds me. I might as well check for freeloaders before I give the engineer the highball."

"Who you lookin' for?" Wendell asked.

"You know, train tramps."

"I'll give you a hand," Wendell said.

"All right Wendell, I'll start at the front and you take the back."

Ruby and Prudy held on to each other.

"This is the last one," the conductor said. "I'll check it and we'll be on our way."

Just then, he slipped and dropped his flashlight. It rolled down a slope, landing at Wendell's feet. Wendell bent down to pick it up as the conductor brushed off his uniform.

"I'll check it for you," Wendell said.

He slid the door open and shined the light inside to find himself looking right at Will and Hanna. He froze.

"Is it empty?" the conductor asked.

Doctor Cooper laid Pansy's letter next to Senator

Blackburn's on his desk and picked up the telephone.

"Operator, this is Dr. Cooper over at Long Pointe, get me the Shultz Meat Packing Company in Chicago." Cooper waited.

Shultz's voice came on the line. "Yes?"

"Drop off the line, operator," Cooper said. "Mister Shultz, I called to tell you Doctor Slayer is dead, so whatever deal you had with him died with him."

"Who are you?" Shultz asked.

"I have to go now," Cooper said, placing the receiver back on its hook.

He jotted on his note pad: REGULAR INSPECTIONS FOR THE PATIENT'S DINING HALL AND ROOMS. INVESTIGATE PATIENT'S TREATMENT.

Will gazed at the acres and acres of virgin timber. Unlike the city streets, the countryside would take years to change. He looked up as he approached the covered bridge. The yellow and red maple leaves were just beginning to fall onto the banks of the stream below.

"Whoa, girl." His eyes stopped when he saw the carved heart W.K. + R.K. He glanced around at the new carvings and smiled. "Git, girl."

Will wrapped the buggy reins around the post. Opening the wrought iron gate, he walked over and knelt on the grass. Pulling out his pocket knife, he cut a small square of sod and began digging out some dirt. He studied the flat stone before he placed it in the hole, then replaced the sod, patting it down firm. Raising himself up, he slapped the loose dirt off his hands. Will looked at the grave marker. "Farewell, my lovely Rebecca."

The church bell gave its final ring.

"Brothers and sisters, I asked Will Krouse to say a few words this special day," Reverend Prater said.

Will stood waiting for the words that had been pent up inside him to come.

"My friends and neighbors, right at this very moment, some young soldier boy is taking his last breath, or thinking about his mother or his sweetheart. Or he's killed so fast, maybe he didn't even have a chance to think about anyone or anything.

"We're born and from then on, our lives are shaped by everyone and everything that surrounds us. I'm not so sure our loves and hates are entirely under our control. One day I was standing in a field of golden wheat, the next I was laying naked, locked down at Long Pointe. Now I stand before you folks once again."

Will ran his hand through his hair.

"Well, when it comes down to it, we're all like seeds someone's planted. Seeds struggling for life. We all have seen some crops grow, and some fail. Maybe it's the weather that's in charge, too much or too little sun or rain. Seeds are fragile, but they do end up somewhere. Same as us. We're no more than seeds of a scattered harvest."

Will looked over at Reverend Prater. He shook Will's hand. 'Amens' came from the congregation.

"What say we open our Hymn books to page 111," Reverend Prater said.

Will could hear the music coming out the windows. "...We shall come rejoicing, bringing in the sheaves ..."

Will took hold of the mare's reins and gave them a crack. "Let's go home, girl."

For old time's sake, he'd brought the twins to Honey Boy's to tell them the news. Wendell looked up at the old railroad clock on the wall. "It's a little after nine o'clock, girls. That freight train headin' west is right on time."

"Oh, Wendell, you and your trains," Ruby said. "What is it you like so much about them?"

"I like the sound of 'em, the clackin' of the wheels on the tracks, the smell of the smoke and iron. And most of all, I like knowin' they're always headed somewhere."

"And where are you headed, Sheriff?" Prudy asked.

Wendell had dodged a bullet and he knew it. Pansy's revenge wasn't satisfied by killing herself and Doc. Even in death, the book remained open on Doc Slayer Jr. Aside from letters suggesting serious medical misdeeds, Pansy had left notes to several people outlining his business dealings. The most troublesome of these had to do with Long Pointe. Wendell believed that there was going to be a big investigation. And since he knew now that the Shultzes, and perhaps others, were in on the atrocities of Long Pointe, the misuse of funds, the mistreatment of patients and so on, the mud was going to splash on a lot of people — but not on him.

"So what's the surprise that you had us both come here for, Sheriff?" Ruby asked.

Wendell did his share of conniving, amongst other indiscretions, but all in all he did right.

"The word's out, girls. The party's tappin' me to run for lieutenant governor," he said.

The twins screamed. "When?"

"Next year."

"So you're goin' to toss your Stetson in?" Ruby asked.

"I wasn't sure up until Doc's death," Wendell said. "But with Doc gone, I'd say it's full steam ahead."

"I'm so excited," Prudy said.

"Me too," Ruby chimed. "Are we gonna be campaignin' for you?"

"I'm countin' on it," he said.

"When you win and go down state, what happens to us?" Ruby asked.

"You two are comin' with me," Wendell said.

"You know, Wendell, you'll be needin' a wife to keep you in line," Ruby said.

"Got anyone in mind, Ruby?"

"Maybe."

"You're also gonna need a son to follow in your foot-steps," Prudy said.

Wendell looked at Ruby and winked.

Grandma Kepler rocked back and forth. Professor Knobbs sat with his arm around Sammy, listening to the rocker's creak. He leaned forward as she spoke.

"Sheriff Gates told me Will's not going back to Long Pointe. Don't that Hanna seem like a nice girl? Did it sur-prise you that Millie's takin' in her Uncle Rufus?"

The professor started to answer.

"Will's gonna get the children back as soon as all the legal paper stops flyin' around them lawyer's desks. I still can't believe you sold your place to Wendell."

The professor finally got a word in edgewise. "Not my entire place, just the house and a few acres. And he didn't buy it for himself. Wendell wanted it for Millie and her uncle," he said, then added, "Rufus wouldn't leave Long Pointe after all those years to come live in town. That man needs room."

"That may be," Grandma said. "But where are you

gonna live now?"

The professor smiled. "That an invite, Martha?"

"Pa, ain't I a bit big to be sitting on your lap?"

"Look, son." Will tapped Aaron's shoulder and pointed to two red-tailed hawks circling the field.

"Damn ... I mean darn, you hardly ever see them in pairs, Pa."

Aaron nudged the large horses into a turn. "I'm sure glad we got our Belgians back," Aaron said.

"Me too, son."

"When Mister Smith took me in, he told me how you saved his cow and calf. Besides, I overheard him tell Sheriff Gates that the Belgians worked better for the Krouses."

Will took in a deep breath. The morning air carried with it the smell of plowed dirt and working horses.

Father and son both looked up when they heard the clanging of the dinner bell. Hanna pushed her blonde braids back over her shoulders as she let go of the rope and waved to them.

EPILOGUE

I felt it necessary to share with you, the reader, the impact that some of my research has had on me while writing this novel. To begin with, I've listed quotes from several authors on their experiences with the mentally ill. No single author has had any more, or any less, influence on me, therefore their work is referenced in chronological order.

"Reformer Dorothea Dix had become the world's leading authority on mental institutions," wrote David Gollaher (1995) in *Voice for the Mad: The Life of Dorothea Dix.* In *The Life of Dorothea Dix* by Elizabeth Schleichert (1991), it was noted that some mentally ill people were auctioned off as farm servants and locked in cages, pens, and pits by their employers. "... Dix emphasized how American asylums had developed farms whose sales of cash crops offset their costs."

From *Under the Cloud* author Anna Agnew (1886) was an inmate in the Indiana Hospital for the Insane for seven years. She told about an exceptionally mean woman attendant who spat on her, and dragged her across the floor by her hair. She overheard a doctor say, "I will break that woman's devilish will, or I will break her damn neck."

In *Ten Days in a Madhouse* by Nellie Bly (1888), Bly writes, "The insane asylum on Blackwell's Island is a human rat-trap. It is easy to get into the place, but once you are there, it is impossible to get out." Nellie Bly had herself secretly committed when she was an American journalist in order to do a story for the *New York World*. She found the infamous Blackwell's Island Asylum dirty, dehumanizing, and abusive.

Finally, in *A Mind That Found Itself* by Clifford W. Beer (1908), he describes an inmate's life: "... the violent, noisy, and troublesome patient was abused because he was violent, noisy, and troublesome. The patient too weak, physically or mentally, to attend to his own wants was frequently abused because of that very helplessness."

There are as many opinions as there are answers as to the whats and whys about our short stay on this earth.

I believe it is to do good, even though we all fail that purpose from time to time.

Thomas Ray Crowel
   Highland, Indiana